The Asparagus Thieves

Also by Eddie Butler:

Gonzo Davies, Caught in Possession
The Hea

EDDIE BUTLER

The
Asparagus Thieves

Gomer

First published in 2017 by Gomer Press,
Llandysul, Ceredigion SA44 4JL

ISBN 978 1 78562 222 9
ISBN 978 1 78562 223 6 (EPub)
ISBN 978 1 78562 224 3 (Kindle)

A CIP record for this title is available from the British Library.

This book is published with the financial support of the
Welsh Books Council.

Printed and bound in Wales at
Gomer Press, Llandysul, Ceredigion
www.gomer.co.uk

To the Boisvert, who sowed the seed,
and to Mbale, master pruner.

Pro-vlog

'No, seriously, I don't mind. Film away. You might say Camera is my middle name, what with all the things I've seen. Of course, the only thing I didn't see was what I thought I was aiming at, but that, as they say, is another story. Obviously, when I say it's another story, it's still part of *the* story... but, you know... am I waffling? It has not gone without being remarked upon that I've been losing the plot a bit of late. But you've got to admit, it's been a... what do they say?... a journey. I'll say. A journey, all right.

'What's that? Oh, it's for the record, is it? I thought you were asking if I had a record. And I was about to say, well, it's been a bit touch and go, but as a matter of fact, and in spite of just about everything, no. So, on the record, then – and at the risk of repeating myself – no. To having a record, that is.

'Say again? Just for "training purposes", is it? I thought you were going to say the needle's stuck. You know, as in "on the record, for the record".

'Anyway, what you're telling me – and forgive me if I'm wrong... wouldn't be the first time... what you're saying is that it's not really a vlog at all, then. Not like a proper one. Not like the ones, you know, that are put out there... for public consumption. Or as I used to say, for "anyone out there". Not a broadcast, then, as such. Oh, well. Whatever.

'Where were we? Oh yes, the camera. The shirt's OK, is it? Not strobing? I picked up a bit of the lingo, you know. I did a bit of it, as you may have ascertained. You know: "Camera, lights..." Vlogging. Online telly on the cheap, you might say. But I had a following, you know. "Anyone out there?" I'd say, as I said. Seems there was. Seems I had what they said amounted to a ripple effect. A right little pebble in the digital pond, me... "Cue the DfL," I'd say to myself. And if I do say it myself, it did all right. It – I, that is – was even verging on what I think, and correct me if I'm wrong... was verging on what they called in the industry, being a "key influencer". The days of the DfL, eh?

'Are those my initials? DfL? No. DfL, just a moniker they gave me when I came down here. I'm about as Welsh as moussaka, me... or so I thought, but it seems I've got history. A tale of the *teulu*, as they might say in these parts. Family, eh? A little bit of previous on that score, it would appear. No question about it, a little form in that department. Not that I'm any the wiser. All a mystery to me. But yes, the DfL days...

'Anyway, you're right, better get a move on. Time is money and all that. And there's a right tale in its own right. On the subject of money, I could bring a tear to my eye. But yes, as you say, let's get down to business. Transfer of title. Transfer of titles, it might be said... life in the plural, eh?

'Just before we start, mind, I ought to mention – if this is for the record, as you say... I should say, when all is said and done, that I'm not really the person to be asking. If truth were known, I was a latecomer to the whole thing. A right little johnny-come-lately. So, if it's the story of what went on before I pitched up – you know, the house and the people that suddenly, like, dropped in out of nowhere – well, to be honest, I can't help you, squire. As I say, it's all a mystery to me.

'You want to carry on, anyway? Fine by me. I was just thinking, though, that if you want the full picture you're going to have to ask them, or find out, as we used to say – well, not so much "we", as the Rev used to say – "via other channels". "We shall be obliged to pursue our inquiries via other channels." That's how they phrased it when they wanted to put the wind up yours truly.

'Not relevant to the matter in hand? Well, pardon my incredulity, I think is the word, but perhaps it should be. Relevant to the matter in hand, that is. I mean, who knows who might crawl out of the woodwork? I did. Minding my own business and suddenly I'm, like, teleported to the other side of the country. Minding my own business being the one person – to the best of my knowledge, limited as it may be, the person I've always been – and suddenly, out of the blueberry blue, I'm another.

'Stick to the formalities? Well, pardon me for being so informal. My name? Well, there's a question. Which one, I may retort? Always liked a retort, me. A right retorter, you might say. Well, as we say in the transfer-of-title game, would you like it with or without the title? I'm still firmly of the opinion, by the way, that you should know the whole truth of the matter. And nothing but the truth of the matter.

'Why's that, you ask? Well, human nature, isn't it? I mean, I've got my – what is it? – my cameo to play, but I'd like to know what the hell was going on. Wouldn't you, now it's about to be yours?

'The paperwork? Just hand it over, Mr P. Where do I sign?'

Part 1

Chapter 1

Dan 'Post' Jones became a professional cyclist on Platform 1 of Rhiwbina station. It happened in the week before Christmas, generally a period of good cheer in the northern suburbs of Cardiff, but not a conventional time for exertion beyond the excessively sociable or conscientious. The days were grey, the nights long and the tread of commuters off the up line trains from Cardiff Central was a mixture of the heavy and the unsteady. Those that trudged still had projects to complete in the days before the festive break; those that wobbled were returning from office parties. Either way, they seemed an unpromising audience for Post Jones on his bike.

His chosen place seemed odd, too. Platform 1 was no velodrome. Its '1' was superfluous, for there was no other at Rhiwbina. And this one was totally unexceptional, a straight stretch of concrete and tarmac measuring 128 of Post's mid-length strides – 132 when he paced it out on a left ankle turned on a rain-drenched run for home one day in July (Bastille Day, he remembered from the diary he had consulted that morning, as he did every morning). In height, Platform One-and-Only rose a few centimetres short of a full metre above a single pair of rails. Post had measured it one day, dangling his rusty 10-metre tape-measure, bought second-hand at Bevan's Bric-a-Brac on Pugh Street, over the edge. His English teacher, Miss Davies, had once told him – with affection, she trusted – after he took her broken interactive board to pieces and repaired it, that he was a couple of inches short of a full yard, and here was the platform, 6.7 centimetres short of a full metre. Not Platform

1, but the one platform on the one and only track. And not standing proud in its exclusivity, but doing its level best to hide from view. A bread lorry, trying to squeeze past a removal van on the bridge on Pantbach Road, had caught a loose poplar branch and that limb had taken out the station sign and for six months anybody unfamiliar with its whereabouts had had to ask for directions.

'Ah, the station,' was the invariable response. 'Behind the library, love. Watch out, though; you can miss it.'

The whereabouts and the dimensions of the railway had little to do with Post turning pro as a cyclist – except that they were slightly out of kilter and likely therefore to divert him. They were distractions and he was prone, as he noted each time they happened, to being distracted by them. He needed to concentrate on his project. He had to be single-minded, not deflected by extraneous detail. It would be for a short time only. He knew he was not going to be long in the saddle. Cycling was not his future, merely a way – a cycle path, as a cyclist might say – of changing course. And that was what Post was after, a break. The future was everything, but he was anchored, with both handlebar brakes fully applied, to his past. It was time for this past, he told himself, to be consigned to the past. Post's past. And what followed in the future would be Post's post-past.

He mused on such things, absorptions that usually ended with a swerve to avoid running into a delivery van. He had once been talking to Charles II about wig-making in the 17th century when he found himself halfway to Cardiff Bay, five miles beyond his intended destination, Dewi Patel's Farm Shop on Rhiwbina High Street. He'd broken off his conversation about periwigs and the plague and pedalled back for his wholemeal loaf and half-a-dozen free-range eggs.

So, he ordered himself to concentrate now. Head down, Post,

and don't allow yourself to be distracted from this moment of transition, this event on the platform that was going to mark the end of what he described as his pause in life – his hiatus, born of confusion, his inertia that had come with being orphaned. This phase of indecision had somehow extended into years rather than weeks, but the beginning of its end was heralded when, concentrating fully, he rode to the station, with the side-panniers of his customised butcher's bike bulging like never before – and he rarely went anywhere without packing certain tools, of which the mole-wrench bearing the stamp 'Invented in Newport' was his favourite – and with a front basket so full that he had to keep one hand on the protruding equipment to stop everything from spilling.

All through the afternoon and into the early darkness of the last Monday before Christmas, he worked on the platform, unloading bits and pieces from his bike, putting them together and then putting the bike itself on top of his construction. He was ready half-an-hour before the first train of the rush hour – Rhiwbina didn't really do surges – arrived. He briefly thought it would be just his luck if a railway official in a high-visibility jacket now deigned to visit the station, having caught this unlicensed work and possible trespass on the CCTV that had to be up there somewhere, but whose whereabouts Post had never detected. He had wondered what to be seen looking for the unseen would look like on screen, but all remained quiet until the trains began to bring the commuters home. Concentrate, Post.

He began to pedal. Head down, legs pumping, he didn't move his bicycle an inch. He had built a contraption that didn't go anywhere but made electricity, his bike wheels spinning on rollers that drove the dynamo that turned on the coloured lights, salvaged from a skip outside the Rhiwbina Ecumenical Association's headquarters on Heol Brenin, reconditioned in the garage attached to Post's house on Park Crescent, and now draped along the fence and over the shelter on Platform 1. Post Jones, power generator.

The passengers, at half-hourly intervals from the 17:34 ex-Cardiff Central onwards couldn't help but notice him, however weary they were from work or bleary from their parties. They raised their heads and even a smile as they walked on by. The last passenger dropped a pound coin on the platform in front of the cyclist.

On the second evening, four days before Christmas Day, they all smiled again and paused as a man in a suit went up to Post and asked him: 'Is this for real then?'

'Sorry?' said Post, still pedalling.

'Are you having us on, like? Are you on the mains... or is it really you doing this? If you stop will the lights go out?'

Post stopped and off went the lights, to a low murmur of disappointment from the passengers. He restarted and they came back on, to a small cheer.

'Good on you, mate,' said the man and walked away, followed by all the others.

On the third day before Christmas, a woman still sporting a party hat swayed slightly in front of Post and asked if she could have a go. Post dismounted and the lights went out. The woman wiggled and hauled up a foot of her long skirt to a louder cheer, climbed on the bike and started to pedal. The lights glowed and faded, flickered and then shone faintly for a few seconds before going out altogether.

'The party spirit lives...' panted the woman. She placed a big kiss on Post's cheek and tottered off.

On the second day before Christmas, passengers on the 17:34 formed a line in front of Post. A plastic sandwich box was put on the platform in front of him, and coins and notes began to fill it. Every passenger alighting from that train and those that followed until the 20:09, including the man that had asked Post if he was for real and the woman with the party hat, made a contribution. The later the trains and the wearier Post's legs, the larger the denomination of the banknotes that filled and re-filled the sandwich box.

And on Christmas Eve, Post and his bike and his dynamo and his lights were gone. His professional career in cycling was over and a low sodium glow returned to the station after dark. Passengers after the extended holiday soon fell back into the silence of habitual commuters, but for a few days in early January they talked about the nights of brighter lights at their station and how their Christmas had been not only illuminated but also somehow enriched by the strange human turbine.

Chapter 2

Many years earlier... when the entire nation's electricity supply was new...

When the newly ennobled Sir Gordon Tallis-Brown unveiled his plans for The Sanatorium, his wife, Lady Phyllis, thought it was proof of her husband's divorce from reality. To commission a hospital in the grounds of their family home, Tallis Hall, was bad enough; to consider such a thing at a time of mounting international tension was pure folly. Even in the depths of rural Pembrokeshire, where the Tallis-Browns had resettled after Sir Gordon's resignation as a Liberal Member of Parliament on the grounds of ill health – a weak heart seemed to run in his family, down his father's line – and where Lady Phyllis found herself surrounded by the Welsh language that she did not choose to use, there was no escaping the rising clamour of the march towards war in the spring of 1914. To commit money to an experimental treatment centre for the consumptive and generally weak of chest at such a time was, in Lady Phyllis's view, irresponsible. The workers at the Tallis-Brown factory in Hen-felin were hardly more susceptible to pulmonary degradation than anybody else in the tinplate industry. In fact, with the works being situated fifteen miles west of Tinopolis, the concentration of the tinplate industry around Swansea and Llanelli, it could be argued – and Lady Phyllis stridently did – that Hen-felin's workforce breathed in air of a better quality than most in their sector.

'Out in the open, my dear, yes, I'll grant you,' replied Sir

Gordon. 'But they work indoors, where it is a different matter. You can fair hear the rattle in the chests of the older workers.'

It still made no sense to his wife. As an MP, Sir Gordon had paid no more than lip service to the campaigns, despite their ascent into the mainstream of politics, to improve conditions in the nation's factories. Ever since being knighted, however, he seemed to be on a one-man crusade to improve the common lot and thereby contribute to the eventual bringing down of his own class. Lady Fierce, into which Lady Phyllis had transmuted below stairs – and even in Sir Gordon's bed chamber, four doors removed from his wife's – was firmly of the opinion that if her husband paid a little less attention to the noises in the chests of the wretched and a little more to their own, far more corrupted, balance sheets, then perhaps he would understand that now was not a propitious moment to embrace altruism. Hen-felin was failing.

Lady Phyllis had given birth to three sons and had buried two before they reached six months. The Tallis heart was weak while hers, a durable Brown pump, was tough. She now hardened it, even towards sickly John, the one child that survived. Perhaps she saw in her offspring a future so enfeebled that it might be for the best if the last son went the way of the first two. The end of the line did not appear to cause her any regret. If the ruling class were to survive, it would need hardier stock than Sir Gordon and she could beget.

Lady Fierce was still upright of bearing and graceful of movement from the chin down. She was an indestructible specimen, a third daughter of a family of landowners from Breconshire. She had been bred and stiffened for a place in society, but thanks to her father's financial imprudence, by the time her sisters had been married off, she could offer no dowry to Gordon Tallis other than her looks. It had been enough for him at the time, back in the late 1880s, and he willingly tagged her Brown to his Tallis for a bit of double-barrelled clout. Thirty years on, the moving parts of her face were frozen tight. A blink was as much as she registered for weeks on end. She lived in general without motion or emotion. It was said in the house that the only pleasure she took was in her expressionlessness and lack of kindness. With never a word on the subject, she handed John into the care of the Downstairs Joneses. In healthier times, she might have deemed this arrangement unsuitable – they were Welsh-speaking servants – but these Joneses now served her purpose of having the child minded.

Unsusceptible to sentiment when it came to her kin, Lady Fierce did care for the family fortune, or what was left of it. Even she was aware that such a thought should remain unspoken, but she sometimes wondered if the impending war might not be good for them. The family line was doomed but war might save their wealth. Tinplate could only do well in a time of conflict, couldn't it? She rather willed the world to get a move on. If men had to have their foolish way, then better it were over and done with quickly. She wasn't sure the Tallis-Browns as a going concern could hold out much longer without it.

In Lady Phyllis's eyes, there were worse things than wars. Wards, for a start. And if this accursed hospital of Gordon's weren't bad enough, there was a new folly – a herd, no less, of Holstein Friesians. German cows. What little was left of the notion of peace was being shattered by this latest introduction – this invasion – into the fields surrounding the sole remaining house from a once-rich collection of Tallis properties. This last Tallis Hall, built into a fold of the Pembrokeshire landscape blasted by the winds off St Brides Bay, and partly protected from this exceedingly fresh air, dated from the days when the proceeds from the metal works were more than sufficient to fund an occasional residence near the coast. The Hall sank beneath the skyline for protection, but was a little bulge on the Landsker

Line, the division of Pembrokeshire into its Little-England south and its Welsh-speaking north. Lady Fierce saw her house, this protrusion, as a fortified salient of Englishness, she being its fortification. But Welsh was spoken by the Joneses beneath her feet. The Landsker line shifted around and even through Tallis Hall.

Worse than any Anglo-Welsh language debate, the Hall was now a full-time home to be shared with one hundred German cows. Clean air and fresh produce and Teutonic mooing. Was there no end to Gordon's nonsense? Lady Phyllis blamed the Temperance Movement for his loss of reason. From the moment he had joined, it was as if he were walking around in a drunken haze. Sitting in her salon one afternoon, not long after the arrival of the Friesian cows, she blinked. A new sound had interrupted her musings on a life turning to ruin – the clatter of a heavily laden wagon. Sir Gordon looked up from his latest set of plans and walked briskly to a window.

'Splendid,' he announced. 'Don't you think, my dear? The first delivery of bricks.'

'The lowing of your cattle and the groaning of your workers… it is a dissonance that will be our undoing,' she replied.

In the end, the herds of cows and patients never met. Before he could mend the chests of his workers, Sir Gordon's own ailing heart gave out. Lady Phyllis found him slumped over the same plans one morning, slightly adhered to the top page by a patch of dried saliva. She hoped it was the only seepage from her late husband, detached him carefully and made plans for the funeral.

Within days, Sir Gordon was deep in the ground, alongside his two infant sons and, within a few months, Hen-Felin was safely in the hands of new owners, a consortium of tinplate owners from Tinopolis, who truly recognised the possibilities of the upcoming war and who did not appear overly committed to the welfare of the workers, much to Lady Phyllis's relief. They cared only for alacrity in the sale. She, in her turn, saw in their haste – to start the business of turning conflict to their profit – an opening. She conducted the sale herself, a tenacious widow in black and in a man's world. She demanded more, insisted on more again, accepted an offer and then came back for yet more. The purchasers each paid this relentlessly avaricious Lady Fierce a few hundred pounds beyond her final settlement, all the quicker to see the back of her and all the more for her, to see her through to the end of her life in the comfort of her own home far to the west and way upwind of Tinopolis.

In this last-remaining Tallis Hall, she immediately put a halt to the nonsense of The Sanatorium. The bricks remained in their piles, russet-red against the grey stone of the house and the rich green of the sheltered meadows in their fold of the Pembrokeshire countryside not three miles from the sea, a hollow where the Friesians mooed until Lady Fierce had them taken without ado to Haverfordwest market. Their sale as one lot made its contribution, too, to her pension pot. This reserve wasn't exclusively hers, just as the space at Tallis Hall wasn't all hers, but to be shared with John. He was just John to her, but *John Addfwyn* to the Joneses who brought him up. Gentle John, the surviving son of Lady Fierce.

The Joneses from below the stairs were as close-knit as the two remaining Tallis-Browns were far apart. Mother Megan ran what she called Tŷ Mawr, the big house in question being Tallis Hall. She was a widow in her early forties, who had never regretted for a moment marrying her Dafydd, the most local of Pembrokeshire locals. He had worked the land around the house from the day he was strong enough to raise a shovel and was twenty years older than the girl he met at the chapel when she was only just strong enough to carry stacks of prayer books around the pews. He waited patiently for her to reach an age when he could ask for her hand in marriage and became a devoted husband of mild manners and strict routines. He worked hard every day, drank copiously once a week – for some reason generally a Tuesday – and bellowed out hymns in the *Capel Annibynwyr* on a Sunday. Perhaps it was this inclination to do everything exuberantly that cut him down prematurely. He dropped to the ground outside the village butcher's saying, *'Nawr te... nawr te...'*, as if looking forward to what was coming next. He was posthumously renamed after his final words, Now Then Jones, a name that was bequeathed to his son in time-honoured fashion. Now Then Senior's first-born surrendered the Gideon given to him at his baptism and on his birth certificate to become Young Now Then. When this son was old enough not to be Young any more, he became Now Then Jones, just like his late father.

Chapter 3

*A few months before Post turned on his lights...
during his pause...*

Post stood on the pedestrian crossing over the single railway line and turned to face the city centre, fourteen-and-a-half minutes distant on the down line. He bent down and looked between his spread legs. What was now the up line was upside down. His unruly hair was still held in a clumped shape by the damp of exertion and for having been compressed beneath his cycle helmet. Post's bike was resting against a poplar tree by the side of the track, the helmet swinging from the handlebar. Post now shook his head and the clump broke. With his fringe brushing a sleeper and stony ballast, he concentrated on the rails, straight and true, polished by steel on steel, always the same distance apart but seemingly converging. The perspective of his parallel universe.

The line before him – or under him (or even above, it struck him) – went no further than Coryton, two stops away and barely a mile-and-a-quarter deeper into the northern suburbs of Cardiff. And from Coryton station it was only a short walk to two hospitals, the one almost next door to the other. Velindre and Whitchurch. Cancer and Madness. The first had claimed his mother, Christine, when he was seventeen and still at school. Diagnosed at 11:17 in the morning of 16 October, Post had written in his diary, and died at 3:46 in the afternoon of 23 December – also noted. He had counted the pages between the grim consultation at Velindre with Mr Scott, whom Christine thought 'marvellous' to the very end, and the last rites of that end, her funeral in the rain at Thornhill Crematorium: eighty-seven days, including the break for the festive period, when it was deemed inappropriate to fire up the burners. Christine had spent the time of good cheer under wraps in the chill of the morgue.

On Christmas Day, even as she lay there – and a single page-turn in the diary – Post knew that his father, cautious Maurice, was not built to deal with full-blown grief. It wasn't the juxtaposition of funeral and festive season that overwhelmed Maurice; more the complete collapse of all the protections that had made this fifty-seven-year-old man such a mild-mannered model of decency in the often-antagonistic world of tax. For more than twenty years he had gone back and forth between his semi-detached home for his family of three on Park Crescent and the tax office in Llanishen. That these giant concrete monuments of collection were the outstanding features of the northern suburbs seemed to say something about Cardiff. Or about him, Maurice sometimes thought, without being sure exactly what this something was. He now fell into complete silence, a muteness broken only in the following February when he started to talk to himself. Or so his son thought at first. It turned out Maurice was engaged in conversations with people who were not there, and before long he was heading west too, up the short railway line and over the road to Whitchurch Hospital. He was gone by August, four days after his only child and the sole beneficiary of his estate learned that he had gained A* in all four of his A levels.

Offered a place at Cardiff University to study Civil Engineering and a place at Glasgow to read History, Post could now choose to go either forward and build for the future through science or go back into the past. He opted for neither, but decided to stay where he was in the house that had, thanks to Maurice's lifelong commitment to careful financial planning, no mortgage, and to live on the small annuity that the same father had set up even while in the early stages of his dementia. Maurice in the first swirls of madness had somehow still recognised that his son might need to pause and take stock. Perhaps the father had seen the pages in Post's diary, future dates with 'Do something' transcribed from memo-to-self inside his head to blunt reminder, written in thick black biro. These days to come had become days gone by, and nothing else was written to suggest that the exhortation had led to anything beyond the routines of a daily life in a northern suburb of Cardiff.

And here he was, years later, staring between his legs up a railway line. He knew there was deception in their offer of a straight escape, of their promise of travel to a world beyond. They didn't go so very far, and what went up on their single line tended to come back: patients going one way, a consultation closer to their end; commuters going the other, regulars who didn't change at Cardiff Central, onward bound for London a world away, but who went to their offices within walking distance, and who came back. Trudged back. Up line or down line, it didn't matter. The rails took you away and brought you back a little more beaten.

Post shut his eyes. He could feel his fringe tickling the sleeper. Not a sleeper, but an entrancement. He began his rote, his repetitions. Not exactly a railway timetable but a test of memory, of mental dexterity – a man in his early twenties looking through his legs up a railway track in order to ward off what he feared stalked him genetically.

'It wasn't meant to be like this,' he began. 'The railways, that is, Your Majesty – not the dementia. Take the end of the line near the hospitals, the western terminus. It's only two stops from here now, but how much grander it was once going to be. Coryton, named after Sir Herbert Cory of a once-mighty coal and shipping dynasty. This Coryton wasn't supposed to be a full stop, a set of buffers. Nowadays, nothing longer than two carriages rolls to a halt there, but Coryton, Sire, was conceived as a point of penetration into the Taff Valley. Now, it gets a bit complicated here. I know there weren't any trains in your day, but I've told you about them before, haven't I? So, it went like this. The even mightier 3rd Marquess of Bute had a blueprint to open his own Cardiff Railway Company freight line to his mines in the Rhondda. That would have connected his mines to his vast coal port in Cardiff Bay. You had coal for your fires in the palace, right? Whitehall and St James's? But imagine this – walking all the way from Treherbert at the distant head of the Rhondda Fawr to Barry or Cardiff on lumps of coal in train trucks.'

Post stood up for a moment. He knew he was talking aloud and knew that it – he – would look and sound a little strange. He checked nobody was coming his way across Caedelyn Park and began talking again. 'Surprisingly for a family with so much land and money, the Butes were halted – in their tracks, as it were – by a legal dispute over a thin strip of land owned by the rival Taff Vale Railway. A ransom strip. The great freight plans were derailed and trains since 1931 have gone no further on the Cardiff Railway line than Coryton. I'm going to race through the last bit, Sire, because you may get a bit bored, but it's good as a memory exercise. I reckon I should have been called List, not Post. The Cardiff Railway was soon absorbed into the Great Western network, later reconfigured as a part of the Valley Lines run by the Wales and Borders rail franchise and then Arriva Trains Wales. Amen.'

Post knew his local railway not so much as a train-user on this Cardiff-Coryton line, but as a crosser of its track. He preferred to travel by bicycle, usually as fast as possible – although the machine was for the moment leaning against its poplar tree. This was his thing, it seemed. His 'Do something'. For the moment, Post told himself with an inward sigh, it would have to do.

He had customised his machine with his own hands and it had grown into a butcher's bike built for speed, perfect for the exercise he deemed necessary for a young adult male of average weight for his height – 1 metre 81 centimetres, or the imperial 5 feet 11¼ inches to which Post felt historically attached – and for shopping. The bicycle was light and yet sturdy, with bulging panniers and a protruding basket. It was a machine that could take him places. To see the world. To leave. One day.

Until then he was hefted. It was a word he liked, one of the things that had stuck from his studies into the last outbreak of foot-and-mouth disease. Another study, another list... more data absorbed. 'Foot and Mouth – *aphthae epizooticae* – led to mass slaughter, Your Highness. But the killing of upland sheep threatened to eradicate the flocks' instinct to stay within their boundaries on the hillsides without the need for walls or fencing.'

Post had been barely beyond his toddler years, but had been absorbed by the spread of the disease, had charted its progress into Wales, pinning flags into a map on his bedroom wall of where the pyres burned, where the cows and sheep were stacked in their piles, legs pointing rigidly at the sky, licked by flames and turned to oily ash that fell wherever the wind bore it. Some of the research had stuck long after the map curled at the corners, overcoming the last adhesive strength of the tape.

'I am urban-hefted, conditioned to stay within my known environment,' he said.

He had been on family holidays, going over the years from Barry Island to the Gower Coast and later to Pembrokeshire in a slowly expanding bubble of exploration. Maurice had even packed up the third-hand Vauxhall one summer and driven them to Brittany, a public servant in Llanishen rather ill at ease on the right-hand side of the road in France. Christine and Dan – not yet Post – had stayed tightly bound to Maurice in their forays, collectively willing with their phrase book but slightly out of their comfort zone on the continent. They confessed to being a little relieved when after sixteen nights away they turned into Park Crescent. The bubble was safely home.

Post wondered if the 11:46 might be due. But he kept his eyes closed and his fringe in contact with the ground, for one last burst. 'So, Coryton was, after all, a full stop – a dead-end. And the funny thing is, Sire, it's known less now in remembrance of the Cory family, but more for being a roundabout for those other things I've told you about. Motor cars. Coryton is a giant interchange at Junction 42 on the M4.'

He opened his eyes and found himself looking at neither a car nor an oncoming train but a face, upside down like his.

'Hello, Daniel Post Jones,' said the face.

'Corinthia?' said Post.

Chapter 4

Gentle John Tallis-Brown was eventually removed from the warmth of the kitchen run by the below-stair Joneses and sent away to school in England. If a weak heart afflicted the child down his paternal line, then as adulthood approached, the organ was best treated – fortified, in his mother's view – by a dose of robust schooling. It seemed to have got him this far. Now the boy needed discipline and he needed to be stretched in a range of subjects more suitable than the timetable on offer at the grammar school in Haverfordwest. Lady Fierce deemed that her son needed more British Empire, less Welsh parish. Cheltenham was a spa town closer to the centre of a greener and more pleasant land, and full of doctors. Lady Phyllis, had she ever delved into her imagination, would have yearned for a life for herself in such a place, a town on the edge of the creamy Cotswolds and far removed from the bare domes of the Preseli Mountains and the thin soil and the stunted, leaning bushes that struggled out of the hedgerows of coastal Pembrokeshire. She would have abandoned Tallis Hall without hesitation had she ever imagined she had a choice in the matter of where she should live. She did not. She may have argued with her husband about the suitability of his plans for Tallis Hall, but now that it was hers, it was her duty to stay where she was. On her own, or at least on her own in the quarters of the house where the servants ventured only when summoned by bell.

Gentle John was packed off to a school on the outer limits of town at the age of sixteen. He had made it through childhood and was coming to the same conclusion as his mother. To agree with her did not happen very often, but they both seemed of the opinion that he did not appear to be an invalid. That was as far as they went as one mind. She insisted that he should not stay in Wales for the rest of his days. That would be improper. If ever he were to make something of himself, he needed to know what life held elsewhere, which meant he had to be removed – from the company in the kitchen of the Joneses, or from wherever it was in the fields and woods that he lurked with their Gideon, or in the classrooms among the nearest town's lice-infested urchins, or roaming the beaches with whole families of peasants. A mother's mind churned even if her face did not move. She had a feral child, a Welsh-speaking son. It would not do. Go, boy, go away. Make something of yourself. Do something. Until then, you must be out of your mother's sight.

This mother thought she now had her home to herself, where she could pull herself corset-tight into a salon twilight and, two years before a shot was fired, become a living portent of widowhood behind closed curtains. Much to the amusement of the Joneses, who kept Her Ladyship's fire and stomach fed, this splendid isolation lasted no more than a week. Gentle John came home and quietly told his mother that his Cheltenham school was not for him. She sent him back and he came home four days later and stayed at Tallis Hall for the next two years. If he had inherited his mother's heart, it seemed he had her obstinacy too, a tenacity he now converted from making escape plans to filling his time at home. As war consumed Europe and beyond, he devoted himself to the bricks that his father had ordered for the sanatorium. Tallis Hall would have not a small hospital but a vast walled garden, complete with glasshouse. If it was his mother's intention to spend the war in her penumbra inside the house, John would see to it that daylight was put to good use on the outside.

Now Then Jones, the same age as John, would lead the workforce. Not that a team of builders ever appeared. Gabriel and Daniel, Now Then's younger brothers, helped here and there at first, but they had schooling to complete and, besides, their attention span was short. Now Then shooed them off his site more often than he commissioned them to carry out simple tasks. He preferred to be by himself on the project. First, however, he had to be told what to do. Each morning he would present himself in the first-floor bedroom, converted into the planning office, for the daily briefing by Gentle John, hunched over his drawings. The young master would give his instructions to the servant, the same as ever.

As time went on, though, and as John completed his designs and found himself at a loose end, he began to go down into the garden and offer himself for work. The master was now the labourer taking orders from Now Then, the site foreman. Together – and as a workforce of just two – they slowly and meticulously built their walls. And just occasionally, and without ever making a sound on the stairs, Lady Fierce would go up into the office and look down on the young men at work. If she worried about any strain on the heart of her son as, stripped to the waist, he wheeled barrow after barrow of lime mortar around the site, she revealed nothing. It proved he had her heart, not his father's. And if on these occasions Gentle John looked up at the first-floor window, he saw nothing, for his mother was careful to stay out of his line of sight.

The walls on three sides grew higher and higher, the double layers of bricks reinforced with pillars at regular intervals and topped with carefully cut paving slabs. When the scaffolding came down in the spring of 1915, three symmetrical walls were revealed, ten feet high to protect the future produce within from the wind. The fourth wall, the west side of the rectangle, to face the wings that projected from the back of the main house, was the last to be built. Being only fifteen paces away from these wings, this side enjoyed the house's shelter and would have a carefully measured scoop. This downward curve would allow light into the house's ground-floor rooms and into the new courtyard that filled the gap between the house and the garden. The scoop also granted a view of the entire garden to anyone looking out from rooms on the first floor.

Now Then began work on the fourth wall, while Gentle John began to make plans for the L-shaped glasshouse. He toured the gardens of the grand houses of the county and peered at their architecture, taking notes on ventilation and making sketches of their roof trusses. He consulted *Notes on the Theory of the Greenhouse*, by Professor Robert W Wood and worked out angles of the sun in the early growing season and tested the degrees of reflected heat off the walls. His greenhouse, he concluded, would sit in the north-east corner of the Tallis Hall garden, close enough to feel a glow, far enough away from the brickwork to leave space all around for growth. Growth was the watchword, resistance against the shrinking of his mother's existence and the extinguishing of optimism everywhere. In the sheltered confines of their construction, the boys pored over newspapers, their lime-cracked fingers turning the pages that charted the course of the war. As the extent of destruction on its unprecedented scale was revealed, they unloaded stacks of panes of glass, packed in straw, and carefully set them to one side. They more vigorously shovelled tons of topsoil off wagons, heaps of dark enrichment for the less productive soil beneath their feet. And as Now Then toiled and as John toured and researched and unpacked and shovelled, his mother sat in the shadows, calculating the cost of it all, her mind going from side to side on the balance sheet of what was being spent against what might be saved.

The glass was still in its stacks as they approached their eighteenth birthdays. The fourth wall was complete but the brickwork of the glasshouse had only just begun – a course or two above ground level. The war from its outset had had an immediate effect on one of the builders. Gentle John, almost to his own surprise and certainly in contravention of the spirit that had made him turn his back on the Cheltenham school – whose very mission was to supply officers to the army – had long felt a restlessness. He now found it hard to concentrate on his domestic project and for days that turned into weeks he prowled the corridors, preferring indoors to out, sitting only to read everything he could about the war's progress, its retreats and its stalemate. The more it became bogged down in France, the harder he found it to keep still.

Now Then was less obsessed. He had more to anchor him to home. But he took it for granted that should John go, then he would follow. It was a pact that they both acknowledged but remained unspoken. John knew that Now Then had good reason to stay – a family to care for – and this responsibility acted as a brake. He held out until the summer of 1915, when they both slipped away to Swansea and headed for the recruiting office.

With regard to the one young man – her own son – Lady Fierce Tallis-Brown could not have been more calculating. By the end of his period of restlessness, she even encouraged him to join up, in contrast to the reluctance she showed when it came to the other. When Megan Jones, stricken with apprehension, came up from the kitchen and informed Her Ladyship that her son, Now Then, was of a mind to join up too, Lady Fierce's lips tightened in disapproval. It was the duty of the Tallis-Browns to do their bit – or at least to pretend that it was so – even if it exposed the sole heir to mortal peril, but it would be decidedly inconvenient to lose a servant. There were privates in their tens of thousands, that could be sacrificed in the fields of Flanders, but a price could not be put on a good pair of hands in the fields – and the new garden – of Pembrokeshire. All the ground around Tallis

Hall, plus the house itself, needed to be managed, tended by people with deep-seated knowledge of what worked in – and of what could not be forced on – the wind-lashed and rain-swept extremes of the land. In short, John's absence could be managed; Gideon's could not.

The two sons, still boys in the eyes of their mothers, left Pembrokeshire at the same time but soon went their separate ways. Now Then joined the Swansea Battalion of what would soon be the 38th (Welsh) Division of Kitchener's New Army. He was just what was needed: young, strong, bright enough to read, ignorant enough – or at least sufficiently uneducated – to obey orders without question. Surrounded by Swansea 'pals', the groups of friends and co-workers to whom the recruiters reached out for their very brotherliness, Now Then didn't have one of his own. John was the keenest to enlist and the first to fail his medical, thanks to the family heart. Or at least to the story of the family heart as told by Lady Phyllis to the army medical board. Despite hearing nothing but eminently healthy sounds from the chest of the volunteer, the doctor declared him unfit for service and recommended a life without exertion alongside his persuasive mother. Gentle John and Now Then were thus denied the opportunity to enlist as pals. Even had they been accepted as a pair, would they have counted? As pals? Now Then had known Gentle John all his life but could hardly classify the son of Lady Phyllis as a friend. Friendship was their below-stairs secret, reserved for rural peacetime. With a sense of solitude that the recruiting sergeants had no interest in finding, Now Then was on his own in the ranks, the terms of his unspoken pact meaningless. He was soon on his way to basic training in Abergavenny, Monmouthshire.

Lady Fierce was left to contemplate her contradiction. Unwilling as she had been to hand over Now Then to the army, she had let him go. Unloving towards her son, she had intervened and prevented him from enlisting. Sacrifice and duty. She tightened the muscles around her mouth and the ropes around her heart and retreated deeper into her twilight.

John Tallis-Brown, having been turned down at a first inspection so perfunctory that he immediately sensed the cold hand of his mother on his chest, refused to go home. Caught between rejection by the army and her paradoxical possessiveness – she both spurned him and refused to let him go – he opted to remain in the company of strangers. Startled at first by the activity, the slightly frenzied toing and froing of the throngs in Swansea, he soon recognised that if he stayed still – it was, after all, recommended by the doctors – something might come of it. Here before his eyes was a great tree of people being violently shaken, with the dislodged fruit then being scooped up and carted off. Here were all these volunteers flocking to join Kitchener's New Army in general, all these Welshmen in particular filling the ranks of the army of Wales dear to the more robust heart of the man that was still chancellor but on his way to becoming prime minister, David Lloyd George. But as these fellow-countrymen flocked, holes would appear in the existing labour market, wouldn't they? By hanging around in Swansea, Gentle and watchful John soon found employment at the Post Office. He became not a deliverer of letters and parcels – not, that is, on the Post side of things – but as a trainee administrator, a willing worker in the Office.

Chapter 5

Post hadn't seen Corinthia for five years and her hair was now shorter than his, a dark-brown bob held above the sleeper, but he recognised her immediately, by her voice as much as anything. Only Corinthia Williams knew how to sew irony into the mere saying of a name.

'Dan Post Jones,' she said again. 'You're a bit red in the face. Either you've been the wrong way up too long or I've embarrassed you. Shall we stand?'

Upright, she was four inches shorter than Post. He concentrated on the branches of trees in the background, over her head and past her ears, while she deliberately looked him up and down. 'You're hot,' she said and then laughed. 'The hot Post Jones… yes, or just a little overheated. Still doing your own thing? Pedalling away?' Post swallowed and nodded. Corinthia carried on with her inspection. 'Obviously still scruffy. What's the word? Unkempt, that's what you are. Sweaty and unkempt – so, hot… in your un-hot way. But you look OK.' She dropped her left hand to her left hip and shifted her balance, dipping slightly, easing into the pose of somebody about to be photographed, somebody accustomed to being on display. 'You can look at me, Post.'

He couldn't help it. He tried to look only in her startlingly green eyes but couldn't hold her gaze and found his eyes wandering, taking her all in – loose-fitting T-shirt, loose jeans, but somehow tight. Boots. Cuban heels.

'You look…' he tried.

'I do, don't I?'

He nodded. 'And you're back,' he said.

'Not for long,' she replied. 'Just for a day. Have to be on my way. You know, as you do.'

'As *you* do,' said Post. They did not speak for a few seconds.

'I know. What I do… especially to you,' she said, more seriously this time, before recovering her playful tone. 'Poor Post Jones.'

Before he ever became Post Jones and before Corinthia grew into Corinthia, they found themselves one day in the badlands of Whitchurch High School. This place was no worse than many other schools' muster stations for smokers and the sullen, but it was best avoided by the innocent. Mr Ellis, who taught Spanish and who liked smoking, too, called the zone at the far end of the Science Block *Tierra del Fuego*. Into this no-go zone wandered Dan Jones of Year 8 one day, not quite on his own, because not far behind came the girl that seemed strangely drawn to – or on this day, drawn by – her class's official odd-bod. He was looking for a place without wind to test his new creation, a home-made helicopter. Through reading about the dynasty of the Stuarts in equally home-made History – as in, they weren't yet part of his designated course, but he read about them anyway – he had just started talking to Charles II, a habit that in these formative years he already acknowledged as best keep to himself. These chats took place, to the best of his ability, inside his head, but he was aware that when he was in deep with His Majesty, the Restoration King, he had the occasional slippage through his mouth.

He was explaining the defiance of gravity to the seventeenth-century monarch and was looking for windless conditions for his helicopter's maiden flight – the trouble being, that in looking for stillness, he was not on the lookout for danger. He wandered into trouble in the *Tierra del Fuego*.

He pulled his string and the helicopter rose into the air,

hovered briefly and then came down gently to earth. Post moved forward to pick it up, but a large boot arrived first, its heel planted three inches from the helicopter, its sole held above the fuselage made of balsa wood. The boot belonged to Kelvin Davies of Year 10. Post was surrounded by Kelvin's mates, the heaviest smokers and the sullenest inhabitants of the *Tierra*.

'Who are you, shrimp?' said Kelvin.

'Dan Jones.'

'Which one?'

'Ten, I think… but I might have gone up to Nine.'

'Well, DJ 10 or 9, you're not supposed to be here.'

'Is that strictly true?' asked the Year 8 trespasser. 'I know I've strayed from my… my comfort zone, but…'

'Ah, a smart-arse,' said Kelvin. And he raised his foot and prepared to stamp on the helicopter, at which point Corinthia – who was still Coryn – burst into the circle.

'Well, what have we got here?' said Kelvin. 'Shrimp 2.'

'Party time,' said Owen Baines. And the circle closed a little tighter around the Year 8s.

'You want to hear me scream?' said Coryn. 'I'll burst your eardrums and you'll be on the sex offenders register before you can say… help me here…' And she nudged her classmate in the ribs.

'Excessive levels of testosterone,' said Post, wondering how she knew so much about life beyond the reach of most in Year 8.

'Are you kidding?' Corinthia was thinking the same thing.

'Just testosterone, then.'

'Before you can say, "testosterone".'

'What the…?' said Kelvin and stamped on the helicopter. Corinthia screamed and the circle burst apart, allowing the prisoners to flee.

'Thank you,' gasped Post when they were back in the safety of their age-group.

'You can't be that dull again,' said Corinthia.

'I know,' said Post.

'I can't be there every time you go wandering off.'

'I know.'

'Who were you talking to, anyway?'

'What d'you mean?' said Post, flustered.

'You were talking to somebody.'

'Oh... him. He must have slipped out.'

'Who?'

'Charles II.'

'Charles II?'

'Yes.'

'So, Dan Jones 10 or 9, talking to Charles II?'

'I suppose so.'

The thirteen-year old Corinthia Williams looked at Post. 'That's cool,' she said and wandered off.

Having begun life in Year 7 as DJ 12, his number shrank every September at the start of the academic year and as older DJs departed to begin their lives after school, until in Year 11, when he was a DJ well into single figures, it vanished for good, his numbers giving way to a new name, Post. His turn had come to give a ten-minute presentation to Set 1, 11P History, on the theme of 'Never Mind The Past; Where Are We Going?', and he'd caught the mood of all those capital letters and put so much stress on 'post-industrial' in his analysis of the destiny of Wales that it stuck. And when the full five syllables of 'post-industrial' proved a little too much of a mouthful, he shrank to Post.

Having risen to the challenge of speaking, the former DJ 12 returned to being an inscrutably reserved student. Post of the 'boffs' – short for boffins. Inwardly he felt both slightly embarrassed by his post-industrial effusiveness and secretly pleased with the new name it seemed to have spawned. 'Post' was concise and likely to elicit a question: 'What's all that about, then?' – a question he was inclined to think he would do his best to duck. Even if people assumed it must be because he was as thick as a post, he didn't mind.

'You don't fool me, Post Jones,' said Corinthia to him much later in Year 11. Post's classmate, as vivacious and dyed-blonde as he was contained and dark, knew about names, but had gone for expansion not contraction, from Coryn to what she told her friends was 'exotic.' And Corinthia in this expansionist mood was toying with the notion of getting to know Post Jones, the rather mysterious Post the Boff.

'I know there's a wild side to you,' she told him.

Post hoped Corinthia was right. He knew she certainly had one and had always hoped, without ever articulating his wish - and certainly not to the girl who seemed absolute of power when it came to the matter of boys - that he might feature one day on her list of conquests. She was on his. Well, not his list of conquests, but his list of wishes, posted at the end of a more firmly detailed menu of things to do, or at least try, that he carried in his head. As he grappled with his reserve, he had 'Do something' swirling in his head. In firm mental pencil, he had etched: oboe, football, drama(?), ski-trip. And with a much lighter, less sure hand, he had the elongated Corinthia down as CW, branded in his brain, faintly written as a hope in his diary.

'I read this thing last night,' said Corinthia. 'In a magazine. It was all about "burgeoning potential". And I wondered who might have it. And strangely enough, I thought of you, Post. Weird, right?'

'I...'

'Like, I know something's going on. You and growing and all that. A bit more muscly than a boff should be... so, I'm caught in two minds.' Corinthia paused. 'I mean, I take it you'd be up for it...'

'Well...'

'We all face choices, Post. That's what the magazine said. So, it's either you or... I'll let you know.' And with that, Corinthia walked away to Welsh, while Post headed for Maths.

She was waiting for him at the bike sheds after school. She stepped aside to let Post insert a key into an old-fashioned padlock and then drop the heavy chain into the front basket. 'I've heard about this machine of yours,' she said. 'Let's see what you've got.' She put one hand firmly on Post's shoulder, hitched her short skirt up with the other and swung a leg over to sit in the saddle. Her feet did not touch the ground and Post had to take a firm hold of the handlebar and crossbar to make sure the bike and Corinthia did not fall over. 'Well, this is dead comfy, I've got to say,' said Corinthia. 'A saddle built with passenger comfort in mind. Broad and well-sprung...'

'Chafing is a pet hate,' said Post.

'Oh, I bet it is,' said Corinthia and they both laughed. 'Come on, swing your unchafed arse on board and let's go.'

It took a bit of doing, but Post managed to get a leg over the crossbar and stood astride it in front of the seated Corinthia, both his feet on the ground and fingers tight around the handlebar grips. 'Ready?'

'Let's go.'

Post pushed off and with a bit of a wobble they were under way, Corinthia in the saddle with her legs dangling to the sides and her face close to his back. She wasn't sure what to do with her hands, but as they gathered speed along the street leading away from the school she planted them on Post's back and felt his muscles move as he worked the pedals. Once he'd worked the gears and found a rhythm over the flat surface, she felt the tension ease and the wheels turned regularly. He avoided main roads and kept to the quiet streets of Cardiff's northern suburbia, where the streetlights were already on in the early gloom of mid-October.

'Did you really build this from spare parts?' she asked.

'I suppose so,' said Post, ever so slightly out of breath. 'The frame is sort of two bits welded together... and everything else came from all over.'

'Welded? How do you know how to do that stuff? Don't go all technical on me, but how did you become Mr Oxy... whatever it is.'

'Oxyacetylene.'

'Whatever. Point is, I can't remember doing welding in class, or taking bike-building courses.'

'I've always liked taking things apart and putting them back together.'

'It's a boy thing.'

'Maybe.'

'Even so, how do you know?'

'Trial and error, mostly.'

'Ever go wrong?'

'Oh, I've nearly burnt the house down a couple of times.'

'For real?'

The street they were on began to climb gently, heading even further away from the city. Post began to breathe a little harder. 'I was explaining to Charles II about electricity, and things got a little out of hand.'

'Him again. Still getting you into trouble.'

'I just got a connection the wrong way...'

'No, the other bit... Charles II.' Post said nothing and seemed to slow. Corinthia thought she heard a low groan. 'No, come on,' she said. 'You've got to tell me.'

'It slipped out.'

'Well, he's out now. So, tell me everything.'

'When we stop.'

'Is it a mystery, Post Jones? Are you a right weirdo?'

'I talk to dead kings, that's all.'

'And I'm on the back of your bike. Jesus, I knew I was taking a risk.'

'I'll tell you when we stop.'

'Tell me now.'

'Can't. Too out of breath.'

They cycled round the outside of the empty Llanishen Reservoir and stopped at the adjacent Lisvane Reservoir, still full. It was nearly dark now and Post first pulled out a red rear light and a white front light from the basket. 'Battery powered and/or dynamo… sorry,' he began as they dismounted. They ended up in a bit of a tangle of limbs and the bike fell to the ground. Corinthia held on to him and then kissed him.

'Tell me more of your secrets and I'll kiss you again,' she said.

On the return journey, Corinthia held her hands flat against his back again, but as gravity pulled them faster towards their homes, she lowered them and placed them on his hips. Post began to turn the pedals again and they went faster and faster, the dynamo whirring against the rear wheel, the light ahead bouncing and bobbing a fraction of a second before the same tremors were absorbed by the sprung saddle. Corinthia, cushioned on its softness, still felt all the vibrations that accompanied them home. Faster and faster they went and Post's long hair flew horizontally behind him. Corinthia looked to the side and her eyes began to stream. She tucked her head back in and pressed her cheek up against Post's blazer and pressed tighter with her hands. He stopped so sharply after racing into her street that there was a twin squeal of noise outside her house, from the brakes and from Corinthia as she was thrown forward into Post's back.

'What's the matter with me, you dare ask? You forgot to pick your sister up from dance club,' said Corinthia's mother. 'That's what's the matter with me.'

'Shit,' said Corinthia.

'And don't swear. You look cheap enough, climbing off that boy's bike in that skirt...'

'Look, we only...'

'I was showing clients round a house. And I get this phone call: 'Bethany hasn't been picked up, Mrs Williams.' How do you think that made me feel? And it's not the first time.'

'What? That other time wasn't my fault. The bus was late getting back to school. You really hold that against me?'

'It's not asking much. To pick her up once a week after school. But oh no, you can't be bothered. You're off with that boy... look at the state of you. I dread to think what...'

'Where is she? Beth.'

'As if you care. She's upstairs. She saw you too, coming down the street like that. I heard her crying.'

They stopped and stared at each other: the red-cheeked, dyed-blond daughter in front of her mother, Irene, greying of hair and blotched of face. They both heard a car pulling into the short drive outside their house and both knew that Vernon, Corinthia's father and Irene's husband, would be able to see them in the small bay window. The curtains were not yet closed and there they were, for all to see – and not just the sub-manager in a freight-haulage company, wondering what he had done so wrong to deserve a wife that he no longer loved and a daughter he could no longer control. He sat in his second-hand saloon, pulled hard on the handbrake whose cable needed tightening, turned off the engine and stared ahead, but not so straight that he couldn't see into his house from the corner of his eye.

'D'you need a drink, Mum?' said Corinthia, knowing exactly what would happen next. Her mother's eyes narrowed and she hit her daughter. Because at this precise moment and maybe for quite some time now, she resented her Coryn and she did want a drink.

Corinthia's hair was so windswept it covered most of her face and the blow landed not so much with the sharp slap of an open hand striking a cheek, but more as a thud, more like a half-inch-thick dossier, dropped on a desktop. Like the delivery of a submission into the current state of play at number 56, another addendum to the case-file of the Williamses of Pentre Close; another day, another row. Vernon sensed the blow out of the corner of his eye, but saw it with greater clarity in his mind's eye. He could have sworn he heard it through the double glazing fitted by a gang of cowboys four years back – the rip-off had sparked one of their early rows – and through the passenger window of the Ford, that he kept open half an inch to help clear the car of the smell of the cigarettes he was not supposed to smoke. Perhaps he didn't see or hear it at all, but he knew exactly what had just happened. And he did not flinch. He stared ahead. He did not believe there was such a thing as a file compiled by Social Services on his family. He did not think for a moment that what went on with a dull thud in his home warranted special attention. He suspected that his family was not so very different from many others in Pentre Close. He pressed the catch on his seat belt and wearily got out of his car and went into his house.

Post went home to Park Crescent and stood outside the back door, not because he didn't want to go in but because he was still hot and he knew it would be cosy inside. Besides, he just needed a moment to relive in his mind the ride to the lakes. His heart was thumping because he had just ridden home on his bicycle made for two. His heart was thumping because of contact with CW. Corinthia Williams, a wish that might come true. He waited for his pulse to slow. He checked it by placing the index finger of his right hand against his left wrist and counted the throb of his blood supply against the tick of his wristwatch. He waited until the sweat on his shirt under his jumper began to chill. He walked into the kitchen and was just about to go upstairs to take a shower when he heard his father's voice.

'Is that you, son?'

Post went into the warm front room to find his mother and father sitting together on the sofa. Maurice had his arm around his wife and she held his other hand in both of hers in her lap.

'Come and sit down,' said Maurice. 'We've just come back from the hospital. We saw Doctor Scott.'

'Mr Scott, I think he is,' said Christine. 'He's very nice. Very thorough.'

'The results of the scans.'

'Not very good, it seems,' said Post's mother. 'Not very good at all.'

Neither Corinthia nor Post attended school the next day. The day after that, Corinthia appeared, jet-black of hair and no longer vivacious but vacant. Her last words before retreating deeper into remoteness were to Post in the corridor: 'Sorry, Post. I thought I'd give the dark side a go. See you.' Corinthia had gone Goth and Post was left with nothing more than the memory of the lingering kiss planted full on his lips. Perhaps there was something else, a prod to self, stemming from vexation, that he should do something to keep her close to him.

'I can help,' he would have said.

'The great mender,' she would have replied. 'You can't fix this. This is a living nightmare, Post; not talking to ghosts.'

He felt too numb to do or say anything. If he was a mouse to be knocked with casual cruelty between Corinthia's claws, then what was there to say? He tried to stir himself: tell her that although this wasn't a problem shared, but a problem doubled, they could work their way through it. The mender couldn't always mend and living nightmares could arrive in pairs, but perhaps they could still help each other. How could this happen to them both? How could she do this to him at such a moment?

Don't worry, Corinthia, he thought instead. What might have been was so far removed from real life that it didn't matter. Nothing mattered. No mending. No sound emerged from his mouth. He opened it but, speechless and powerless, he watched her go. She did not find out about his mother until it was too late. Too late? There was nothing she, or anybody, could have done. His mum was going and Corinthia was going. He would never know where their might-have-been would have gone.

Having turned her back on daylight, Corinthia Williams left before the end of term. Her parents proved resolutely unhelpful when it came to tracking her down and the school even alerted the police. They made a few inquiries but had no reason to suspect foul play. Chronic loss of feeling within the family group was far from rare and hardly a reason to start a search for a missing person. Besides, it wasn't long before one of Corinthia's old classmates reported seeing her at Christine Jones's funeral. She'd been on her own and had spoken to nobody and the friend – or ex-friend, because Corinthia, well, she'd just, like, vanished, hadn't she? – had seen her only because she was running late and the crem was full and she'd spotted the loner in the rain. But she was sure it was her. And before everybody came out of the service, she was gone again.

Post spent his last two years at school in a remoteness of his own, not deliberately chosen but simply where he seemed to be parked. CW had vanished from his list, struck off like all the other wishes: oboe – two left hands; football – two left feet; drama – stage fright; ski-trip – snow fright.

Corinthia didn't go far at first. Her time as a Goth was brief. She was too short of patience to apply all the make-up. She tried leaving her black coatings on overnight, but her skin erupted, and red-eyed and spot-flecked Corinthia became instead a devotee of nothing but water and soap. She had no plan other than to stay away for as long as she could, and was prepared to be less than pristine when it came to her clothes and even her hair, but when it came to her face and body, Corinthia set out on her adventure with soap at the ready. Whatever she encountered, she would be clean of pore.

She edged out of Cardiff, stepping no further afield than Caerphilly, no more than a short bus-ride from home. She would have laughed at herself – at this as a definition of going out and seeing the world – had she not decided that permanent sarcasm was no position from which to start afresh. 'Great start, girl. Nothing like the long haul,' she would have sneered at herself. Not now. Corinthia didn't want to be earnest – she couldn't see herself ever leaning into a conversation to listen more intently – but she needed to be less snide. She wished to put her put-downs behind her.

Drawn then into the company of strangers in Caerphilly by her looks rather than her wit – she was aware that it was a fall-back position that could be both positive and dangerous – she joined them in a pub near the castle and found herself on the move with them. A musical beer tour, they called it. They ended up in Blackwood and she joined them in a squat in Pant Farm Street. Far from being part of some bunch of bohemian oddities, she found they blended into one of what the *South Wales Argus* newspaper called the Youth Communes that were springing up in the Valleys. These collectives were populated by itinerant locals, who simply went from room to room in their own town, never too far from home but wanting to live less formally than with their parents. They found space in houses

49

occupied by students, who found the Valleys so much cheaper than Cardiff. They had neighbours, migrant workers accepted by the young but not necessarily by the older people of the town. People seemed to swirl from room to room, up and down Pant Farm Street. Shared between these groups of house-occupiers, there were always travelling musicians from anywhere, loosely bound combinations that came and went but who seemed to glue everyone together. Music was a permanent accompaniment: gentle acoustic sets that became pulsating head-banging sessions, either played live in pubs or as the backdrop to the casual sex that took place in the bedrooms throughout the commune.

Corinthia lived and loved like this for a few months in a three-bedroom terraced house whose mattresses were never empty. In older times, bedrooms were permanently in use as lodging miners came and went according to their shifts; now rotating communards filled the beds, with work featuring low in their priorities. As far as she knew, she was content with the arrangements – or the complete lack of them – in her life. She had no money, but drinks appeared when she went out and there always seemed to be something in the kitchen – a little mouldy perhaps but generally on the right side of edible. She would have sworn one day that she was at ease, but the very next a familiar restlessness appeared. She would have called it her itch were it not a word she used for a different affliction. She was constantly inspecting herself for signs of bites. When it came to food, it seemed she was it. She was as much at risk of being consumed by bedbugs as any furry corner of cheese in the fridge was of being turned into rarebit.

One evening she went to The Navigation in Garw Row, the pub nearest to her squat.

'You all right, Mike?' she said to the landlord, a lugubrious man in his forties, who had once imagined himself running an altogether more genteel establishment. He was staring at the band setting up on the low stage and at his clientele, nursing their pints – and the secret shots of vodka, sourced not from Mike's cellar but from the shed behind the Polish car wash. 'Full house,' Corinthia went on. 'Another night of rock and roll and profit.'

'Profit? What would you know?' said Mike. 'You lot want to see it from my side of the bar.' He turned away and began to serve lager and the packets of crisps that were the only solids he ever sold. He had let his last barmaid go a month earlier and was trying to cope on his own.

The next day Corinthia appeared at The Navigation at five o'clock. She had gone to work with her soap and even shampoo. She was in clean clothes, having been to the laundrette and shared a wash with Lydia, a part-time communard and fully committed student nurse at the University of South Wales in Pontypridd. Lydia had sat on Corinthia's knee and run a finger down her cheek.

'You've got lovely skin,' she said. 'Medical miracle – that's my professional opinion.' Lydia removed one slightly waxy end of her headphone and worked it into her friend's ear and, with one earbud apiece, they nodded to music and watched Corinthia's jeans and tops going round and round with Lydia's uniform. Corinthia at The Navigation was now presentable – slightly un-ironed but fragrant.

'It's a deal,' she said to Mike.

'What are you on about?' he said, bleary of eye. He reached up, served himself a large neat gin and tossed it back.

'I'll see it from your side,' she said. 'I'll do a shift.' He immediately held up a hand in protest. 'Don't worry about paying,' she said. 'We'll see how it goes. As we say in the pub game, this one's on me.'

She was strict with the customers, refusing to give them free drinks and suggesting they adjust the ratio of paid-for pints to illicit vodka in favour of the landlord. The regulars frowned at that but paid up. There could be no denying that Corinthia brightened up the place and she certainly brought a new efficiency. And because money was never such a problem for the communards who supplied the rest of Blackwood with weed, they responded by not only putting more cash in Mike's pocket but also by spreading the word that The Nav was on the up. The landlord in turn paid Corinthia and the runaway became a model of working respectability, saving her money, counting the notes hidden carefully in the pub cellar and making plans for what to buy. She became like Lydia, a part-timer when it came to their wild life, the future more important than living the moment.

One day, she had just folded a wad of £20 notes into her stash when out of nowhere she thought of Post Jones. She had always liked him for being apart from the rest. She'd found out about his mum through a blanket text message from school – she still received them – and had gone to the funeral. Or stood outside. She'd wanted to speak to him but the very thought of having to go into his inner circle on a day like that and to try to explain… she wouldn't be able to say anything other than she was sorry. And he'd be hearing enough of that. She stayed outside and she slipped away before Post emerged.

And here she was, not a rebel after all, but fast becoming part of the service industry. It was time to move on. Post had been the witness – and perhaps even a part – of her need to change. But surely, after all this time, he couldn't be a reason to stop and go back. Having wondered for a moment what he might be doing, Corinthia eased him out of her thoughts. She told herself she needed to see a wider world, not revisit his remoteness, and having thus spoken firmly to herself, she told Mike that she was off. She collected her money from the cellar in Garw Row, her single bag from Pant Farm Street and left Wales.

Chapter 6

By the New Year going into 1916, Private Now Then Jones was in France with the 38th Division. Partly to their relief, but also partly to their frustration, they were not marched directly to the front but were given more training in the ways of trench warfare. And more. The new soldiers were not held in high regard by the top brass of the regular army, the commanders of the new fighting force considered to have been appointed on political rather than sound military grounds. These Welsh needed to be prepared more thoroughly. They were moved again. The soldiers of the 38th knew all this and passed enough columns coming back from the front line to know what lay ahead and to be grateful to be spared for the moment. On the other hand, they also felt the slight and wanted to prove themselves. They trained in the rear and they repaired reserve trenches to fuel their impatience, and they spent enough time close to Ypres to know that they were still blessed to be out of it. And then they began to make their way south, out of Belgium and back into France. They all knew the score: the Big Push was coming. The weather was warm as they marched towards the Somme.

Gentle John was in France, too, by early 1916. The Army Postal Service was having to handle millions of letters going back and forth between the Western Front and home, and recruited workers from the civilian Post Office. John Tallis-Brown immediately volunteered and, without going back to Tallis Hall, found himself in the military at last, with the Royal Engineers, Special Reserve, Postal Section. He went briefly to London, to the new parcel depot that covered five acres of Regent's Park, but within two months was lurching over the Channel in a mail ship, bound for Boulogne and from there by equally lurching delivery van to the Advanced Base Post Office in Amiens.

Letters in all states passed through his hands. By merely skim-reading post cards from the front, or the pages of letters that had escaped their envelopes for a thousand reasons in this world of destruction, Gentle John had as clear a picture of the Western Front as anybody. Even if the censors' pencils blacked out the details of the fighting, he could tell by the volume of mail and by the tone of the writing what was going on where. He knew in June 1916 that the Swansea Battalion of the 38th Division would soon be sent into action for the first time.

During the second week of the Battle of the Somme, Now Then took his place among the 676 soldiers of the Swansea Battalion and attacked Mametz Wood. The initial attack of July 7, involving not the Swansea but the Cardiff Battalion, had been repelled, Major General Ivor Philipps had been relieved of his command of the 38th Division and now it was the turn of the Swanseas. By the time they were relieved on the 12th, 400 were dead or wounded. Now Then walked out, covered in mud and the blood of others – of the enemy engaged in hand-to-hand fighting and of comrades who were shot while advancing by his side or in front of him, or over whom he had to walk, or who simply vanished in shell-fire, with no remains left save for what was sprayed over those, like Now Then, who were not hit, but who staggered on. His only wounds were splinters in his hands from when he was sent sprawling against the leaning remains of a sweet chestnut by the body of a German sniper, snagged on – and swinging from – one of the few branches still attached to a trunk in the biggest wood on the Somme front.

Immersed in letters by the million, Gentle John had to make time to read. And through his fiction, it struck him just how easy it would be to reinvent himself by written word. The letters of condolence were so common, the losses so huge that it would be easy to vanish – not to desert, but to redeploy himself, to emerge elsewhere. He could disappear and reappear. In a world of pens and ink and paper he could write himself a new life, starting with his own death. He could write the letter that began with the 'regret to inform you', his mother, that her son was missing, not in action but while carrying out his duties close enough to the front to be exposed to shell-fire. Gentle John spent enough time going between Amiens and the field post offices to know what damage could be done by stray shells. It could be his imaginary good fortune to evaporate and present himself with forged credentials and references somewhere down the line.

As the Battle of the Somme ground towards the day it was called off in November 1916, such was the shortage of men that Gentle John did not have to forge anything. He simply and routinely requested a medical and surprised the doctor by seeking not grounds to be discharged but a clean bill of health for active service. There was no Lady Fierce to influence the outcome here, and the doctor heard only the beat of a sound heart. Before Christmas 1916, Gunner Tallis-Brown of the Royal Artillery was handling as many shells in an ammunition column as he had letters in the Postal Service.

The 38th Division was stood down for a year, their performance at Mametz Wood marked less than exemplary at General Headquarters. They were sent to lick their wounds, to be brought back up to strength and reconditioned. The familiar mixture of relief and frustration set in again. In this time of little engagement for the mass of men, other than the occasional trench raid, Now Then was taken aside and given a new role. The army had been reassessing its attitude towards sniping for some time, its disdain for this 'unsportsmanlike' way of purveying death having given way to an acknowledgement that German snipers had been singularly effective in inducing instant panic and a creeping loss of morale in the British trenches. It was time to make amends. Jones of the Swansea Battalion was known for his accuracy of fire and the patient private now volunteered to put to military use his knowledge of the land, his feel for it, his experience of shooting rooks that would peck out the eyes of struggling ewes and their new-born lambs. He was sent to Scouting, Observation and Sniping Training School and teamed up with Harry Williams – Harry the Eyes, a farm worker from Talgarth, who became his spotter and the keeper of the log, Now Then's record of kills. The sharp-shooter was now armed with a modified Lee-Enfield. They were coming late to the business, but Now Then and Harry the Eyes set about making up for it. The pair returned to Belgium in August 1917 and went with the 38th Division to Pilckem Ridge, the assault that served as an opener to the Third Battle of nearby Ypres. Passchendaele. Privates Jones and Williams blended into the contours of Flanders, covered themselves in its soil and when that turned to mud that threatened to drown them, crawled unseen through the ruins of farms to find their spot and lie still until the moment came to kill.

Gentle John had advanced up the ranks quickly, from Gunner to Bombardier and now Sergeant – the number one – of a battery nearby. While Now Then painstakingly prepared his shots, seeing his target through his sight, Gentle John rained as many shells as his 18-pound field gun could manage down on an unseen enemy. Shrapnel, high explosive, smoke, mustard gas – he sent them all as fast as he could into the distance, planning their flight and their landing with the same attention to detail he had once invested in his garden wall. Walls now were for flattening.

Now Then went about his work with the same calmness of mind and steadiness of hand. And when they met for the first time in over two years, in a village a mile back from the new front, they simply stopped – white eyes staring out from mud-caked faces, no flicker of emotion, not even a double-take as they realised who was who.

'Now Then.'

'Sir.'

And then they embraced, in a hug so tight that dried mud cracked and fell from their uniforms.

'So, guns and a rifle,' said Gentle John after they had told each other what they were doing. 'We've gone our separate ways, and yet here we are.'

'This is Harry Williams,' said Now Then, introducing his observer. 'Harry the Eyes.'

'I'm the eyes and he's the trigger,' said Harry and Gentle John immediately saw their professional bond. And in seeing their togetherness, Gentle John felt a yearning for times past. Times lost. Times best left unremembered. Instead, the trio briefly talked about rations and the rain, but they mentioned nothing about home and certainly nothing about the future, not even making a plan to meet up again. They rather formally shook hands after twenty minutes and said goodbye. Pembrokeshire in the past did not exist. Tomorrow did not exist.

Chapter 7

Corinthia stayed away for three years, the time in which Post finished his schooling and proceeded to do nothing. She went from city to city in England, seeking students and sharing their lives in all things bar the studying. She worked in pubs and restaurants, earning, saving, upgrading her sleeping arrangements until she found herself in a room of her own in Leeds, paid for by herself, with a small basin in the corner where her own bar of soap lay permanently at the ready, with a spare in the cupboard beneath. This small cupboard also concealed an untidy recess with a couple of bricks partly prised out to accommodate the pipework, over a loose board. She wriggled the board free and made a home below for her money.

Occasionally, Corinthia shared her mattress with a student, or a musician – and once with a lecturer in archaeology – but she never invited them back for more and certainly never let them inspect what lay behind her strangely locked little door in the corner under the washbasin. The gaps between her workouts in bed – she coined the term to strip them of any affection or sense of attachment – were growing. She was ready to move again.

The offer came almost immediately. New openings were always being dangled before her, but most came with such an obvious leer that it was easy to bat them away. This one was more intriguing. Having worked her way north for three years, this was for a job in the south. Not the south of her known universe but a south beyond.

'Come and work for me,' Mr Coslett, one of her regulars – her very best tipper – had said. 'I've got clubs and pubs everywhere, me. Could do with someone like you. I mean it. Proper work for a good worker. Think about it.'

She had. And three days later, after Mr Coslett had finished off his *tarte Tatin*, told his business associates he would see them in the car and drawn her to one side, she told him she would like to take him up on his offer. They had shaken hands and he had initiated a form-filling process that seemed out of proportion with the bar work she imagined she would be doing. She told herself that her new employer was trying to make an impression, but he insisted it was required now that she was going to be on his payroll in Mallorca.

'You'll be legal,' he said by way of reassurance, although it made her wonder: 'legal', as opposed to what, if she didn't fill in the forms? She hardly knew this man. Where was he sending her?

The doubt made her think of Post. Three years away and she still consulted him. Two hundred miles distant and she still asked herself what he would do in such a situation. What would he say? Well, obviously, having never been outside Cardiff except on family holidays, he would advise extreme caution. And the very thought of such sensible, risk-averse counsel made her all the more determined to go. At the same time, the very thought of going to work on an island in the Mediterranean made her want to go home and see him. Mr Weirdo. Perhaps for the last time. Who knew?

First things first, Corinthia packed in her job at her restaurant, on the very day that the manager was thinking of promoting her. He didn't tell her. In fact, he packed her off with less cash than she was owed. Corinthia didn't rail against him, but waited until he returned to his desk. She gave him five minutes, then went to the bar and took a case of red wine. Back in her house, she kept a couple of bottles for herself, left the other ten as a farewell present for the students in the house and headed for the station.

'Rhiwbina, one way, please,' she said.

'Sorry, love,' said the ticket-seller. 'Say again.'

'Rhiwbina. Can't believe you haven't heard of it.'

'Poor Post Jones,' she now said on the crossing over the railway line. Actually, he looked much better than she'd expected. Not poor when it came to his structure. A bit confused maybe and certainly a bit flushed but... he looked good. 'By the way,' she said, 'you know there's a train coming.'

He still did not respond. Poor dab. Stop saying 'poor'. 'No, I mean it,' she said aloud. 'There is a train coming.' And she pulled Post off the track.

Attaching herself to his left arm – his right was now pushing his bike – she didn't let go for the rest of the day. As they walked away from the station, she found herself not talking but listening to the ticking of a strand of brake-cable against the spokes of the rear wheel, a metronomic sound that normally she would have found irritating but that for now was hypnotically soothing. Far from overexcitedly filling the silence that might have been awkward – she had after all once walked out on Post – she dropped into a companionable hush. They ticked their way across the small park and into Rhiwbina's parade of shops, at the end of which she drew him into a coffee shop, placed two hands over his one and drew an update out of him. It didn't take long. What had he been doing since leaving school? Very little. What was he going to do next? And she felt his hand tighten as he said he wasn't sure, but that he was making plans. Slow plans, uncertain half-steps to be taken towards a future as yet undefined. He tried to withdraw his hand, but she squeezed.

'Look at me,' she said.

'I am,' he said, because he was.

'As if you mean it,' said Corinthia. He frowned and she released his hand and cupped his cheeks with both palms, her index fingers slipping through his hair and touching the tops of his ears. He blinked twice. 'Who do you talk to?' she asked. He shook his head and lowered his chin, but she tilted his head back into position. 'Are you still talking to your king?'

'Charles II,' he said quietly. 'You're the only person I ever told.'

'The boff who talks to dead kings. And how did I extract this information?'

'You said you'd kiss me if I told you a secret.'

'And did I?' He nodded. 'So, tell me more.'

'It was a long time ago, Corinthia.'

'I know,' she said. 'I remember History, too. Charlie boy, the Restoration King. After... what did you call it? The Interregnum. Three hundred and...'

'The kiss,' said Post. 'The kiss was a long time ago.'

'But you remember it.'

'Of course.'

'So, tell me more now. Come on, Post. It's our thing.'

'Our thing... they're just fleeting instants, Corinthia. Flashes. Revealed and then gone. Like you.'

'Just tell me.'

Post sighed. 'It was an age of discovery. Of science. Of Christopher Wren. Boyle, Hook. And the king took an interest in it all. It was an age of danger – of plague and the Great Fire and of emerging from the time of Oliver Cromwell. But it was also this age of enlightenment... and so I talk to the king who was curious to know. I tell him about the internal combustion engine and taking to the sky and electricity and... well, all sorts of things. Bikes.'

'The king's curiosity,' said Corinthia. 'You're a curious person, too.' She took a sip of Post's tea and grimaced. 'You're too young to be a tea-drinker. Especially without sugar.' She offered him the last of her Coke – she had asked for a bottle not a can – and when he shook his head she sucked on her straw and noisily slurped up the last drops. She laughed and gently, without it being anything like a belch, blew out some air. 'I'm going away,' she said and paused. 'I was going to say, "Why don't you come with me?", but that would frighten you, wouldn't it? So, Post Jones, here it is – my suggestion. Why don't you have a think about it? And come and find me.'

'Where are you going?'

'You have to find that out. You're the one with all this curiosity. Find out and make a plan.'

'When are you going?'

'Soon. So soon you'll be cursing me for doing it to you again. A right little tease, aren't I?' Corinthia reached into the front pocket of her jeans and pulled out her phone. 'Don't tell me you don't have one of these?'

'I do,' said Post and put his own on the table between them. 'Not that I use it much.'

'May I?' she asked and picked up his phone. 'Quite up to date. Password secure?' Post nodded, took it from her and tapped in his code. Corinthia held out her hand again and he handed it back to her. She went into his contacts and swept her thumb up once. 'This is insane,' she said. 'Five… no, six contacts… and one of them's your own number. Cycle shop, dentist, doctor, doctor, doctor and you.'

'I know. I must get out more.'

'Seriously, Post, you must.' Her fingers danced on his phone.

'Are you in there now?' he asked.

'No, I've sent yours to me.'

'So, I have to wait for you. As usual.'

'Be curious. Do something.'

'Like what?'

'Something. It'll come to you,' said Corinthia and stood up. 'You look good, Post Jones. On the outside. But, you know…'

Post nodded. 'You look good, too,' he said.

'Well, there's a start.' Corinthia leant down and kissed him on his right cheek and then on his mouth. He longed for her to stay but knew she was about to leave. She stood, put her phone in her pocket and walked out without looking back. Post sat back and began to explain to Charles II how a mobile phone worked.

Chapter 8

In the months that followed Gentle John and Now Then's departure, very little moved at Tallis Hall. All work stopped outside the house and weeds sprang up in the walled garden and especially over the great mound of topsoil. Now Then's younger brothers, Gabriel and Daniel, left on foot every morning for school, four miles away in Haverfordwest, and came home at the end of the afternoon. Soon, young Daniel was going on his own. Gabriel simply left the classrooms behind as soon as he could – or even before he was allowed to – not long after Now Then and Gentle John left. He preferred to be at home, waiting for the day when he would be conscripted. All the talk was that this conscription would soon be introduced – and it was, in early 1916. What was the point of learning or doing anything when all Gabriel would need to know was marching and killing? And dying. He knew the score. The film that was made about the Somme and shown in the new cinemas across the country was supposed to stir patriotic feelings, but Gabriel saw only futility. He would have to go, but he would not go willingly. He shut himself away in Tallis Hall, a brooding presence downstairs, every bit as still and unblinking as Lady Phyllis upstairs.

His mother, Megan, was by day the only sign of life in the house. Work was her refuge and she busied herself, more like a curator of statues than a keeper of the house's inhabitants. She bustled from her warm kitchen to feed the fires in the parlour where her son sat, and in Her Ladyship's room upstairs. She carried trays of food to them and took their plates back to the

64

scullery. Not a morsel was ever left on Gabriel's plate, while Lady Phyllis's was hardly touched. She pecked at Megan's pies and cuts of meat without interest, while Gabriel wolfed them down. He drank, too, helping himself to the cellar, to the stocks that should have been out of bounds to him. Megan told him he shouldn't, that he had no right, that it was plain wrong, that this would help no one, but he stirred himself from his father's carver to take the key from the heavy iron ring that Megan kept on the back of the door to the old butler's room, and helped himself anyway.

Born in early 1899, he was two years behind Now Then and one year ahead of the new century. He was at his worst in the bleakest year of the war, 1917. He sat waiting for the letter that would call him to arms, knowing that his invisibility in the darkness of Tallis Hall's downstairs and his inebriation could not truly hide him or protect him. He drank no more than usual on his eighteenth birthday and certainly did not celebrate, but merely began to count down the days to his departure.

Megan had letters from her oldest son, short missives that on the surface told her nothing except that he was alive. She knew her Gideon – her Now Then – and sensed the pause in his pencil over the page, its reluctance to say what he truly felt. How much he missed her. She knew it was too painful to say, that he dared not think, let alone put down on paper, that one day he might come home. She read the brief nothings that replaced what he could not say, and felt to her very soul all that went unwritten. Even when he did come home on leave, he was unwilling or simply unable to tell her about the war. He was not silent or brooding but he could not discuss what he had left behind for a few precious days.

The only surprise came in the late summer of 1917 when he wrote that he had met the master. He could not mention his name or what he was doing in wherever it was Now Then found

65

himself, but it was the first time in three years that word had entered Tallis Hall that Gentle John was alive. Megan did not rush to tell Her Ladyship, but three days later, while retrieving a lamb chop and boiled potato, from each of which the smallest single mouthful had been taken, she took a deep breath after the little outbreak of tutting that went with every removal of these barely-touched meals and spoke.

'The day is fast coming,' she announced, 'when I'm going to open the curtains more than the inch you permit and let some proper light in. Open a window for some fresh air. Pardon me for talking out of turn but it's what this place needs. What you need.' She was accustomed to receiving no response, and had long given up worrying about being ignored. 'Anyway, just so you know. And as for this,' she said, indicating the plate, 'I know I say it every day but this is… well, it won't do. Won't do at all.' She put the tray on a small console and began to plump a couple of cushions on another chair, that hadn't been sat against for years. If this fussing was more extended than usual, there was no indication from the shadows that it had registered. Lady Phyllis was immobile, but there were still signs she was alive: the flutter of an eyelid; the slight rise and fall of her chest.

Megan stopped and pulled the letter from her pinafore. 'You may have reason to eat after all,' she said. 'I've had a letter from our Now Then. He says he's met the master.'

Megan was watching her. Just for a second, it was as if Her Ladyship froze, as if all the faint tremors of a heart still beating stopped. For an instant, and no more, her eyes caught Megan's. And then she looked away and her hand rose from the arm of her chair and gave a fleeting backhand flick of dismissal.

Somehow, the call never came for Gabriel. Megan suspected at first that Lady Fierce had intervened again. She knew from Now Then's early letters, written from basic-training camp in

Abergavenny, about Gentle John's failed medical in Swansea. She thought that perhaps a case had been made – invented – for the middle son, that as a worker on the land he belonged to a reserved occupation. She thought she had heard somewhere about an exemption from military service on those grounds, but could it be true? If only they knew how little Gabriel did on the estate, that all the work was being done by Daniel, who with a greater reluctance than his brother had put down his schoolbooks and stayed at Tallis Hall. Not drinking like his brother though, but out there every day, checking the animals in the fields, working on the hedges, fences and ditches – and, of late, entering the walled garden.

It was young Daniel, seventeen at the turn of 1917 into 1918, who drew Gabriel from his stupor, told him to thank his lucky stars and put that good fortune to better use than feeling sorry for himself. Impervious to Megan's entreaties, pleas that had faded with time, exchanged for the disapproving silence of a mother out of patience with – and quite possibly out of love for – her second son, Gabriel stirred himself from his father's chair. At first with a bottle in his hand, he came into the garden to watch Daniel at work, mockingly at first, but then with interest. With the same barrow that Gentle John had used to take mortar to Now Then and his trowel, young Daniel was spreading the topsoil over the garden. On the third day, Gabriel appeared without a bottle and waited until his brother was on his hands and knees, knocking nails into retaining boards that further increased the height of the soil. When Daniel looked up, the barrow was full again and Gabriel was rubbing his hands, warming to the task of returning to the land.

'*Ble 'rwy' ti moyn e?*' he asked in Welsh. ('Where d'you want it, then?')

'*Fan hyn, ar y gwely uwch,*' said Daniel. ('Right here, in this raised bed.')

Gabriel tipped the soil and went back for more. At lunchtime Megan appeared with a tray of bread, cheese, raw onions and a large jug of water. She said nothing, but she smiled at Daniel and nodded at Gabriel. At the end of the first day, Gabriel's palms were blistered and his face flushed. He winced as he plunged his hands into a water butt against the north wall.

'Teimlo'n dda?' said Daniel. ('Feel good?')

'Paid dechre bod yn gall,' replied Gabriel. *'Dyw'r boen ddim mor drwg fel na alla' i roi clowten i ti.'* ('Don't be too smart now. I'm not in too much pain to give you a clip.')

'Ddaliet ti byth mohona i.' ('You'd never catch me.')

Gabriel scooped out water in both hands and threw it at Daniel and with a roar began to chase him. His brother was laughing so much that he allowed himself to be tackled into the middle one of the five raised beds. They wrestled until Gabriel was exhausted and he lay back, covered in soil. He spat out a mouthful and raised himself on an elbow.

'Ar gyfer beth ma'r rhein?' he asked. ('What's this for?')

'Y gwelye uwch?' asked Daniel. ('The raised beds?') Gabriel nodded. *'Merllys.'*

'Beth ddiawl yw merllys?' ('What the hell's merllys?')

'Asparagus.'

'Iesu. 'Asbaragws' yw'n gair ni, glei?' ('Jesus. Don't we say asbaragws?') Gabriel looked across the rest of the garden. *'A fan'na?'* ('And there?')

'Tato... panas... moron... ac mae'r brassicas yn mynd draw fan'na.' ('Potatoes... parsnips... carrots... the brassicas go over there.')

'Brassicas, yfe? Shwt wy' ti'n gwbod hyn i gyd?' ('Brassicas, eh? How d'you know all this?')

'They left a plan. Gentle John and Now Then. They had it all worked out. Until...'

'Ay... until...' Gabriel lay back.

Daniel looked at his older brother. 'It'll be all right, Gabe.'

'No, it won't, Dan. No, it won't.' He put his hands down to push himself up. *'Mae'r blydi dwylo 'ma'n hanner fy lladd i,'* he said. ('My bloody hands are killing me.')

They worked throughout 1918, teetotal six days a week, but on Fridays presented with a jug of cider at the end of the day by Megan. Now Then Senior had enjoyed a drink – and a long one at that – one day a week. His sons could enjoy it too, she thought, in moderation. It was as if she was weaning Gabriel off the booze and introducing Daniel to it. She watched Gabriel carefully as he lifted the heavy jug, but he caught her eye and took a short swig, handing it to Daniel. *'Gan bwyll,'* he said. *'Ma' tipyn o glatsien gyda'r stwff 'ma.'* ('Go easy. It'll knock our heads off, this stuff.')

He dried out and his hands hardened and by early spring the young men – Megan's boys, as she still thought of them – were sowing. Pride of place were the five raised beds, three of them prepared for asparagus, but not for an immediate crop. It would take time for the plants to become established and produce their edible shoots. This was planting for the future, as close as anybody came to making plans for the time, if ever it should come, beyond war.

Chapter 9

Post was aware that there was a limit to the money left to him by his father. He knew that Maurice had planned this allowance carefully, this annuity that allowed Post to pause. Maurice had been careful in his calculations and Post was equally careful in his budgeting. There was money left for a final few months of contemplation and assessment. What neither could have foreseen was the conduct of Maurice's old friend, Arthur Davies, tax inspector of 40 years and trustee of Post's fund. Or at least he was until, in his seventh year of retirement, he packed up and went to Greece – or so he told his neighbours – taking with him the proceeds of not just Post's, but three entire trust funds, set up by colleagues and acquaintances who had chosen him for his absolute probity. Arthur disappeared and so did the last of Post's pot of money.

This sudden end to financial security coincided with the arrival – a rare ping – on his mobile phone. A text message: 'Magaluf. C x'. Post typed out a reply: 'On my way... where specifically? x', but hesitated before pressing Send, hating himself for the indecision. He told himself that he was resolved to go – to do something – but that he needed to be sensible. He scrolled through his contacts list and found the number of his bank, only to discover by automated reply that his local branch had closed. He had been riding past it for weeks, oblivious to its fate. He was offered alternative branches, all situated more towards the centre of Cardiff; he was invited to consult the online service if he was thinking of applying for a loan. He was and took to his laptop for the application process. How much did he require and which repayment schedule might he prefer? What were his outgoings and what was his income? And here Post ran into trouble. He had only the house. He cycled down to the High Street and went into an estate agent's to be told that, of course, they could put the house on the market, but that at the same time, to be perfectly honest, their advice would be to wait. The market was flat. Nothing was moving. Unless it was a fire sale, their recommendation was to sit tight.

Did Post want to sell under any circumstances, at a knock-down price? He cycled slowly home. He phoned the police and then tried the bank emergency number, fished out of his Emergency Number folder, and was told that any investigation would take time and there was no immediate prospect of compensation. He cycled to Arthur Davies's house, thinking that he would find clues that the police had missed. He went around and around the respectable detached house and thought for a moment about breaking the back-door window. He knew he wouldn't.

'There's nobody in,' said a voice from the drive, making him start.

'I know,' said Post, turning to see that he had been startled by a tiny woman in her seventies.

'They're saying terrible things about him, you know. Can't believe it… always seemed… so nice.'

'He didn't say anything?'

'Not a thing. Well except, "How are you, Enid? And the cats?" Last thing he said – seemed so normal. Put a small case in the car and was gone. Haven't seen him since.' She paused and took a step closer. 'Are you one of the… you know?'

'I suppose I am,' said Post. 'One of Arthur's victims, yes.'

'Well, well, well. It goes to show, doesn't it?' said Enid. 'You think you know somebody all these years… and his wife was lovely, you know. She'd never have put up with this, I'm sure.

Janet, she was. Ever so kind. She'll be turning in her... bless her. Well, well, well. Turns out she married a right bastard.'

Enid turned and walked back on an ailing hip to her house next door and Post cycled home to stew for two whole days. Finally, he stirred. Unable to think of what he could do to make it happen, he picked up his phone, found his message to Corinthia and pressed Send.

Corinthia flew to Mallorca at the start of the summer season and began to work in The Bulldog, a single-storey flat-roofed drinking den on the outer reaches of the area of Magaluf known as the Strip. If the surprisingly detailed terms of her employment confined her to serving – beer and shots, rather than cocktails – she was still required to wear as little as she was paid, but without actually ending up as naked as the girls who worked on either side of The Bulldog in a pair of lap dancing bars, the Naughty Naughty and the Big Blue. She worked hard into the increasingly steamy Mediterranean nights, exposed but protected by the expat workforce that included a couple of bouncers, Des and Joe, who after midnight were the busiest pair in the pub, pointing the excessively inebriated – by the score – towards the overworked emergency clinic nearby, or simply towards the nearest drain on the street. The slightly less unsteady were steered towards the clubs on either side, where a more aggressive security reigned. Rarely did Des or Joe have to turf out troublemakers. There was an excess of noise, but in the main the flows of drink and humans remained smooth night in, night out.

The workers all lived in single rooms in a jaded apartment block three streets back. The air-conditioning units whirred, but with the faint crunch of too many bearings failing at the same time. The Bulldog shut late and opened early, offering a full English breakfast not long after the last of the night trade had been eased out. Before this replenishment service began, the establishment had to be put back together again, its tables and chairs inside and out rearranged, and the floors brushed and mopped. The toilets had to be cleaned, by far the worst job that the rotating workers had to do. Rubber gloves were as precious as cigarettes in prison, delivered by the box load but immediately snatched up and dangled at a price before those going on the early shift. They called it Marigold fever.

The Magaluf town beach was serviced slightly later in the day. The local police tried to keep excess off the sands but every morning there was debris all over it, in human form or as food wrapping and coloured bottles by the hundred. Every mid-morning the municipal cleaners moved in, easing the barely conscious out of the way of the machines that swept back and forth across the beach until it was returned to pristine condition, a beautiful strand facing the small Isla de sa Porrassa in the middle of the bay. The clean-up on the beach was not as frenzied as the rush to make the Bulldog presentable in time for breakfast. Sun-worshippers tended to stay by the sides of the pool, if their accommodation offered one, or head later in the day to the Wild West water park on the outskirts of town. The sun-loungers of the beach were for the slightly more staid visitors and these were few in number in high-season Magaluf. Most of the tourists, old enough to drink, young enough to do it every night for a week, slept through the entire day and emerged to start all over again when darkness fell.

In the couple of hours of morning downtime afforded to the toilet detail after they had peeled off their gloves, Corinthia bucked the trend and went to the town beach. She liked seeing the cleaning machines at work, the banter between the drivers, their endless patience at going through a ritual that would have to be repeated the next day. They cleaned their town and the tourists trashed it. Occasionally she would come across an even more contrasting activity – members of a running club going through their paces, old and young doing their circuits and their shuttle runs on the raked sand, devotees of physical exercise in the same place where only minutes before bottles and condoms had been strewn.

On her full day off, Corinthia liked to walk further afield, around the headland to Cala Falcó, to the small beach bar where she would sit with Kaja from Estonia, one of the lap dancers from the Naughty Naughty. The bar was frequented by whole families of locals, who soon greeted them warmly as regulars prepared to try out a little Spanish – even the odd word in Catalan. Corinthia and Kaja loved the volume of normal life: the laughter and debate and arguments and the crying of children that unfolded against the faintest lapping of the tiny waves that came into the inlet, all so far removed from the unrelenting bass pulse that couldn't be avoided on the Strip.

Above all, they liked being in a place where they not pestered by drunk young men. It wasn't the drunkenness so much – in fact, they quite often tottered away from Cala Falcó in quite a state themselves. It was the young men, they decided, that made them seek out this haven. There was simply too much leaning and leering where they worked, too much testosterone and too much lechery. Kaja said she felt more removed from it than Corinthia, performing to a largely all-male audience, unlikely to incur the wrath of a girlfriend who hadn't come all this way to be jilted for some tart behind the bar.

'Thanks a lot,' said Corinthia.

'Sorry,' said Kaja, a couple of years older than Corinthia and just as dark of hair. 'But you know what I mean, no? Your Des and Joe, how many times is the trouble for them caused by women going crazy?'

'Nearly every time,' said Corinthia. 'Women, eh?'

'Drunk women… let's drink to them.' They clinked their rum and Cokes and took a long pull each.

'Do you get used to it?' asked Corinthia. 'You know, the stripping…'

'You know, sure, I hated myself for it at first. But you know, I was better when I was a little scared – the men sensed it. The innocent stripper. I had big tips then…' Corinthia raised an eyebrow. 'I said tips, you dirty Welsh woman…'

'And is there a man, somebody who might not like what you do?'

'Like a childhood sweetheart back in Tallinn, you mean? No, there is nobody.' Kaja put her drink down. 'Sometimes I see big Joe…'

'Our Joe? Bulldog Joe?'

'Yes.'

'I never knew. You and bouncer Joe…'

'Big Joe, yes.'

'Big?'

'I mean big.' And they collapsed into laughter, making the families all around them burst into laughter too.

'And you?' asked Kaja.

'What, me and… who, somebody like big Des? No…'

'Maybe a boy back home then?'

And this time Corinthia put her drink down and stirred the ice cubes. 'Well, there is this one bloke… I don't know what he is. We're old friends, which sounds really bad, doesn't it? An old friend is somebody you've outgrown. Maybe I have. It's just that I speak to him. In my head. Still talk to him.'

'He's sounds like a special old friend, then'

'Sort of.'

'What's he like?

'Well, he's certainly not made to be a bouncer.'

'Not… big, then.'

'Give over, you Estonian stripper. I don't know,' said Corinthia. 'I told him to come and find me, you know. But…'

'But what?'

'He doesn't know where I am.'

'Well, tell him, then. This Estonian performance artiste says that for a beautiful bright girl, you are pretty stupid...'

So, Corinthia took out her mobile and sent her message: 'Magaluf. C x'.

'Is that it?' asked Kaja, looking at the message upside down.

'He's a bit different...'

'He must be a mind reader.'

'I'll send him more clues.'

'Please do. I want to meet him, this old friend of yours. Who is he? Sherlock Holmes?'

'Not quite...'

Two days later, Corinthia was on the town beach early in the morning. The athletes were out, waiting for the final stripes of restored cleanliness to be made by the machines going back and forth across the sand. They stood in the shade of the trees on the promenade, chatting and stretching beneath a sun not yet glaring. As they danced on to the beach, twirling and laughing before starting their workout, Corinthia felt a slight pang. She checked her mobile phone, but there was no reply from Post. She looked again at the athletes and again at the phone. And then she ran towards the sea, stripped to her underwear, put her phone in the middle of the pile of the clothes she left near the water's edge and threw herself in.

She was not a strong swimmer and she stayed well within her depth, but she liked running her hands across the top of the sand underwater, disturbing it in little clouds. She took a deep breath and sank again, daring to turn on her back and face the surface, remembering to blow out through her nose. Bubbles mingled with a blurry vision of the sky. She waited until she really needed air and pushed for the surface. The beach was empty, the runners having taken to the smooth rocks at the far end for a circuit of push-ups and sit-ups. Corinthia waited, lying on her back, staring up at the sky, kicking with her toes and swirling her hands by her waist until she was breathing normally again. She sucked in air and went down to the bottom again. She took a few strokes towards the shore and then stood. She was only up to her waist.

She shook herself at the water's edge and wiped off as much water as she could with her hands and then carefully picked up her top. And then she rummaged more vigorously through the rest of her clothes. She looked up the beach. Her footsteps were visible in the raked sand, the imprints of a swimmer running towards the water. And there was another track: deeper footprints, farther apart, made by somebody running across the beach. And stopping to go through Corinthia's pile of clothes and take her phone.

Chapter 10

In the spring of 1918 both Gentle John and Now Then began to move. They had spent plenty of time over the past two years marching up and down the Western Front, and sometimes went into battle to try to push it forward. The line itself had barely shifted. But now it did begin to move, and at first in the wrong direction. The Germans had launched their Spring Offensive and had broken through. Now Then found himself in Bouzincourt, the same short distance north-west of the town of Albert as Mametz Wood was to its south-east. He was back where he had started. He had fought in the First Battle of the Somme and now, with the German supply lines stretched to breaking point and their advance at a halt, he would fight in the Second.

Now Then and his observer were transferred to the 33rd Division and ordered south. They went from company to company, not really caring where they were or who they were with, but unsettled by how little time they spent anywhere. Stalemate suited their job; to be on the move impaired their accuracy. The confusion was noted.

'You're a sniper, Jones,' said the captain who was ordering him to a new position. 'You work on your own – or in your small team of two. You and Private Williams. Why the knitted brow?'

'It's this, sir,' said Harry the Eyes, holding up Now Then's trigger finger. Now Then said nothing.

'Your point being…?' said the captain.

'Exactly that, sir,' said Harry the Eyes. 'He points and he fires. And if he's going to hit what he points at, he has to know what's out there. The Huns' trench systems, the contours, no man's land… to know what may have changed overnight. Where the enemy sniper might have set up. It takes time to find his loop-holes and his hiding places and he has to wait – choose the moment for the shot. He's got to be settled, isn't that right, Now Then? Sorry, sir. Private Jones. He doesn't mind if he's a Royal Welch Fusilier or a South Wales Borderer… but it's the chopping and changing of the ground, sir. He's a bit… unsettled. And he doesn't aim so well. Sir.'

'Point taken,' said the captain. 'But you have to obey orders and the orders are to move. Haven't you noticed? Everything is on the move. Look, you're being ordered to change position. You're not being asked to change sides…' Neither Now Then nor Harry smiled. 'Look,' said the captain, 'you're still in the company of Welshmen, yes? That will have to do.'

'He likes a bit of Welsh, sir.'

'What?'

'He likes to hear a bit of Welsh, sir. Makes him calm. Makes him steady. Never misses when he's in Welsh, sir.'

'Dear God, Williams. Then speak to him in Welsh.'

'Don't speak it myself, sir.'

'Then we'll find somebody that does.'

'Permission to speak, sir,' said Now Then. 'Private Williams is the best spotter, sir.'

'Then learn Welsh, Williams. Dear God, we do not have time for this. Move, the pair of you.'

Megan Jones thanked the Lord and cared not a jot about the reasons why her second son, Gabriel, was not conscripted into the army. She had feared that it would be too cruel for her to bear – imagining, as she did with every day that passed, that he had been saved from himself and made whole again by Daniel, merely in order to go to war. Having Now Then out there was almost too much for her.

Gabriel thought it was an oversight that would soon be corrected. Any notion that as a worker on the land he might be exempt from military service, he treated with contempt. He was a drying-out gardener, with nothing to show yet – no fruit of his labour. He was no more qualified for exemption than a junior clerk. He was grateful and he was wary. In the hours before the arrival of the post he dreamt of the letter hitting the bottom of the post box. He thought of how he could spare himself the anxiety. He could return to the bottle, but such was the turnaround in his life that he rejected the temptation. The outdoor life that had replaced alcohol suited him and he enjoyed his increasingly muscled appearance. Or he could bypass conscription by volunteering, just as his brother had done. Gabriel did not want to go to war. Now Then had survived the Somme but it hadn't spelled the end of the slaughter. Passchendaele had been just as costly. The need for men was as urgent as ever. Gabriel stayed within the walled garden of Tallis Hall. Something nevertheless nagged at him. He heard the drop of the letter in his mind and there he saw white feathers, too. The mark of the coward floated his way. He buried himself by day in his manual labour, never discussing his situation with his young brother. He took Daniel's orders without question and worked and worked, seeking the exhaustion that might carry him through the night.

The days of the teams of snipers in his sector were numbered, but before they were disbanded and before Now Then was sent back to his original company, he and Harry the Eyes worked on their own, so quiet that no language in any tongue was spoken aloud. If Now Then heard anything, it was the occasional snatch of German, so close did he crawl to their lines. Accurate up to a distance of 250 yards, the Lee-Enfield was deadlier when used at shorter range. Now Then edged to within half that distance, seeking to eliminate as many of the factors, such as wind drift, that might affect his aim. If he made a sound, it was the hum of Welsh hymns as he nursed the stock into his shoulder and patiently went through his firing routines.

Most of the time, what he saw was in miniature, even through the telescopic sight. And it wasn't as if he ever had whole soldiers to aim at. There were only glimpsed parts, a shoulder, half a helmet, or sometimes nothing visible at all – just an imagined head behind the protection of a steel loophole. Now Then's new higher-velocity rounds could penetrate the shield, but he liked to be sure of his shot.

One rare day, a little drama played itself out in full view. Now Then and Harry were lying on the remains of a twisted duckboard in a shell crater, their bodies raised an inch above filthy water. It wasn't strictly no man's land – a leaning, swaying strand of barbed wire marked that particular boundary – but they were forward of their own trenches by a few yards. Two hundred yards away, a German soldier suddenly appeared on the parapet of the trenches opposite and with a clearly audible roar held out his arms and stood stock still.

'Another one,' whispered Harry. 'Gone mad. Asking for it.'

Now Then made no move except to ease his finger into position. He waited. There was another commotion and the sound of interest in the British trenches behind them.

'Stay down, you men,' barked a British officer to his men.

Almost immediately, and as if in direct disobedience of this order in English, three German soldiers climbed into view and moved towards their comrade, still standing stock still. They tried to pull him back. Another head appeared and a second later Now Then heard the sound of an order in German. The three soldiers stopped and two immediately returned to their trench. The third hesitated and the officer's head popped up again. Before he could repeat his order Now Then shot him. He could have taken down the two remaining soldiers, but instead watched them scramble back and disappear.

Harry the Eyes squeezed Now Then's arm and wrote 'Officer – head shot'.

'*Di iawn, Nawr Te*,' he whispered.

As the sun of 1918 began to warm the land and as Gabriel's recovery continued, Daniel and Megan, who had been following an unwritten schedule that always left one of them at Tallis Hall, began to leave the house together. Monitoring Lady Phyllis and Gabriel had a wearing effect on the oldest and the youngest of the Joneses. If the Hall had been built as a country retreat, it also served now to trap them and they both needed a break from the confining walls of the bedroom and the garden. Mother and her third son missed each other's company, and they both welcomed the chance to talk or simply share in silence the slowly passing countryside, or spend five minutes – they knew it would court misfortune to dwell any longer – on the absent *Nawr Te*. To be out together offered a few hours' respite from Gabriel and Her Ladyship. Cow parsley was starting to flower in the steep verges beneath the hedgerows, plentiful on the side that caught more sun, less conspicuous on the more shaded side of the lane. The wild growth was a contrast to the rectangles and uniformity of the garden at home, where sticks of hazel and lines of string were more conspicuous than any abundance yet in the virgin dark soil. Megan and Daniel slowly clip-clopped towards town in the old trap – more a cart converted to carry a passenger, a throwback to the days when Lady Phyllis ventured off the estate – drawn by Seiclops, the old Welsh cob with a milky eye. The further they were from home, the more they found themselves giving in to a little irreverent humour at the expense of Lady Fierce and No-angel Gabriel.

'It still preys on his mind sometimes, Mam,' said Daniel. 'If he thinks about the war – about going or not going… if he strays from a straight way of thinking about everything at the same time as… oh, I don't know… *yn gosod ei res o dato, ma' peryg yr aiff y cwbwl… wel, nid honna fydd y rhych tato cynnar fwya cywir yn Sir Benfro, glei.'* ('…when he's putting in a row of spuds, it's liable to go all… well, it won't be the straightest line of earlies in Pembrokeshire.') And Daniel drew a careful line in the air, that suddenly squiggled.

'Siawns nad yw'r tato'n becso a ydyn nhw'n dod mas mewn llinelle syth ai peidio,' said Megan. ('Don't suppose the spuds care if they come out in straight lines or not.')

'We'll see,' said Daniel. 'What do they call the kink in the line? *Yr elin. Tato Elin Gabriel.'* ('The salient. Spuds from Gabriel's salient.')

Megan laughed and immediately put a hand to her mouth. *'Ma' ofan arno fe,'* she said. *'Wyt ti'n meddwl yr aiff e?'* ('He's frightened. D'you think he'll go?')

'Not now,' said Daniel. 'But I don't think I'll be so lucky, Mam. And if they send for me, you know I'll go, don't you?'

'Duw a'n helpo ni,' said Megan. *'Paid, paid â gadel iddo ddod i hynny, wir.'* ('Dear Lord. Please, please don't let it be so.')

Gentle John was rushed to man his guns closer to Ypres for a time, taking part in the Battle of the Lys. He heard all sorts of languages. Soldiers of the Portuguese Expeditionary Force, allies caught in the battle before they were ready for combat, retreated through his guns. He was then assigned to the French army, to provide cover on their flank, before he was sent back to the British sector for the Hundred Dars Offensive, the last push of the war. Without ever seeing Now Then, Gentle John moved forward with the redeployed 38th Division, advancing from river to river, from the Somme to the Ancre, the Selle and finally the Sambre in early November, 1918.

The field guns and the siege guns poured their shells down on the retreating Germans. Years before, in the early days of trench warfare, when Gentle John and Now Then had been building their brick wall in Wales and waiting to be old enough to join up, the guns in France had pounded away, their co-ordination unsteady, their accuracy never trusted by troops about to go over the top. When the guns had stopped and the whistles had blown, the soldiers walked forward. Far from obliterated, the enemy before them had returned to their machine-gun positions. Now, in the closing phase of the war and with the two young but war-weary soldiers very much part of the fighting, the guns did not stop, but continued to fire, adjusting their sights, tilting their barrels, their redirected shells landing ahead of the troops on the ground. Their fire could never be perfect and to almost the very last salvos, men fell under friendly fire, but Gentle John's guns were more precise than any. Ground was now being taken by the mile but his accuracy to the nearest yard took and saved lives. Hit the Hun, miss our men.

Late one morning in early summer, while Megan and Daniel were on one of their escapes into Haverfordwest, Gabriel was thinning the seedlings and weeding in the carrot patch. He hadn't minded the heavy work of preparing the whole garden, the humping and heaving that were perfect for his recovery. He had had a sense of purpose in the first days of spring, supplemented by the rigours of toil. They pushed aside his guilt and the desire for a drink. Labour was his substitute for his craving. If his mother knew how strong the lure of the bottle was she would never entice him, tease him with her thimblefuls of cider – the weekly dousing of the weak. He wondered if his father, *Nawr Te* senior, had shared this lust. He presumed he had. Gabriel had seen his old man drunk often enough and seen the mask slip to reveal a red-ringed despair in his eye, for which no amount of honest endeavour and hearty hymn-singing could compensate. Gabriel, like his father – passed down from his father – was cursed.

He hated thinning and weeding. On his hands and knees, using only the muscles of his fingers, he hated the detail of this work. Sometimes, after finding the healthiest young carrot and removing all its fellow kind and picking out all the nascent dandelions and yarrow, all the buttercups and cat's ear, to leave it single and full of potential, he deliberately ground it back into the soil with the palm of his hand. One for good-boy Daniel, one for cider by the sip, one for being stuck here, trapped.

In the main, however, he worked methodically up and down the rows, leaving piles of wilting debris behind him. The sun was on his bare back and he was low to the ground, protected. Nobody was trying to shoot him or gas him or bayonet him or blow him apart.

'*Bore da,*' said a voice behind him.

He was so startled that he almost dropped flat into his carrots. Instead, he recovered and jumped to his feet. '*Bore da, f'arglwyddes.*'

Lady Phyllis was only six feet away, in the middle of the walled garden, which meant she had walked twenty yards without him being aware of her. Perhaps she hadn't walked. Perhaps Lady Fierce had simply appeared. She had disappeared, hadn't she? Why couldn't she just reappear wherever she liked? She'd been more ghost than human for years.

'*Mi wnes i dy ddychryn, de,*' she said. ('I gave you a start, then.') And Gabriel swore the corners of her mouth twitched. Nobody had ever seen her face move and it may have been more a grimace than a smile, but there had been an upward twitch, and Gabriel was speechless. '*Wyt ti'n fud, fachgen? Rwy'n siwr y byddai dy fam wedi dweud wrthyf.*' ('Are you mute, boy? I'm sure your mother would have told me.')

'Ry' chi'n siarad Cymrâg...' ('You speak Welsh...')

'I'm full of surprises, it would seem.'

'Ac ry' chi... mas.' ('And you're... outdoors.')

'Again, so it would seem. I have always been suspicious of the open air. So full of benefits, they say. But not for me.' Gabriel noticed what she was wearing and remembered his mother saying long ago that the mistress had withdrawn into black. Goodness knew what she was doing out of the house now, but she didn't seem to have stepped out of widowhood. *'Mae angen i ti wisgo crys, ŵr ifanc.'* ('You need to put a shirt on, young man.')

Gabriel was suddenly conscious of his bareness to the waist. Part of him resisted, willing him to disobey and to remain on his own two feet in front of this crone. There was still the serf in him, though, the peasant that bent down, took his shirt, draped over the handle of a fork, and covered himself.

Lady Fierce watched him closely and saw the flash of rebellion. Megan Jones's troublesome boy. 'I say it not because... *Rwy'n ei ddweud e oherwydd fod dy ysgwyddau di'n goch.'* ('I say it because your shoulders are red.') She moved to one side to reveal a basket, the one Megan used to collect eggs from the coop outside the walled garden. There was a loaf and some cheese in the basket, and a bottle. 'I thought we might have luncheon,' she said. Gabriel looked at the basket and back at Her Ladyship. *'Rwy'n gwybod ble mae'r pantri,'* she said. *'Yn fy nhŷ fy hun.'* ('I do know where the larder is. In my own house.') She took the bottle from the basket. 'And in my own house I know where the cellar is, too. What was laid down and what should still be there. What has been taken and drunk.' Gabriel tried to hold her eye but he felt his cheeks flush and looked down. *''88 claret yw hon,'* said Her Ladyship. *'Rwy' am i ti ei hagor.'* ('This is an '88 claret. I'd like you to open it.')

Megan and Daniel returned to find Gabriel slumped and fast asleep against the north wall of the garden, an empty bottle by his side. He was the biggest pile of debris in the garden, Daniel thought. The smaller heaps of weeds and seedlings in their line were evidence of a short time spent on work. At least Gabriel had had the... sense was not a word Daniel could apply to his brother, but at least he had displayed a trace of self-preservation and put his shirt on and saved himself from the sun. From the window overlooking the new garden, Lady Fierce looked down as Megan and Daniel made their discovery. She watched without expression as the mother tried to wake Gabriel, and then her mouth opened a fraction as Megan, with an audible cry of maternal exasperation, slapped Gabriel hard on the cheek. It was the end of any forays off the estate by the mother and youngest son on their own.

Lady Phyllis reappeared only once, at the end of the summer. The broad beans and peas had been picked and their beds had already been cleared and dug over, but the late potatoes still shone dark green in their rounded raised lines and the runner beans stood at their tallest in their rows, concealing her entrance from Daniel who was sifting through the leftovers of the vegetable cropping – throwing greenery into the compost boxes and stalks on to the bonfire not yet lit. In her black dress, she floated behind the screens of foliage towards Gabriel, up to his knees in the lighter green leaves of the parsnip bed.

'*Bydd angen tywydd rhew i'w melysu nhw,*' she said. ('They'll need a good frost to sweeten them.') If Gabriel was pleased to see her – or what she might be bringing – he did not show it. Instead, his eyes darted around the garden, checking where Daniel was. She ignored these fearful looks. 'Have you heard?' she said. He looked at her. A striking boy, she thought. But so slack of jaw. He shook his head. 'I know we have heard things – been fed things – before. But this time it may happen.'

'*Y rhyfel?*' asked Gabriel.

'Of course, it's the war. Everything is the wretched war.'

'What about it?' asked Gabriel, quick to add, in case his truculence was too obvious: 'Your Ladyship.'

'It would appear that by the time they are good to eat,' she said nodding at the parsnips, 'we shall be having a homecoming dinner to prepare.'

The sweep to victory was so different everywhere from the trench warfare of the past three years. The role of tanks and the protection they afforded to the advancing troops, including Now Then, reintegrated into the infantry, became more refined. Casualty rates among the soldiers on the move fell. Nobody spoke of the day when it might be over, but sometimes they took enemy positions without a single shot being fired at them. Sometimes they could stand and walk around in no man's land. The enemy had disbanded their snipers, too – or they were dead. And the next day, Now Then would push on again, leaving that no man's land behind for the last time. It would not be revisited again, not be picked at by a zig-zagging line of thousands of trench tools racing to build a shelter from the shells that would churn again what had been churned countless times. No man's land was returned to France. The end, never mentioned, was nevertheless in sight. Daniel received his call-up papers in mid-October, but by the time of his eighteenth birthday, the guns had fallen silent.

Having not fired his gun for five days before the Armistice, Gentle John ended his war quietly. Shelling went on to the very end, but not in his sector. Barrel wear, he reported, was reducing his accuracy. He did not write that to be aimless summed up the very pointlessness of it all, perhaps because there did seem to be a point. The war was won, or as good as. He simply made it clear that his guns were exhausted, and just for once somebody seemed to listen. They were ordered to cease firing. He sat with his men and drank tea and listened to the muffled, fading detonations of other guns that worked to the war's very end. When it came on November 11th, they shook hands, ordered another brew and awaited orders.

It was while they were on the move in the final days of the Hundred Days Offensive that Harry the Eyes was wounded, taking a shrapnel splinter to the lower leg. It was a small fragment of metal but it sliced half his calf away. Once he was sedated and out of harm's way, Harry was caught between the frustration of 'catching a late one', as he called being wounded so near to the end, and his relief at heading for home alive, a prospect that he had considered so very unlikely for so very long that he cared not how cruelly close he had come to surviving intact. He had his ticket home and his only remaining concern for what he was leaving behind was for *Nawr Te*, whom he had followed into the infantry.

With two days to go, Now Then was heading out of harm's way too. He was standing at a crossroads near the Sambre river, waiting for transport that would take him well away from the front. He was an escort to two of his lightly wounded company – walking wounded, happy to be heading for home. There was no lighter duty. Now Then had thought about writing to his mother to say he was working his way to safety, but had decided not to tempt fate. He had thought he might beat such a letter home to Pembrokeshire, but shut down that idea too.

Far away, a German gun detachment loaded one last round and, without the slightest calculation, sent it westwards. Slaves to a duty that no longer applied, bound to a ritual that was by now senseless, they had no orders to follow, no instruction to fire or retire or to do anything. They had nothing to gain. They certainly had no cause because that was well and truly lost. But they had a shell and a gun and they had a habit, perhaps an addiction, and they fired. And once it had been sent, they could claim their habit broken. They could abandon the gun and turn their backs on the war, to join the thin columns of the defeated that had already begun to trudge home to Germany.

Their parting shot landed on the crossroads and killed the three soldiers resting there, two of them blown apart and Now Then Jones left seemingly untouched – but just as dead as the two comrades, his life extinguished by the shockwave from the blast.

Part 2

Part 2

Chapter 11

Donna Hopkins missed home not a jot. She liked 'jot'. It wasn't a word she'd have used in the old days. 'D'you fancy 'im, then?' her friend Maxxie might once have asked in her openly inquisitive way. No respecter of a person's privacy, was Maxxie. 'No way,' Donna might have replied. 'Not one bit. Not that it's any of your business, anyway, Maxxie Thomas.' With a load of expletives thrown in, too. Expletives. There was another word that wouldn't even have come to mind. And now 'jot' and 'expletives' did.

'Do I fancy him, did you ask, Maxine? Not a jot.'

Donna tried not to dwell on the old days too much. She looked at her Ian, doing his lengths. She could spell expletive, but how did you spell his diminutive? There, another one. Diminutive. As in: Donna was not a diminutive woman. 'I have girth,' she would say. 'I am a woman of substance.' But he, Ian, was shortened to 'I'. Except 'I' would be I, as in, 'I like it here in Spain, I do.' But 'I' was 'Ee', as in 'he' without the 'h'. And Donna didn't drop those any more. And what was 'Ee', except something in a Yorkshire cartoon? 'Ee' was not on, not for an Eliza Doolittle like Donna, a right Donna Dofuckall, who now had airs and graces and lived the high life. Yes, the high life, didn't you know, old mate Maxxie. A high life without you, Maxxie slag. But with a bloke that, yes, she did fancy. Her 'I' for Ian and his 'I' for insulin. She watched him swimming up and down in their pool, two of the very reasons she missed home not a jot. The good life and this man. 'I', as thin as a rake and doing the full freestyle, up and down their 25-metre pool, and she, Donna, broad of beam and slack of diet, a billboard for the perils of obesity and lack of exercise. But there was an 'I' for irony, eh? He with his Type 2 early-onset diabetes and she, fit as a fiddle, expanded of body and expanding of mind.

She wasn't sure whether she was proud of it or not, but she had been leader of a platoon of Valley Commandos back in the days of next-to-nothing. The band of sisters: Donna and Maxxie, her mate in arms, plus six other regulars and a couple of hangers-on, all crammed into their uniform of red T-shirts, two sizes too tight, with the words in white – 'Valley' and 'Commandos' - swaying among their mounds and folds. They would meet at Pontypridd station for the start of the ten-mile booze-cruise to Cardiff on the days of rugby internationals. The Commandos were nothing if not disciplined, adherents to what they called their strict diet – of two bottles of vodka, downed between them before they reached the capital. And that was just the start of it.

They were at their thirstiest on rugby days, but sport was never their single trigger. There were other times when they headed for the bright lights, straining against the stitching of short dresses, heading not for the rugby temple of mass hysteria but nightclubs. These were Donna's days and nights of learning how to misbehave, of discovering from the miscreant's point of view how trouble was activated and how it was policed. She viewed herself an authority.

She was not the first woman to be ejected from a Wales-England rugby match, but she held the record for the most blood spilt. She was the day's most notorious iconoclast. Roll with that one, Donna. The iconoclast of the *costas*, that's what she was now. The new breed – not your ordinary cheap ex-thief on the run, but a mould-breaking cheap ex-thief on the run. Ex-hooligan, too, and that was a title that took some earning in South Wales. Not the 'ex' so much, because she had simply… she was going to say 'stopped', but that would be little rich, wouldn't it? Forget the 'ex', anyway. What mattered was 'hooligan.' Took something special to receive that particular accolade. Donna Hopkins, Valley Commando and recipient of the lifetime achievement award… for services to Hooliganism. For Valour. Or in need of four Valiums. What was the plural of Valium? Valia? Donna was a little drawn to her Latin primer nowadays. Jot that down, Maxxie. From the Valleys to Valia.

She had always been iconoclastic. Mould-breaking days, bone-breaking days. Take her, for example, at that Wales-England game. The vodka run had led to, well… here was Donna's take… now, of course, she knew the premise – that whatever the cultural differences and the historical rivalries on a day of Wales against England, their conversion into a sporting intensity was supposed to define their limits. Let the hostility be confined to the rugby field. Well, not for Donna. When England scored a try, she kicked a visiting fan, a robust woman in her own right but one raised on the belief that what set rugby apart was the lack of segregation among the supporters, in the back of her knee, causing her to buckle and fall backwards. Donna caught her fall, but only to elbow her in the nose, causing a positive fountain of red over her white England shirt. When the poor woman's friends turned around to protest in horror, the Valley Commandos threw their pints of lager over them.

The difference between Donna and Maxxie – and the rest of the Commandos – was that, come Monday, the red T-shirts and the jutting anti-everything gave way to more conventional attire and a more supine position in the pecking order of working life. These were nurses and classroom assistants and clerks in firms of accountants, whose consciousness of their temporary insanity on the weekend was suppressed, held firmly in check until Thursday, when they began to brew for the weekend, perhaps with a bit of student-bashing in Treforest.

Again, not Donna. She was not to be suppressed. She was 24/7 committed beneath her carapace. Carapace, get her. She went demurely enough to work, but her mind was whirring. Two days at a housing association and one gloriously hypocritical day as a carer to the elderly, leaving a weekend of four days. Three days of work to fuel four of play. Donna thought her work-life balance was Mediterranean. She told Maxxie she was sure she had some Spanish in her.

'Aye,' said Maxxie, 'and about a dozen native Welsh blokes last month alone.'

They said in the housing office that she couldn't have been more diligent. The old folk in her care said she had a heart of gold. Donna skimmed at the first and scammed the second. She was rotten to the core. She had been rotten, she reminded herself sharply. A pluperfect. Pardon her Welsh, but it effing purred off the tongue. Donna Hopkins, mistress of the pluperfect. She had been a cow and now she was a model of self-improvement, prudence itself in the management of what she might once in her roughness have referred to as her stash, but that she now preferred to reference as her primary investment fund. This stake had been accumulated by stealth. Never could it be said that Donna Hopkins was, or ever had been, greedy, other than when it came to chips. And they were history, too. Her chips – and Donna knew that she might be mixing a culinary metaphor here – were toast.

Chapter 12

Post waited for a reply from Corinthia. When none came within three days, he re-sent his message and waited again. He was an old hand when it came to this waiting game, but even he sensed that nothing more was coming his way from her. He had to decide whether to accept the situation – that he was simply on the receiving end yet again of her capriciousness, a victim not for the first time of a change in her heart – or to respond. But how? By doing something. To do so, he needed to raise some money. Post took the plunge. Fully aware that he was heading into the business of being proactive at a headlong rush, he put the house up for sale and found – obviously, typically – that the market was tepid. The estate agents were apologetic. Things had stagnated. It was a time of uncertainty. He did not have a single viewing. He reduced the asking price and nothing happened. The summer turned to autumn and the autumn gave way to the run-up to Christmas. The estate agents recommended he put up a few decorative baubles at least, to create an impression – 'Every little helps,' they said – in the unlikely event of any interest being shown, but Post couldn't be bothered. His rush of blood had clotted. He felt a clot and knew that only a prat like him would call himself a clot. He sat in his stark living room in Park Crescent and wondered how doing something could turn out to be so difficult. Where would Corinthia be now? He had researched Magaluf on the internet and knew that it was as seasonal as apple trees, productive in warm weather and barren in the cold months of the year. She would be gone.

Corinthia thought about returning to Cardiff at the end of the September. The weather had cooled and there was no need now to run the cleaning machines over the beach every day. The parasols had disappeared with the arrival of the winds that whipped up the sea and gave an extra chill to the temperatures. There were still occasional days of warmth and sunshine, but only the locals came out to enjoy them. They had their town back.

She bought a new phone, but no longer had Post's number. It had been so clear in her head, five digits followed by six. She had drummed the rhythm of his number into her own memory, as well as into her Favourites. Post was unforgettable. Except she couldn't remember... She really should go to see him. Her stash of cash was more than enough for a flight home. Instead, she joined a party of workers from the Magaluf Strip, including Kaja and Joe, and set off on holiday to Morocco. They found a hotel that doubled up, much to the amusement of the guests and the bewilderment of the locals, as a donkey sanctuary, run by an ageing Anglo-French couple, halfway between Marrakech and the Atlas Mountains. The young guests lazed by its swimming pool by day and settled down later at the bar, sitting in the open around large log fires that warmed their tight circle in the semi-desert nights. They drank, laughed at the braying coming from the stables next door and smoked too much weed. They brayed back at the donkeys. Although it was all much cheaper than in Europe, Corinthia worked her way through her money.

'Don't worry,' said Kaja. 'We have a plan. Next stop, the Alps. There is good work in the ski season.'

Her wages in Magaluf had always been paid as cash, but Mr Coslett's paperwork suggested that she had somehow been complying with local regulations. In St Anton in Austria she worked in the black economy, with no deductions made for tax, living above the clouds on many days in the high valley, but under the radar. She had to borrow some money from Kaja to take the flight with Joe and her from Marrakech to Zurich, and cross from Switzerland into Austria. In St Anton's Montego Bar, she was paid in cash but even without paying tax, she was earning less for serving the same old rounds of lager and vodka shots by the tray-load than in the Bulldog. Prices of food in the mountains were much higher than in Mallorca. It was hard to rebuild her stash and the plastic bag taped behind the wardrobe in her room contained few euros.

'You can make more,' said Kaja. 'Come and dance with me. My partner, Magda, has vertigo – you'll see why… Don't worry, we keep our clothes on in Austria.'

It wasn't as if Corinthia was unaccustomed to wearing very little. It was just that now she was the centre of attention, part of a double-act in a glass-bottomed cage suspended from the ceiling in the Skimpy, the club that throbbed with music the deepest into the Alpine night. And to this music and in this cage swaying three feet above the most straining hands of the punters, mostly British and posh, Kaja and she gyrated. There were four cages, two for female dancers and two for male, and Kaja and Corinthia soon became the centrepiece of this suspended show that set the Skimpy apart. Crumpled notes, either euros or scraps of paper with the scrawled mobile number of a Rupe or a George or a Bosco appeared through the bars of the cage and fell to its floor. When this carpet impeded the view of the crowd below they bellowed for the bucket and Jurgen, the waiter, would stand underneath with a yellow plastic pail at the ready. The dancers would scoop up all the paper and throw it down and then resume their dancing.

At the end of their shift, not long before the slopes opened, Jurgen checked the ropes and the pulley systems near the ceiling, undid the knots around the hooks behind the bar – well out of reach of the revellers - and carefully took the strain. He lowered the cages to the ground. Kaja and Corinthia cleared the floor for the last time and sifted through the contents of the bucket, pooling the banknotes and pushing the rest of the litter into a black bin bag. They split the money – 'the meat-market bonus', they called it – three ways and Jurgen immediately handed back two-thirds of his share.

'I hold the bucket,' he said. 'You are the ones that fill it.'

'But you are our life line,' said Corinthia, and they handed him an extra note each.

They tried skiing once, under Jurgen's earnest instruction. 'You are dancers,' he said. 'You have a natural sense of balance. So, changing weight on your skis should be easy. But no, you go straight and do not turn. You laugh and you fall.'

They declared it hazardous to their work and didn't move again off the bottom of the valley. At the end of April, the ski season ended and Jurgen left the bar for his summer job in his family's roofing business. Corinthia had repaid her loan to Kaja and replenished her stash. Kaja and she now packed their bags and headed back to Mallorca, toned by their winter work and looking forward to being a little more tanned by the Mediterranean sun. The Bulldog was open, catering for the British families that came to Mallorca at its cheapest before the summer rush of British singles. Eating and spending time on the town beach were serious activities, although everyone knew that the days of drinking and smashing bottles there were fast approaching. For a few short weeks, the sand was extensively and peacefully used by day. The nocturnal wildness lay ahead and in this period of calm, the steel shutters remained pulled down over the frontages of the Naughty Naughty and the Big Blue. The stripping season was not yet underway on the Strip.

It was while Corinthia was high in the Alps and high in her cage that Post began to pedal and light up Platform 1, the one and only, at Rhiwbina railway station. The winds of early December had forced the 'For Sale' sign outside the house in Park Crescent to lean and flap against the dead heads and branches of Maurice's hydrangeas in the front garden, and Post took this as a signal to surrender. He had set out to do something and nothing had happened. He needed money by an alternative method, so he cycled. And as soon as the travel agent's shop opened in the New Year, he walked in and asked about flights to Magaluf.

'And when are you thinking of going, my love?' asked a woman with Deb on her name badge. 'I mean, I can get you there tomorrow, and cheap too, but there'll be nobody there right now.'

'I need to find somebody,' said Post.

'It's what Magaluf's all about,' said Deb. 'The three S words: sun, sea and, well, you know…'

'Sand,' said Post.

'There's a fourth then… what young people are after. Well, not always the so very young…' And Deb, who had not had a good Christmas, what with her Don's mother – her and her cat, down from Tylorstown – outstaying their welcome by a good week, folded her elbows and fixed Post with the look that she liked to think of as meaningful.

'Stability,' said Post. 'Something.'

'Sex,' said Deb. 'Although who am I to say?' Deb was slightly disconcerted by this serious young man. 'But as I said, my darling, there's nobody there as yet.'

'When does the season start?'

'April is for families… but since you're looking for somebody – or your something - I don't suppose that's you then, really, is it? Or maybe it is… who am I to say?'

'No, no family,' said Post.

'Perhaps May then. That's when it gets going – but even that's early.'

'I want to start looking as soon as possible.'

'Have you tried a dating agency?' asked Deb, eliciting another blank expression. 'Only saying...' She concentrated instead on her screen. 'There are,' she said, 'plenty of options. Flights, not dating agencies, that is. And good prices too. Even one from Cardiff on the 4th.'

'I'll take it.'

'And how would you like to pay?'

'Cash,' said Post and unfolded the stack of money made from lighting up the Christmas that Deb hadn't really enjoyed.

'That's unusual,' she said. 'But hey ho...' She booked Post his flight and carefully counted his money – only because she was in no rush for him to go. He was a very nice-looking boy – a man, she should say. She hoped he found the something he was looking for. The somebody. A girl. Maybe a man. Who was she, Deb, to say?

The Bulldog still sat, low and weary, between the two locked and even more run-down strip-joints. They would undergo their annual purge of the rats and cockroaches that wintered there and the walls would be given a lick of paint as usual, to comply with the cursory inspections of the Town Hall, but nothing more. The clubs would need to entice only at night, flashing their neon attractions, their seediness unexposed in their hours of business. Little on the face of it had changed, but behind the scenes there had been more movement than just the scurrying of creatures in dark corners. Mr Coslett was history. It was rumoured he had lost the three establishments in a game of poker, that he had been forced to sign them away as a debt repayment, that he had been dispatched after pulling the deeds – under the duress of a gun to his temple – from his safe. The truth was that he had sold them in a perfectly legitimate fashion, having been offered a reasonably good price. The sale would allow him to retire to the

Yorkshire Dales beloved of his wife, Joan, who had never minded all the nakedness that went with her husband's exotic ventures, but had never felt at home in the sun. Joan Coslett wanted them to retire to a cold climate, pullovers, moorland and hot tea.

Inside the Bulldog, as the greater workforce began to reassemble after the winter spent elsewhere, the exchange of tales from across the continent gave way to more local questions. Who were the new owners? What would become of the workers? Rumours as wild as the stories about what had befallen nice Mr Coslett began to fly. The Russians had come. The Chinese. Malaysians were leaving London and coming to the island. Or was it old London money on the Costa del Sol – the Costa del Crime – that needed to be laundered? The Bulldog was to be the laundrette.

For the time being, it seemed it was to continue doing what it did. A representative of the new owners had flown in, an overarching on-site manager. He called a meeting for the second week of May, at the end of the fortnight Kaja and Corinthia and Joe had spent shutting their ears to the whispers and easing their way back into island life through the quiet inlet at Cala Falcó. They had returned to Magaluf, checked that they were included in the summons to the meeting and, when told that anybody previously employed by Mr Coslett had a right to attend, had then relaxed in their sheltered haven around the corner of the coast from Magaluf, still trying to keep its distance from the resort now gearing itself up for its influx of pleasure-seekers.

The meeting was held in the bar of the Bulldog. Just for once, the sign on the door had been turned to 'Cerrado/Closed' and the workforce had the place to themselves and their new manager, who turned out to be a Mr Hughes.

'Call me Kev,' he said. He was short, with dark hair on top, greying at the temples. He was dapper in chinos, clean deck shoes and a white shirt, its long sleeves fastened at the cuffs.

'And thank you all for coming in. I don't know you all yet, but I soon will.' He looked around at the waiters and bar staff, the short-order chefs and the strippers – all in T-shirts, shorts and flip-flops, that he considered to be uniformly unappealing. 'Dress-sense apart, we are a varied bunch,' he said, 'but we're going to get along just fine.

'Just to put you in the picture, as you probably know, there are new owners. If I say it myself, I am their go-to manager. I've run places for them in Fuengirola, Marbella, Lloret, Benidorm. And now Magaluf.'

'Because… what're they going to do with the place?' asked Koz, the Australian barista who started every sentence with 'Because…' Kev had already talked with this man from behind the bar, because he was the employee that would know most. He liked him. Koz the Oz – 'cos he was - and Kev would require him to keep an eye on things.

'As far as you're all concerned,' said Kev, 'it's business as usual. But just to give you an idea of the bigger picture, this area of town is about to change. Right where we are here has been earmarked for redevelopment. In a year's time, work will start on a new casino.' A murmur went around the staff. 'That's right,' Kev continued. 'All this is coming down. Goodbye Bulldog, hello blackjack. The clubs on the side – gone. As far back as, and including, the accommodation blocks,' – and he pointed at the apartments where the workforce all lived – 'that's all coming down, too. So, it's on a big scale. There will be big opportunities. Exciting times ahead.' He paused. 'In the meantime, there's this season about to get under way and as I say, it's business as usual. Maybe a few things will change here and there, but life goes on.'

Three days later, Corinthia was finishing the first part of her day, the breakfast and cleaning section of her shift – the Brek 'n Vac – and was planning to go back to her apartment to tease some water out of the increasingly erratic shower. Management had been informed about the lack of hot water but it seemed there was little appetite to spend money on maintenance of the boiler in the last few months in the life of the buildings at the end of the Strip. Corinthia had taken to swimming in the sea and using the public showers on the front to rinse off the salt water, but she needed privacy for the soaping and shampooing that were essential to wash away the grime that went with the heat and the job. She didn't think it was asking too much to have hot water in her room.

There was nobody in the Bulldog yet. She had taken off her rubber gloves and was trying to sort out her hair. Tightly bound for work in the kitchen, strands had escaped over the vacuum cleaner and now she was trying to shake it loose and pack it away again, until she could wash it properly. If that wasn't asking too much. She sniffed at her T-shirt. It smelt of greasy bacon and bleach. She looked down at her feet, squelching a bit in her sandals after mopping out the toilets.

'Because he's in early,' said Koz. 'He wants to see you. Manager Kev. Mankev, I reckon.'

'Shit,' said Corinthia, holding out her hands and looking down at herself. 'Where is he?'

'Right here,' said Mankev, strolling out from the kitchens, looking clean and pressed in his uniform: chinos, deck shoes and white shirt. 'Come on, let's go outside and talk.'

They sat at one of the tables on the pavement. 'Drink?' asked Mankev.

'Just some water, thanks.'

Koz had followed them out. He nodded and went back inside. When he returned, Mankev thanked him and then ordered him away with the slightest tilt of his head towards the bar.

'Coryn, right? Coryn Williams. It says here you're from Cardiff.' The manager pulled out Mr Coslett's paperwork.

'Rhiwbina.' Corinthia leaned forward to look briefly at what he was reading. When she had filled in the forms, she had given Post's address, just because she didn't want her parents to be contacted, not even in an emergency. There it was: Park Crescent. It was the first time she had thought of Post in weeks. Longer than that. Months.

'And you?' she asked.

'It's a Welsh thing, isn't it?' he replied.

'What's that?'

'We always ask: "Wherere you from then?" Nosy buggers, aren't we?'

'Kev Hughes. The name, it's a clue… and there's still a trace of an accent. Somewhere a bit further west?'

'Something like that,' said Mankev, tossing the paperwork on the table and taking a sip of his black coffee. 'So, Coryn…'

'It's Corinthia.'

'Corinthia? What's that? You made it up?

'Something like that.'

'Nice one. Anyway, Corinthia… sort of like a stage-name…'

'Or just a name.'

He tapped his finger nail against the table top. 'For a moment, let's hold that thought,' he said. 'Corinthia, a stage name.' He tapped his nail a little harder. They sat there for a moment in silence.

'I'm holding it,' said Corinthia.

'I'm just thinking: well, in that case, let's put her on the stage.'

'What stage?'

'Our stage. On either side of us. We're a regular little theatre company here. Stages everywhere.'

'Now hang on,' said Corinthia.

Mankev tapped the table top harder. 'Look,' he said. 'We don't need bar staff here. We need artistes.'

'You've got lap dancers coming out of your ears,' said Corinthia.

'True, we've got plenty of girls. But not many like you, Corinthia.'

'Hang on, hang on…' said Corinthia. 'If I'd wanted to be a lap dancer I'd have applied…'

'Just think about it. The money's better…'

'Stop…'

'As you know full well from what you did at the Skimpy…'

'How did…?'

'All I'm saying is, have a think about it.'

On their next morning off, Corinthia and Kaja went to Cala Falcó. Children waved away the waiters and held the hands of the two foreigners and steered them to a table near theirs. Families shouted their welcomes and several parents came and kissed them on their cheeks. They ordered rum and Cokes.

'Don't do it,' said Kaja.

'Really? I thought you once said you…'

'Don't do it,' repeated Kaja. 'You know all that shit about business as usual. Well, that's exactly what it is – shit. How long have we been back? One week, and you know what? The clubs have changed – on both sides. It's not like it was. Haven't you seen the same at the Bulldog? The punters are louder. There are more drugs, especially at the clubs. Harder stuff. Joe knows – he sells it at the door.'

Perhaps the atmosphere at the Bulldog had been a little more raucous – if that were possible. Or was it even a little more hostile, with less intervention from the bouncers when the finger-jabbing and the squaring-up began? Was there a little less filtering of the incapable as they staggered from the pub either into the night or towards the clubs next door? Corinthia had been too busy to pay attention. But had she been pawed a little more than usual on her way through the throng?

Two little girls came and stared. They held up their arms and Corinthia and Kaja reached down and picked up one apiece and sat them on their knees, letting little fingers tease their hair for a few minutes and spin the ice cubes in the glasses until the toddlers' mothers called their daughters back with a wave of apology. Corinthia and Kaja waved back to say it was no problem at all.

'I mean it. It's different.' said Kaja. Nobody on the beach spoke English, but she still lowered he voice. 'There's more groping – hands everywhere. And nobody gives a shit. Security are under orders to sell more drugs, care less about keeping the crowd under control. It's like, what do you call it, with drunk cowboys…?'

'The Wild West.'

'That's it. The bloody Wild West. That Kev Hughes and the new owners, whoever they are, they're running the place down – to make a fast buck and then knock it all down. You say no, my darling. You stay away.'

They stayed under the shade and had another drink and then left with everybody else to walk back in the hottest part of the early afternoon to their apartments, where the hot water didn't always flow. Corinthia lay down on her bed and waited for sleep to overtake her. She was not due back at the Bulldog until the evening. She was just dropping off when suddenly, with a rush of adrenaline, she was wide awake. She went to her sink and opened the cupboard door. She felt inside. Her stash of money was gone.

Chapter 13

Donna watched Ian complete his lengths. He was still tall, but a little stooped now, still slender but with a little paunch. He towelled himself off and disappeared inside. He'd be testing his blood sugar levels. Double 'I' for the irony of insulin. The devotee of physical exercise was failing, while in a double slap by fate, she, Donna, was blooming on doing nothing. It fitted neatly into her zero-balance view of her known universe, that improvement in her would be counterbalanced by malfunction elsewhere – but how typical it was that it would be in one so close. It would have been easier if her advancement was countered by, oh, some bloke in the Amazonian Basin taking leave of his senses and going walkabout in the jungle. But no, she was on the up and her 'I' was suffering. Ian had no truck with her view of a cruelly equalising hand of fate. He had diabetes because it happened. End of.

She had met him in her primordial days at his bar at the end of the tourist zone of Fuengirola. It was called Ian's, which smacked a bit of a lack of imagination, she thought at first, and made it sound just like any of the other English-themed drinking dens in the resort. He wanted it to be different, however, thinking he had an eye for development, that he had identified this end of town as ready for a little upgrade. His music was restrained, the food he served was fresh and uncoated in grease. It was the very last place in town that the VCs – the Valley Commandos, not the Viet Cong (although Donna had a grudging respect...) and certainly not Victoria Crosses – would have chosen, and Donna and her sub-platoon of Maxxie and three others were far from what he was seeking as a more discerning class of customer. They were fresh from taking their jolts – their vodka shots – on the beach and seemed to have taken a wrong turning in their haze, to find themselves in the wrong part of town, the dead end of the resort. Ian's would have to do until they got their bearings. As for him, these valley Amazons would have to do until the elusive new breed of finer diners discovered his alternative venue. Ian, he had to face it, was the only person in Ian's.

'Welcome to Ian's,' he said. 'Now then, ladies, what can I get you?'

They immediately identified him as posh Cardiff, which he was, from Cyncoed, perched atop Penylan Hill above the eastern side of the capital. This was leafy Cardiff with views over the Bristol Channel and the other way, towards the valleys to the north, whence came people like this to give grief to people like him. They were nevertheless on best behaviour, not wishing to be locked up on the first day of their away-break. Or rather, they were not on worst behaviour, which meant that they could still give the Cardiff bartender some stick.

'Fancy that, eh?' said Maxxie. '"Welcome to Ian's", is it? And are you him?'

'What you doin' 'ere in Spain, tall boy?'

'Long way from home, like.'

'Wales not good enough for you, is it?'

'Five San Miguels and a round of vodka.'

'Is this yours, then, skinny Ian? Doesn't exactly roll off the tongue, does it?'

'Make any money?'

'Have one yourself, skinny ribs. You could do with a little meat on the bone.'

'Would have to be dead careful with you, thin man. Imagine, girls. Go for the big grapple and… snap.'

'Don't think this place is making you much money at all.'

'What d'you think, Don?'

Donna let the Commandos take their turns. They'd be waiting for one of her Pol Pot specials. A killer line. She decided to wait. The others shrugged and talked among themselves – about Ian, no longer to him – and downed their beer and shots. They had time and they were going nowhere. They were taking some well-earned R&R away from the front line of home. They'd be going back soon enough and Ian feared it wouldn't be too long before he was back in Wales with them. The thought chilled him. He had borrowed to cut out on his own. To make a go of it. Soon he would be slinking home, defeated and battered, leaving Ian's liquidated and shuttered. He was respectable, decent Ian and he was about to surrender. 'No,' he would have replied. 'This place makes me no money.'

He could also have replied: 'No snap, unless by my hand. Little do you know...' Respectable, decent Ian kept quiet.

Neither would be able to remember how they drifted into a conversation for two, away from the five-on-one ordeal, but somehow Donna and Ian were soon talking on their own. Perhaps it was the age-old relief of recognising a known accent, a little echo of home, that prompted defences to be lowered and confidences to be shared. These women were visually intimidating but they were fun in their mocking way. Ian could take it. 'Befriend the ringleader' might have crossed his mind. Isolate the strongest predator. Skinny Ian, with a history of being bullied, had defences of his own. What previous experience couldn't prepare him for, though, was the chemistry, a strange mutual attraction. He immediately liked large Donna and she put aside all her put-downs and found herself intrigued by this rake of a man and his failing bar.

'Are you two gonna get it on, like?' asked Maxxie two rounds later. ''Cos he's awful skinny, Don.'

'Maybe,' she said. 'Not now though.'

'Makes a change,' said Maxxie. 'Are we off, then? 'Cos it's awful quiet 'ere.' She looked at Ian. 'No offence, like.'

'I'll be back,' said Donna.

'Like the Terminator,' said Maxxie. 'My advice is to keep running, mate.'

She didn't return during the six remaining days of their break. The Commandos doubted they would find the place again. They moved into Fuengirola at its more lurid and stayed there. They were ejected from four pubs and one nightclub and returned home exhausted, just as they should be. It was what R&R was all about. Normal life resumed, the balance between good and bad behaviour more or less under control, the route between Pontypridd and Cardiff as well-travelled as ever.

Donna played her part, leading the charge from the front, their public figurehead. Inwardly she was making a more private plan. She gave up her two part-time jobs and within three weeks of their return and without telling any of her platoon of Commandos, she was gone. She had to move quickly, before the discrepancy in the books, the imbalance in the accounts between the time when Donna Hopkins was around and the time after her departure was noticed. It took the housing association and social-care office longer than she thought, perhaps because she had never cheated on a grand scale. But when the trickle-feeds were accumulated, it came as a decidedly unpleasant surprise to discover that heart-of-gold, diligent Donna was a downright villain.

However inadvertently she had led the pack into Ian's, she remembered on her return exactly where it was, and headed straight there. She did pause to wonder if its Ian would still be there. He was, a month closer to closing down but still going – still the only person in his bar. She placed a bulging supermarket bag on the counter.

'As long as you don't mind where that came from, it's yours,' she said by way of a hello.

It was Ian's threshold moment. He could cross or he could stay. 'Is it… is it…?'

'It's not hot, but it may be a bit warm,' said Donna. And Ian crossed the line, reaching out and looking at the contents of the bag, the bundles of banknotes.

'And you?'

'I'm your new partner,' said Donna. 'When I said, 'It's yours,' I meant it was ours.'

She was an equal in the business, the fiddler of accounts who became the scrupulous keeper of the books. She had an eye for detail and a nose for trouble, quickly sniffing out the little scams in the kitchen, the little rip-offs among the suppliers, that damaged the business. She was an old hand when it came to trickle-feed losses and immediately knew where to place her fingers – for a poke in the eye here and to plug a leak there. 'Stop taking the piss,' she said with a wagging digit. 'I know your game. You're taking money that a bar without customers – that even a bar with customers – cannot afford. Instead of taking, make it work. Work with us. And we'll all make more than you'll ever pinch.'

It wasn't her finest team-talk, but the leeching stopped. Perhaps it was young Jaime's bloodshot eye that proved most persuasive. By whichever tool of persuasion, the assistant chef stopped taking meat from the fridge and the example was followed. The books grew more balanced. Ian's neither lost nor made money. Donna's money kept them afloat until they became the chosen haunt of a group of expats that lived in Fuengirola for twelve months of the year. They stepped into Ian's in the autumn, when the shutters were down in town and the rains were coming in off the Mediterranean. They came and they stayed. Donna worked front of house, the very picture of the buxom barmaid, but a shrewd analyst of the clientele, never forgetting a name, never forgetting who liked which tapas, as prepared by Ian and Jaime in the kitchen. Ian's was Donna's. And as the following spring drew nearer, she could claim the worst to be over. She used the word 'consolidated' for the first time.

They gave themselves space to enjoy their working life, choosing not to advance by sheer unremitting toil, but by optimal use of their time and careful assessment of their market. They let the staff run the place on two days of the six days a week it was open, while they explored other establishments. They were already thinking ahead. They weren't so trusting that they left the bar totally in the hands of a workforce that had been less than honest in the past, but brought in Kevin Hughes as an under-manager. He had been part of the original gang of expats that had come to Ian's and saved it, but he was too young to have joined the majority in full retirement. He did a bit of this and a bit of that in the chorizo business, but his main sphere was security. 'Sausages and secret surveillance,' he said were his interests. He had a controlling influence in a little company specialising in CCTV. He offered a discreet service and Donna liked the phrase. The staff knew who he was and what he did and thought they were under constant supervision, which they weren't. Donna and Ian did nothing to convince them otherwise and their new under-manager used his own eyes to make sure Ian's course stayed true.

The families of the other expats began to appear, more colourful of attire than the full-time residents. This was a more transient trade, not so committed to a single destination, but Donna lowered the lights and raised the volume – discreetly, as she put it – and introduced live music. She didn't blast out a sound but wooed her customers. They stayed, even when the lights of town came on and the long nights beckoned. Or at least they stayed until Donna closed up, affably bustling them out of the door and shooing them the way of the thumping music in the distance. She needed her rest and she needed her time for self-improvement. Donna time. She read so much that she could soon call herself voracious. She scoured the internet for fulfilment courses, locking herself into lifestyle exchanges on social media, seeking counselling on such matters as achieving one's goals in life.

She was heading upward and in keeping with her views on a zero-balance universe, something had to go down. And she knew by now that she needn't look further than close to her new home. Ian, in full knowledge of what he was doing, had opened the bag and had crossed the threshold. He was going with gravity. But just as Donna's upward trajectory was front-of-house visible, his debasement was more disguised. In his kitchen, he was the consummate professional. His dream was coming true and he poured himself into the process of salvage and renaissance. His bar and its maid. Their bar. He was made. And when they became partners in bed, too, he could ask no more, a Jack Sprat and Donut Donna who now worked and slept together.

But how he fell and how he tumbled in his fantasies. Snap, something in him had gone. Ian had a sexual appetite that made Donna reach for her adjective of the moment. He was voracious. She hoped she would never have to go any further, but she suspected that he was heading towards vicious. It was as unexpected as their mutual attraction had been in the first place. Opposites, she supposed. But what if they were more like-minded than either of them had imagined. She had a history of amorality that she was trying to bury. But did it linger? Could it have ignited a latent depravity in her man?

115

It was enough to test a person's resolve. And Donna was truly resolved to make herself a better person. She was in love, wasn't she? She was less sure about this more abstract element of their relationship. The notion of love, for heaven's sake. She had felt and she could define contempt and hatred, but did she believe in romance? She wasn't sure about things she couldn't grab. Sentimentality was – had been – to be scoffed at, but because she was embarked on a broadening of herself on the grandest scale, she let herself go with it. Onward, on with self-discovery. She opted to encourage her new man and tolerated his ever-more demanding needs. Out of love, she supposed. And because she was learning on her improvement courses that openness was a key to a lasting relationship, she asked him about his desires, his increasingly disturbing inclinations. And he in turn told her all, and she accommodated him and them as best she could, until they became too much for her to handle on her own and she arranged for others to cater for his needs. And she watched. She was making progress in life and business, but in her private life Donna was turning into a voyeur, turned on by her husband's wickedness. She had been going one way – upward – and he was falling in the other. What had happened when they met at that point, their moral crossroads? What had she pluperfectly done? Sailed on past, heaven-bound? Not quite. Donna had performed a U-turn and fallen in with him. Fallen with him. It quite upset her zero-balance universe. Perhaps his diabetes was the revenge of some thwarted controller of fate's balance sheet. Donna couldn't yet work it out.

It stayed out of sight. In public, they entered the uplands of profit and they expanded, buying another bar in the area that did, after all, have its upgrade. And when Ian's Too began to outdo Ian's Won, as the original was renamed, they sold them both and bought a club in downtown Fuengirola. It was business on a bigger scale, but they approached it with the same attention to detail and the same rigour in the accounting. It also appealed to their dark side. There was seedy promise in the nightlife. They did less of the hands-on work. They managed and they watched. Soon they had clubs along the *costas* and they paused. To consolidate.

Chapter 14

The homecoming meal of late 1918 never took place. Gentle John came west by train, travelling the breadth of the land from Folkestone to Pembrokeshire via a London clad in bunting still but beginning to balance the joy at the war being over at last against the cost of it all. He noticed how the capital was without railings, removed to be melted down and serve the war effort. He knew it could surely not have been, but what if he had been killing with urban adornments, recast as an 18-pounder? He wondered if his exhausted guns would return the favour – be made molten and re-forged as decoration in the weary city. He imagined not. He left and headed for the isolated tip of Wales, passing towns whose parks were still packed with temporary buildings. There were hospitals everywhere. Makeshift barracks. Huts as post offices. How it had all started. He stayed overnight in Swansea, having arrived too late there to catch the last connection to Haverfordwest. Swansea, where it had all started: from garden man to man of letters, to man at arms, one no more ludicrous than the others.

The next morning, he was up early and on the first train west. He had written to Megan from France, a letter of condolence with a short note appended, telling her the date of his departure. He had not followed up with a telegram with more precise details of his return. Telegrams came with a shudder, he knew. He would find a way home somehow. He was still in uniform – still officially in the army – with no civilian clothes to his name. What he had worn to Swansea nearly three years earlier had gone the way of so many things. Lost. They were from a time now in the past. He doubted he would fit into them anyway, being slim, he supposed it would be called. He thought he might be merely reduced. Big men make better targets, they had been told at the front. It might have been a rule of thumb in the trenches, but he had never been too sure about it from his firing position, being a purveyor of death by shells that cared not for human size or shape, and that were much more effective in the killing process than even a machine gun. If he had dwelt on such things in the countdown to the end of the war, it was with the same numbness that had crept through him during the many bleaker months of 1917. These were the days of doubt, that had preceded the turn of the German Spring Offensive into the final one hundred days, and in them he had lost feeling, as if he had been breathing ether. Mustard gas for the Germans; anaesthetic for himself – and in double doses since he found out about Now Then. *Nawr Te* Junior, as gone as the clothes they had worn to Swansea. But the closer he was to home, the more acutely he sensed the return of feeling. He wasn't so numb after all. *Nawr Te*'s death and the return to see his family at Tallis Hall were activating a terrible grief.

He had not known surprise for ages. Shock, yes, that was turning agonisingly into this sorrow. But not a little jolt, triggered by the unexpected. He was nevertheless taken aback on seeing Daniel waiting for him in the horse and trap outside Haverfordwest station. He couldn't help it when Now Then's youngest brother, no longer the runt but a strapping young man that would have been ready for action had the war not ended, jumped down and stood before him. 'Sir…'

'No more "sir",' said Gentle John. 'Ever.' And he embraced his servant and felt the tears pour down his cheeks and into the rough wool of Daniel's thickest gardening jumper.

'How did you know?' he asked as they made their way back to Tallis Hall, his kitbag that contained almost nothing – and certainly not his working uniform, stained by gun oil and mud and thrown on a fire before he had boarded the ship at Boulogne – tossed into the back of the trap.

'We sort of worked it out, Mam and me, from your letter,' replied Daniel. 'Well, we guessed, I suppose. And not very well, at that.' He held up his hand holding the reins to indicate the horse. 'Seiclops is exhausted. He's been going back and forth for three days now.'

'What? You've been going to the station…?'

'To be honest, there's not much else to do. The garden is frozen over…'

'Now Then told me what you've been doing…'

It was the first mention of Daniel's brother and they both fell silent.

'I can't help thinking,' said Daniel after a minute, 'that if Gabriel and I had gone, then the third brother would have been sent home. To work the land. He could have been saved.'

'You were too young.'

'I could have lied. It would have been easy. And Gabriel should have…' Daniel could not continue.

'He was spared,' said Gentle John.

'He doesn't deserve to be lucky. If anybody deserved good fortune it was *Nawr Te*… I should have gone.'

'You were spared, too. And the important thing now is to make it count for something.' The trap's wheels crunched through an icy puddle in the lane. The air temperature had risen above freezing, but nothing at the bottom of the banks, untouched by the thin sun, had begun to melt.

'Aren't you cold?' asked John, deep in his great coat, looking at Daniel in his jersey.

'I'll warm soon enough when we're home. There's a bonfire on the go. Look.' From the depths of the lane they could see little of what lay ahead, but a thin plume of smoke rose in the distance above the hedgerow.

'And how is it at home? How's your mother?'

'It's a sad place. And she's sad. The Hall has been like it for years, but Mam kept a corner of it warm. And now she's… she's broken by this.'

They rounded a long corner at the end of a shallow incline and they could see over the top of the hedgerow. The sea lay slate-grey in the far distance. The roof of Tallis Hall, of even darker slate, came into view, almost the same colour as the sky.

'It may snow,' said Daniel.

John said nothing until they turned through the gates of the estate. It looked as if they had not been shut since he had been away. The driveway was rutted and pot-holed. 'And my mother?' he asked quietly, looking straight ahead.

'Mam sees her… and I think Gabriel may have seen her. But I haven't seen her for ages. She stays upstairs…'

They pulled into the courtyard between the walled garden and the house. Nobody came to greet them. John looked at the back of the house and then made for the doorway built into the scooped wall of the garden. He looked across the expanse of Now Then's monument. It looked even bigger now that the soil, last seen as a mound, like a small waste tip at a coalmine, had been spread and divided up into beds. Nothing had been touched since the news of Now Then's death and the runner beans hung, blackened and limp, against their supports of hazel. In general, though, everything elsewhere was neat and tidy, the brown of the topsoil lightened by its coating of frost, a cluster of Brussels sprouts a rare patch of green.

Gabriel was standing by the bonfire of dried stalks supplemented by logs from the store. He was warming his hands and made no move to go to John or Daniel. Instead they went to him and John held out his cold hand and shook Gabriel's warm one. John and Daniel then rubbed their hands in the heat, watching the smoke rise vertically into the still air.

'I'll leave you to it,' said John after half a minute. 'We'll speak later.'

'Welcome home,' muttered Gabriel as John turned and headed for the house.

Upstairs or downstairs? He headed for the kitchen and found Megan sitting by the range. She struggled out of it as she saw him.

'Master John,' she said. 'You shouldn't be down here.' She looked shrunken. 'I've had a fire laid in the front room for days. I'll light it. In an hour, it'll be...'

'Stay here,' said John. 'And come here.' And he pulled her into his arms and held her tight as she shook.

'You're thin,' she said at last, and broke from his embrace to look at him at arm's length. 'And pale.'

'So are you,' he said.

She pulled a handkerchief from the sleeve of her cardigan and wiped her eyes and her nose. 'How silly,' she said. She looked at him again. 'I've heard so little,' she said, folding the handkerchief in her fingers and then screwing it into a tight ball. 'Can you talk?' she asked. 'I've heard there are many that can't when they come home.'

John nodded. 'Give me a minute,' he said and raised his eyes towards the upstairs. 'Is she...?'

It was Megan's turn to nod.

'I'd better...'

'I'll make tea. Unless you're hungry now... I can prepare something soon enough.'

'Just tea. Thank you,' said John. 'I don't imagine I shall be long.' He turned to go.

'She's... she's...' said Megan to his back.

'I'm sure she is,' said John, heading for the stairs.

'So, not a postman after all,' said his mother's voice from the shadows of her bedroom.

'No, not a postman. Not for long.'

'But you were.'

'For a time.'

'All those letters you must have seen. And not one for your mother.'

'Letters go both ways.'

'How would I ever have known where to find you?'

'You'd have found a way. If you'd wanted to.'

'A gunner, then.'

'You knew.'

'Of course, I knew. A gunner who stayed away. I take it they gave you leave? You chose not to come home.'

'No.'

'Not once.' She moved a hand on the chair and in the gloom, he saw fingers tap against its end, thin bones against worn material. 'Gideon came home.'

'Now Then had a reason to. A welcome.' Gentle John couldn't then believe his ears. A sound like a stifled sneeze with a whimper came from the chair. His mother was laughing.

'You've changed,' she said.

'Perhaps,' he said. 'Have you?'

This time there was no sound from Lady Phyllis. 'Open the curtains,' she said eventually.

The heavy curtains were already a quarter open on one side. He pulled them fully apart. He turned to see his mother holding up a hand against the grey light that hardly flooded her room. 'This room needs air,' he said.

'One thing at a time,' said his mother, lowering her hand. 'Yes, you have changed.'

This time it was Gentle John who gave a short laugh. 'And you haven't. Living in the dark has... preserved you.'

'And how would you know how I have been living?'

'Of course, I knew.'

'Touché.' She placed her hands on the ends of the chair's arms and pulled herself more upright. He thought she might be about to stand. He thought for a moment she might approach him, but she relaxed her grip and remained in a stiffer sitting position. 'What are your plans?'

'Already?'

'You must have a notion of what you are to do.'

'I am home. Will that not do for the moment?'

'The gunner who came home at last.' He saw her face tighten and knew the barb would come next. 'The light has returned.'

'No,' he said, 'you haven't changed. Perhaps it is your acid that has preserved you.'

'Acid…' she said. 'Acid does not preserve. It corrodes. So, think on this: your home, but Gideon – who returned when he could on leave – has not now… come home. What corrosion follows hereafter?'

She eased herself back into her chair. He was dismissed, but instead of walking away he went over to the chair and looked down on her. He leant down and she turned her head to accept the kiss, but at the same time kept moving so that his lips made only the most fleeting contact with her surprisingly warm cheek.

Chapter 15

'Of course,' said Make. 'Let's call it an advance.' He opened the safe in the wall of the back-office at the Bulldog and then turned his head towards Corinthia. 'What'll tide you over?' He looked at the pile of Austrian euros, no longer crumpled but in a carefully counted and pressed pile. Minus a bit of commission – the fee for the theft – they came to a couple of grand. 'A thousand now and if you're still short in a month or two, the same again? Would that help?'

Kaja had not been able to help with a loan. She had steadily worked her way through most of her own wad of savings during the fortnight of readjustment to Mallorca. They were back on local prices and the rent for the apartments was too reasonable for any complaints about the shortage of hot water to be strident, but without any incoming cash, stocks of euros were running low. It hadn't mattered because soon they would all be back at work. Business as usual. Except it wasn't and the early reassurances from the manager had turned into growing concerns among his charges that there was now a disregard for what Mr Coslett would have called 'proper standards'. Cheap and cheerful was now mean and menacing. Word soon spread that this end of Magaluf, earmarked as it might well have been for redevelopment into something far more auspicious than a Brit-themed pub and a pair of strip clubs, was in freefall. It had never been a desirable destination but now the Bulldog was a magnet for undesirables. Kaja at the Naughty Naughty was being constantly mauled and insulted. Men predominated in her audience but there were plenty of women too, and they were the most provocative in their insults, deliberately goading the dancers and the watchers, stirring the juices of sweat and drink. Joe had been transferred to the Big Blue, manning the doors on the other side, where it was even more obvious that nobody in charge gave a damn any more. If the punters could pay their way, they could have their way. Joe was no angel, but things were getting out of hand. There was something about the gear they were selling that was very iffy, he told Kaja. Girls were falling unconscious over their drinks; boys were spewing everywhere, or fighting. And then puking again. Sweat, alcohol and vomit. The place was a cesspit. Joe and Kaja were rebuilding their bag of euros, planning an exit. They could not help Corinthia.

'Thank you,' said Corinthia to Mankev, who apparently could. 'That'll help no end.'

'A bummer,' he said, his back turned. 'To be burgled like that in broad daylight.' He counted out a pile of crisp new euros and at the last moment replaced a couple of new twenties with more tired notes, that looked as if they had once been crumpled and thrown. Screwed up in the Alps, unfolded in the Med. The wonder of the single currency, thought Mankev. You unscrew them and you press them back into service. Euros were euros. He doubted she would ever notice. They would be spent in no time, without a glance, without a care for their provenance, but he considered it a neat touch, a clue, should she ever have the wit to wonder.

He held out the notes that Corinthia took without looking and certainly without counting. He smiled. 'Of course,' he said, sitting on an old swivel chair behind the desk, whose top was scratched and stained by countless cups, 'we'll have to discuss repayment terms.' He surprised Corinthia by leaning back and putting his feet up on the desktop. He eased his heels out of the deck shoes, to let in a little air. 'Blisters,' he said.

'What, like interest?' asked Corinthia after a pause. 'How much?'

'Nothing you can't afford, don't worry. No, it's not so much a question of how much... more of how? As in, how you earn your money with us.'

Corinthia nodded slowly. 'Like, take you up on your job offer.'

'That would be an option, certainly.'

'And what are my other options?'

'Well, I'm sure you'd find a job somewhere else without too much bother.'

'I meant here.'

'Well, let me rephrase it. These are the options for you: keep the money and work; give the money back and leave.'

'Why can't I keep doing what I'm doing?'

'That is not an option. That job...' and Mankev waved his hand in the air and softly snapped his fingers, '... vanished.'

Corinthia said nothing. She held the notes and, without looking, abstractedly ran a thumb across their edges. She did it again, feeling the slight change in the movement at the point of insertion of the old notes, sensing the tiny air pockets between euros that were not silky smooth from the cash machine, but used and greasy. She should listen to Kaja and leave. Walk away. She had a whole history of leaving at short notice. Magaluf was nothing to her, a name sent once as a clue, that had led to nothing. She looked Mankev in the eye.

'OK,' she said. 'I'll do it.'

On the mainland of Spain, long before Ian and she – but principally he – bought the Bulldog and adjoining clubs in Magaluf, Donna found the Namelesses. They were working as divers in Puerto Banús – not in the tourist trade but in the business of security. A different kind of security. Not like their manager's, but Mankev Plus. The Namelesses were retained by a whole raft of owners of superyachts to check the harbours and docking berths for anything untoward underwater. Because they were professional to the last drop of sea water on their wet suits, they repeated their operations scrupulously, even though they could have sat on the waterfront and ticked the form that guaranteed to the incoming Russian or American or Saudi or Chinese that such-and-such an inspection had been carried out and this or that sector of the port had been scanned and blah, blah, blah, the water beneath the keels was safe. They could have but they didn't. They were fully aware that they were part – a small part – of the show of wealth. They were employed to be discreet but they were also employed to be on display. Part of the scene; important to be seen. So, they propelled themselves by flipper under the hulls of the floating palaces and shook themselves off on the dockside. They were unimpeachably reliable and if they had ever answered any·question – which they simply would never have done – about job satisfaction, they would have declared themselves bored out of their minds.

Donna was doing her own little recce of Puerto Banús, having been offered an option on a bar there. She wouldn't be taking it up. This was all a little sanitised and overpriced. Donna and Ian needed rock and roll, not some oligarch sending the heavies round because his mistress couldn't sleep for all the noise. Her mind was made up in a very short space of time, but they were enjoying the stroll, happy enough to mingle in the parade of admirers before the beautiful young things sunning themselves on their decks. Ian, she had no doubt, was thinking terrible things. She in her turn was drawn to the two men hanging up their wetsuits. They were obviously part of the circus but they were clearly apart from it. She watched them and they saw her. Obviously not a yacht owner; patently not here just for the gawking.

She came back on her own the next day and they watched each other again. And on the third day, she offered them a job – or at least, to begin with, a sideline. She also gave them names, happy to play along with their reluctance – their refusal – to provide details about themselves.

'I get it,' she said, 'the whole thing.' They were to be her anonymous helpers. As club owners on the *costas*, Donna and Ian were coming across certain escalating difficulties. Their managers could resolve most day-to-day issues and there were always bouncers on hand if resolution required a dose of heavy-handedness, be it a rowdy clubber or a local official pressing for a larger kickback. There was, however, the more serious matter of being able to fend off the emissaries – quite possibly from the very yachts before them – that came with a false smile and real menace and an offer to protect the clubs. Donna needed a little protection from protection.

'The Namelesses who need names,' she said. 'I'll call you Anon and you're the Mouse. I'm Donna.'

Corinthia danced with Kaja at the Big Blue, a reworking of their old act in the Austrian cage, except that this time they took off what few clothes they wore at the beginning of their routine. The first time of shedding the last item hardly registered. There was no gasp from the floor. Perhaps a drunken cheer came from a group of first-timers to the club, but the surrounding noise and the music were so loud and the visual experience so common that being another naked dancer was completely unremarkable.

Kaja was even less engaged with their work. She took a little blue pill half an hour before their first turn of the night and sank into a daze, sufficiently alert to writhe, but vacant of expression. On Corinthia's inaugural night, she offered her a pill too, but her dance partner declined.

'Jesus, Kaja,' she said, 'if I'm on the road to damnation, let's take it one step at a time, eh?'

'They're not the ones they sell at the door,' Kaja said. 'These are the private supply. They're safe.'

'It's not that,' said Corinthia.

'Then what? Are you ready for what it's like up there?'

'It's just… look, it doesn't matter… just not for the moment, all right.'

Kaja shrugged and put the pill in her mouth, throwing her head back and swallowing without water. And it became their routine. Together, but in their differently induced states of detachment, they took to their stage. Corinthia, stone-cold sober and Kaja, floating and empty – both feeling nothing.

It was Kev who had the idea to make the unremarkable remarkable. There was a peak time at the Big Blue, around 1:30 in the morning, when the club was at its loudest and most throbbing. The dance music to which the drinkers nodded their heads and swayed and to which the dancers stripped was the same across the bars and clubs of the resort – of the island, and across mainland Europe. The continent as one thumped to the same sound. One night, a fortnight after Corinthia's first turn, Kev changed the routine. Instead of drowning the din of the club at its busiest with Euro-music at its most pulsating, he turned everything off. Silence in the speakers induced silence in the crowd. Suddenly aware that they were shouting to be heard against nothing, men and women as one shut up, too. It would not last. In fact, the protest was already welling in their throats when Ravel's *Bolero* began to play. It was nothing new. In fact, Kev had chosen it because everybody would know it. But it was different. All the other dancers slid away, leaving Corinthia and Kaja alone on the catwalk leading to the raised dais in the middle of the club.

The protest at silence turned to a gathering mutter of discontent at this classical intrusion. The music was still loud, however, and its insistence kept the crowd at bay. And then the dancers began to move, and seventeen minutes later, on the last note, fell naked together to the floor, to the sound of drunken rapture all around.

Bolero night became *Bolero* nights. Word spread that in the clapped-out end of town there was something worth seeing and the revellers came in their droves for the 01:30 happening. Mankev could start to charge money at the door and Joe was busier than ever, taking cash not only for the drugs that he now dispensed wholesale, but also as the revenue from the hottest tickets in town. The money rolled in. Other clubs soon began to put on specials of their own and classical music for a time in the early hours replaced Magaluf's electronic bass pulse. Free drinks were offered in bars elsewhere, a late-night happy hour to keep the trade locked into the centre of town. Nothing could stop the haemorrhage after the stroke of one o'clock towards *Bolero* at the Big Blue.

None of the extra money came the way of Kaja and Corinthia. Their working day – their night – consisted of their seventeen minutes on stage. They did not have to dance at any other time. They did not have to suffer the intrusions that other dancers faced. Mankev had feared at first that the reverence with which the dance was greeted would not last, only to have to put extra security in place as soon as it was clear the routine was pulling in customers from all over town. The supplementary bouncers were soon removed from view. The respect endured. During *Bolero*, nobody from the audience went near them. *Bolero* had an exclusion zone around it. *Bolero* was out of bounds.

'You're free to do whatever you like twenty-three-and-three-quarter hours out of twenty-four,' said Mankev as he turned down their request for more money, 'No brek 'n vac, no mopping the toilets… and you come asking for more money. Quite frankly, girls, I am, to put it mildly, disappointed.'

'We see the money you're making out of us,' said Kaja.

'They're coming to this dump from all over town,' said Corinthia. 'Because of us.'

'It's only fair…' said Kaja.

'To get a little more,' said her partner.

'I'll tell you what's fair,' said the manager to Kaja. 'It's fair enough for your employers to expect you to turn up for work not looking like you've swallowed an ICI chemical works. I see what you're taking, don't think I don't. And I see what it's doing to you. Your little dream sequence up there. You're out of it. How long can you go on, spaced out like that? And you want more money? So you can take more of your little blue space pills? Well, here's your welfare officer speaking. You clean up your act and I'll think about paying you some more money.'

'Clean up our act…' said Kaja. 'We're strippers, for Christ's sake.'

'Exactly,' said Mankev. 'What did you think you'd turned into? The Bolshoi Ballet?' Kaja was about to say more but he put his hand up. 'And as for you,' he said to Corinthia, 'sure, I can give you more money. As much as you want. Let's call it the second part of the loan.'

'The loan?' said Corinthia. 'I've more than paid you back that grand. One *Bolero* and you've got it back.'

'There's the interest.'

'I knew it… I knew it… How much?'

'Until I say.'

'Screw you,' said Corinthia.

Mankev smiled. 'Screw me? You know what *Bolero* is? Ravel said he'd written this piece that he thought would work… seventeen minutes of it - but he also said there wasn't any music in it. No development of the theme, no intricacy, no playfulness… it's about a flamenco dancer who gets up on the table and drives men wild. But not this man. Screw me for more money? Screw you.'

'We'll leave then,' said Kaja.

The smile stayed on Mankev's face. 'Oh, you could. You're hot property, sure. But my advice would be… well, I really recommend that you don't do that. Now, why don't you go and enjoy the free time we give you?'

That night, he opened the strictly private video-link to the mainland. It wasn't the ideal time, thought Mankev, what with the whiff of rebellion in the air. Or perhaps that made it the perfect moment. Bolshy *Bolero*. Bolshoi *Bolero*, after all. The owners would appreciate it. Donna and Ian. This would be their foretaste. The nutters' foreplay. Mankev was sure his masterpiece would bring them to Magaluf for a live show.

Two days later, Kaja and Corinthia were at Cala Falcó. It was mid-morning and they had the beach bar to themselves.

'I'll tell you something,' whispered Kaja.

'Why are you whispering?' said Corinthia.

'Because you know what? I think that little bastard Mankev can hear everything I say. See us wherever we go.'

'That'll be the drugs,' said Corinthia.

'What are you talking about?'

'The paranoia.'

'Shut up, Welsh woman.'

'You're doing a lot, you know. He's a twat, but he was right there.'

'Twat. It's better than bastard for Mankev, is it?'

'I reckon.'

'And what is he to you? The money. He is your banker.'

'Well, it's true he lent me some money.'

'And you can call your banker a twat?'

'Or I can just call him a banker.'

'What?'

'A right banker. Doesn't matter. Twat will do.'

'But seriously… he was right. I'm in a mess. Look what we're doing. *Bolero*, it's shit. This life is shit.'

'Let's do the season and then we can go. Wherever we like.'

'Sure, but…' Kaja swirled the cubes in her iced coffee. 'You know, there's talk about us.'

'What d'you mean, 'talk'?'

'Why aren't the other girls mad at us? We're the "special ones" …but they don't want to do *Bolero*.'

'Well, the money's no better.'

'But Mankev said it. We only work quarter of an hour. No, there's something else. What does "grooming" mean?'

'Being got ready for something… bad.'

'"Mares being groomed". That's what I heard.'

'Like I said, that'll be the drugs.'

'No, not drugs, Corinthia. Listen,' and Kaja dropped her voice to a whisper again. 'I'm telling you because you may need to know… We're getting out. Joe and me. He's been keeping back cash. Loads of it. They're making so much at the door they don't even notice. We're going.'

'Are you sure, Kaja? You heard what he said. And he put on his best scary voice too. Shit, Kaja…'

'As he said: 'Exactly'. We're strippers. This is shit, Corinthia. I'm going to die if I don't get out of here.'

'When?'

'When Joe says. When he has enough. When he has a plan.'

Chapter 16

Gentle John told Megan as much as he knew about Now Then's time in France and Belgium and about his end, but it was in truth very little. He needed to fill in the gaps, to give a grieving mother as much detail of a son's life cut short. Megan betrayed such a yearning for knowledge only to him, sensing in Gabriel and Daniel mixed emotions about the war: guilt and relief in the second son; frustration and resignation in the third. Gabriel had never had any desire to go anywhere and now settled without resistance – to say that he happily accepted his lot would have been an exaggeration – for a life without exposure to questions. What did you do in the war? I lay low. And to avoid saying so, he determined to stay lower.

Daniel sensed a chance lost to see somewhere beyond Little England. He was conscious that as a Welsh-speaker in the southern sector of Pembrokeshire, he was a little out of line, if only by a matter of yards, but that did not strike him as a claim to be a person of interest. The war had ended and with it the chance of a life elsewhere. Would he ever have opted for change? Would he have marched off at eighteen, never to return, had the war not ended? He wished he had been put to the test. He had no choice now. There were worse places, he told himself, but how would he know? On what grounds did he base his assumption that he should be grateful to exist in such a place as *Sir Benfro Saesneg*? English Pembrokeshire. The only grounds he knew now – the only runes to read – told him he would be going nowhere. He could not leave his brother or his mother. He was stuck.

Gentle John tracked down the one person that might help paint a picture of Now Then's wartime life. Harry Williams had returned to Talgarth and quickly resumed a working life of sorts on the sheep farm two miles out of town and a further quarter of a mile up the mountain. He was back on his feet but walking with a limp, one of his calves calf shrivelled and scarred. He doubted he would ever have the strength in this leg to walk the slopes above and tend the flock, but there were plenty of other chores to do on the farm, and its owners, the Morgan family, were pleased to see him back – with only one piece missing – and were prepared to be patient. As long as there was lamb on the table, Harry was welcome to stay.

Thirteen weeks into his convalescence, he received a letter from John Tallis-Brown. The Morgans encouraged him to go west to see the family of Now Then Jones, at the invitation of the artillery officer Harry had briefly met – and whose offer to cover Harry's train travel was much appreciated. The Morgans would be as accommodating as they could be – Harry could stay indefinitely here in Talgarth and it would undoubtedly do him no harm to go and offer succour there in Pembrokeshire – but times ahead looked tough on the land and every penny saved counted for something, it couldn't be denied.

It wasn't an easy journey and Harry was jostled at the station and in the streets of Swansea, where he had to kill time before his connection. He was wrapped in his greatcoat, although the spring weather in the deep lanes between Haverfordwest and Tallis Hall was a good two degrees warmer than on the hill farm. He didn't know what to expect at journey's end, but he was surprised to find the master of the house waiting in the trap outside the station. By the time he had had tea in front of the range with John and been introduced to Megan and made plans to tell all around the large kitchen table over supper, he wasn't so surprised to see Gentle John excuse himself to go and check on work outside. There was seemingly no end to the master's denial of his position in the house.

Under orders from Megan to rest his calf, that both ached and stung, Harry had gone only in the late afternoon into the walled garden, built by – and so dear to – Now Then. He watched John and Daniel at work there, their sleeves rolled up, a team of two on the raised beds. The master was making drills for seeds and Daniel came behind him, sowing parsnips. Wooden trays filled with bean shoots lay under frames whose panes of glass, once destined for the grander greenhouses never built, were pulled aside to let the young plants taste the air. Boxes of seed potatoes were stacked against a wall, where there was already blossom on a south-facing peach tree. Asparagus, planted years before, now pushed their tips towards the sun, offering the hint of a first crop.

Gabriel had been redeployed to the greater estate, to mind a small herd of Herefords. He was old enough to remember the brief stay of the Friesians, when Sir Gordon had been alive, but knew nothing of Lady Phyllis's distaste for the pre-war project. He was not aware that they represented a change of heart. All he knew was that minding her beasts suited him better than working in the garden.

Strangely enough, Harry found Gabriel the easiest to talk to. He wanted to know about cattle because the Morgans, too, were talking of diversifying into beef. Gabriel, relieved in the main to be away from the presence of Gentle John, but glad of some sort of company, was the only one reluctant to talk about the war. The subject was on hold until its moment came at the kitchen table, but it was obvious that everybody bar Gabriel was eager to know more. Gabriel was happy to talk about anything other than the damned war. He was hardly a chatterbox at the best of times, but he opened up to Harry on the matter of winter feed giving way to grass and about increasing the size of the herd and its meat yield, and Harry replied with his observations on the contrasts between the farms. What he was seeing here was lowland work, toil on the flat to which he would have to adapt. He had always been more a general labourer than a shepherd on the Morgans' farm in Breconshire, but he had always worked at an angle, with one foot higher than the other. His chatter helped pass the hours.

Megan cooked the meal that she had not cooked when Gentle John came home. Winter had turned to the first spring of peacetime and it was not as hard to put food on the table, and she was not as grief-stricken. She was achingly sad but not overwhelmed any more. She had rolled up her sleeves and now she was putting a leg of pork in cider into the oven and setting the table for five, the size of her family once, with master John and Harry replacing the two Now Thens in her life.

'Make it for six,' said a voice in the passage between the kitchen and the stairs. Megan stopped in her tracks, at the same moment as the men came into the kitchen. They too froze when they saw Lady Phyllis. 'Come, come,' she said. 'Don't look so startled. Do you think I can't find my way around my own house?'

She picked at her slice of pork and she pushed her potatoes and parsnips around the plate, but she listened. And she watched. This stranger in her home; young Daniel spellbound by his every word; Gabriel trying to listen but thinking more of the bottle of claret that Megan had opened for John and Harry – and half a glass for Her Ladyship. She watched her own son as he listened, attentive but not enraptured like Daniel. Gentle John kept his distance, as if he had been too close to all that Harry was describing. Except that he hadn't been so very close, her son the gunner. Not close enough to hear the enemy talk, to see their heads. Her son, the merchant of death from afar. Lady Fierce knew all about the war and she knew she was being absolutely, unforgivably and malevolently wrong about her one surviving child. She knew full well that the artillery on whichever side was specifically targeted by that on the other, and that casualty rates among field gun detachments were high, from the start of the war to the end. She knew all that, but he was the living embodiment of detachment, of living at a distance and she had nothing but contempt for this mirror of herself.

'I followed events as best I could,' she said as her first interjection, over a pudding of apple tart and thick cream. 'And Gideon told me, when he was here on leave – after training school and before his return to the front – that he would be expected to keep a record.'

'That was my job,' said Harry.

'And would you have it?'

Harry looked at Megan. It was not the sort of logbook a mother might wish to see. 'If you have it…' she said, and he pulled the battered notebook from his back pocket.

Daniel couldn't resist reaching out for it. He held the filled pages between finger and thumb. '*Iesu…*'

'Dear Lord,' said Megan.

'This one… right here,' said Daniel. 'This must be his first. Tell us all about it.

'I… I can't remember them all,' said Harry, looking again at Megan.

'But the first one,' said Daniel.

'Dan, *bach…*' said Megan.

'I should like to hear,' said Lady Phyliis.

And so, Harry began to go through the kills. And it seemed he did remember them all. And he soon lost his coyness, because at about a dozen stories in, he began to chuckle as he described the circumstances of each incident, or framed the scene through a tunnel made with his hands, as if he were looking through Now Then's sight. He told of the wounded put out of their fading misery, or the healthy deliberately wounded – not killed – so that others might hear their rising pain and despair. He re-shot Now Then's victims: the advancing, the retreating, the stationary, the hidden, the standing, the crawling, the scared, the petrified. Each target was a tale for Harry to tell. Daniel urged him to say more and Lady Fierce and Gabriel listened to every word.

'Dear Lord…' repeated Megan and rose to clear the table. Gentle John helped her and saw her wipe away the tears. 'Dear, dear Lord above… what did they make you all do?'

When Harry was finished, Daniel still thirsted for more. 'Was it like that for you, John?' he asked. Lady Fierce visibly winced at the familiarity. Her intake of breath and the slightest tightening of her already-rigid self silenced the table.

'No, Daniel,' said Gentle John eventually. 'It wasn't like that at all.'

'But you can tell us.'

'Not now.'

'But one day…'

'One day, perhaps… but not now.' It was said so quietly that Lady Fierce missed the last part. She was about to tut her irritation at being mumbled at when John raised his voice and said: 'Today is Harry's day. So, thank you for coming, Harry. A toast…'

'Wait,' said Lady Fierce tapping her glass. Megan poured until she was ordered to stop with a flick of a finger. And a further flick ordered her to pour a glass for Gabriel.

'To Harry,' said Gentle John.

'To Harry,' said the table, except Lady Fierce, who, incapable of being so informal with the servant class – even after descending the stairs to their world – merely raised her glass to her lips.

'And to *Nawr Te*,' said Gentle John, and this time his mother did take a sip.

Harry left early the next morning in the trap driven by Dan. Having spoken so much the night before, the former observer was quiet and the clip-clop of Seiclops was all he could hear until Dan started to hum.

'What's that tune?' he asked.

'"Steady My Hand, Oh Lord",' said Dan.

'He'd sing it… you know, as he prepared. It soothed him. "Steady My Hand Oh Lord" …'

'"That I might smite thy foe…" You speak Welsh then, Harry.'

'He taught me – only a bit. All part of that steadying of his hand… "two hundred paces", I'd say. "One-fifty yards…" He'd never miss. "Three hundred… "That was a long shot. "Light wind from the left… "Bang. "Dai iawn, *Nawr Te*," I'd say.'

Harry left and never returned. He went back to his farm above Talgarth and coughed and spluttered for a week. The Morgans wondered if the trip had been good for him after all. He was soon up and about on his one-and-a-half legs, however, and did not have a day of ill health until the one on which he died. He worked for the Morgans of his time and the next generation, a general handyman best kept off the upper slopes. He preferred life in the shed, mending machinery and doing general chores. The Morgans laughed at him for being the only man in the county who pegged washing on the line. He did it for Anne, the local girl he married. They had two children and lived what they all called 'a good life'. He died in 1938 of pneumonia brought on when he went out into a blizzard to dig out a dozen ewes buried in snow. *'Da iawn, Nawr Te'* were his last words.

Gentle John wondered if it might have been lurking in Harry's greatcoat. More likely, it had been picked up in the jostling crowds of Swansea. Whatever the means by which it arrived at Tallis Hall, it hit the kitchen hard three days after the guest left to resume his life in Talgarth, the third and last wave of

Spanish Flu in early 1919 made it all the way to Pembrokeshire. A wave that almost reached the sea. It knocked Gabriel down and put him in bed for five days. And with her defences possibly weakened by knowing the details of her son's war and by the re-opening of grief at its most acute, Megan went down with it too. Three days later she died.

Chapter 17

Corinthia and Kaja were back at Cala Falcó a few days after Kaja revealed her plans to escape. Life had gone on, split into its seventeen minutes of work and the long hours of waiting. They had been unsmiling days, but it appeared that the more they approached their routine with sullen defiance, the better it went down. Their haughty indifference was the bait. As for the rest of her nights and days, Kaja waited badly, fidgeting and pacing and craving. The temptress on her dais was falling apart off-stage. Stripped of her make-up, she was bruised black and red around her eyes by stress and fatigue and chemicals.

'*Pero, chica, qué te pasa?*' asked one of the local mothers, unfolding the pushchair she had carried over the ten metres of sand between the only road to the inlet's beach and its only bar. She shook her head and held Kaja's face in her hands and turned her to face the group of other mothers. She rattled off her concern and, having inspected Kaja from their chairs, they all gave a burst of agreement. The mother patted Kaja on the cheek and went to join the others. Their conversation was animated but restrained, full of chuckling, with an occasional outburst of laughter. Their children took to the sand and the only raised voices were to warn them not to climb too high on the rocks or to stop them squabbling at the water's edge. It was a typical morning at Cala Falcó.

A taxi came down the hill from the direction of Magaluf and pulled up on the edge of the sand. Most cars that stopped tended to edge into the shade of the pines, but this vehicle rolled to a halt in full sunshine. What was also unusual was that instead of a paying customer alighting, the driver's door opened and a figure slid out, moved quickly into the shaded parking area and got into a blue Seat that eased away and up the steep road, leaving Cala Falcó in the other direction.

The mothers glanced at the taxi and ignored it. Kaja and Corinthia were barely aware that it was there. For twenty minutes, it sat in the sun and then a Belgian couple from the boutique hotel – almost the first place outside the greater Magaluf conglomeration that wasn't down-market and British – had to go around it on their way from their exclusive accommodation to the quiet beach, the very two things that had attracted them to Cala Falcó and persuaded them to take the risk of holidaying so close to the neighbouring town and all that made it so notorious. As they walked around the taxi they noticed that there was somebody in the back. Perhaps they sensed that to be there in the heat would not be at all comfortable, and they paused to look more closely. And when they saw what was inside, the woman stepped back sharply. More cautiously, her partner opened the door. And he too stepped back, because Joe spilled out. Joe the giant bouncer, afraid of no one; Joe, Kaja's lover and planner of their escape from Magaluf. He had been leaning against the door of the taxi and now he fell on his side into the dirty sand, with his feet still in the car. His hands were bound behind his back with what looked to the Belgians suspiciously like a woman's thong, stretched so tight that it was biting into the victim's wrists. The features of Joe's face were distorted, his eyes had disappeared beneath grotesque swellings, his nose was flattened and his lips were split. They knew he was still alive, because as he landed he gave a grunt as air left him and a groan as he tried to breathe in, expanding his chest against fractured ribs. It was even harder to breathe because his nose was blocked with blood and into his mouth had been stuffed a fistful of small-denomination euros. The Belgian man, not without having to fight back his revulsion, inserted a finger into Joe's mouth and freed the crumpled notes, whose every crease was smeared with saliva and blood.

The Belgian woman had cried out when Joe fell to the ground. Her sound made everyone on the beach turn her way and soon there was a crowd around the taxis. The mothers took one look and recoiled, clutching at their children to stop them from going any closer. There was a horrified jabber. As they stepped back it opened up a bit more space around Joe, a gap filled by Kaja, who fell to her knees and pulled Joe's feet from the car. Corinthia felt a strange detachment as she knelt down too and felt for a pulse. She then tried to undo the knots on the thong. Trying to be gentle at first, she couldn't even get a grip on the knot with her fingers. She lowered her head and used her teeth, eventually freeing Joe's hands. He groaned as blood surged back into his hands.

Kaja had raised his head and placed it on her legs as she knelt in the sand. She began to cry, tears from her black-ringed and reddened eyes rolling down her cheeks. Her nose ran and she wiped her mouth with the back of her hand, covered in sand and dirt. She watched Corinthia finish the job of releasing Joe's hands and they stopped for a moment, the one's face smeared with mucus and blood and dirt, the other's coated in sweat, with a stripper's thong in her shaking hands. Everybody had stopped talking. Corinthia looked up at the crowd around them, at the faces of the families she knew. They looked back in silence, no longer seeing foreign friends with whom they had laughed on their beach, but a couple of whores and a pulped black man, all part of the great sewer over the hill, a leakage of filth into their home.

Mankev was very understanding. The clubs had an arrangement with the clinic in the next street. The doctors appreciated the income generated by a flow of intoxicated tourists, as long as it remained controllable, and they supplemented this late-night treatment of the tourists with regular check-ups for sexually transmitted diseases among the workers. They had never seen anything like Joe, though, and did not have the facilities for a long stay or the orthopaedic expertise the patient required. His left arm and right leg would need to be pinned and they thought he would have to undergo reconstructive surgery to his face. Mankev gave the go-ahead for Joe's transfer to the Son Espases Hospital in Palma.

'You can go with him,' he told Kaja. 'Just as long as you're back to dance tonight.'

'Please...' said Kaja. 'I can't.'

'Oh, but you can,' said Mankev. 'Oh, but you must. The show, as they say...' He stopped himself. He was turning into a cliché. *Bolero* turned and turned in his head. It was driving him mad. He stood and went to the safe. May as well go the whole hog, he thought, and complete the cliché. Play the part of the boss with a soul, the crook with a conscience. Four, five, six... he counted out the 50-euro notes, drummed his fingers and put two back. Let's not overdo it. 'There,' he said. 'You asked for more. Think of this as a loyalty bonus. But remember – be there tonight.'

'I can't.'

'Let's not start repeating ourselves, shall we? Repetition can be so dull. We wouldn't want to see anybody else get hurt, would we?' Kaja looked at him through her dulled eyes. 'Would we...?' said Mankev. Christ, he was repeating himself. Come on, you dumb Estonian bitch: get it. She nodded and reached out for the money. He pushed it across the desktop but kept his hand firmly on it. 'This is not for your little pick-me-ups.' She kept her head lowered. 'Right?' She nodded again, a tiny motion, a ripple of lank blond hair on her shoulders. 'This is to get yourself sorted. For tonight.' The hair moved again.

'I get it,' said Kaja.

'Good. Now run along. There's a good girl.' There's a good girl. He couldn't believe he'd just said it.

They picked Corinthia up at the town beach. Mankev knew where she'd be. So much spying on her paid off. The CCTV cameras at work. Following her. Her dirty little stalker. Mankev knew his girls and he knew Corinthia in particular. He'd sent for the two Namelesses again, the owners' security consultants. He'd had to 'consult' them before and had to admire them for their efficiency, but Mankev felt a call to them was always an admission of failure on his part. It meant that he had not been able to manage a situation. Kevin the non-manager.

He guessed they had to be ex-special forces, but knew they would not tell him. He had once thought of following them to find out more but since they were experts at that very sort of thing, he suspected that he would have been easily rumbled and he was absolutely sure that to be on their wrong side would be unwise. The point was, he supposed, that they were here again. For a second time. That counted as two failures. The second time he had requested back-up – it was his NYPD touch – had been more routine. He had told head office on the mainland that he would like the Namelesses to run a sweep before the arrival of the owners. It was a standard request. The owners liked a little ceremony, and the pre-check by the Namelesses was part of their ritual. A little ostentatious, Mankev thought. A little presidential, but that was their style and who was Kevin Hughes to question it? He should be grateful to be in their employ. And he was. But he could have done without having to make the first and more urgent request. The Joe thing. The Joe episode. A point had had to be made. He knew and accepted that. But why the excess? Make the point. Joe would get it. Mankev wouldn't have believed how pointedly it had been made, had he not seen it with his own eyes. Big

Joe taken down by just the one, the Mouse. Felled with such nonchalance, while Anon stood casually by, and then savaged. A point emphatically and repeatedly made. And made not just for Joe to understand – to within a whisker of his life being extinguished – but for Mankev too, he feared. Anon, the bystander, had made a point of his own – of looking more at the manager than at the victim of the punishment beating. He, Mankev, was meant to manage such matters and avoid the likes of this.

Mankev could have expressed his indignation at being inculpated, his outright fear that his head too might somehow end up being bounced back and forth, but he knew the circumstances precluded a defence of his good name. His reputation did not matter. Better to suck it up, as he had learnt to say. The owners were on their way. Hadn't that been his mission? Did he have doubts now? He had to weigh it all up. He couldn't be anything other than thrilled that they had been drawn his way, and by the *Bolero* no less, his very own creation and quite the talk of, if not the entire collection of Spain's *costas*, then certainly of his stretch of the Mallorcan coast. And because they were coming, the Namelesses were back too, requested by him out of respect, a little extra insurance. To make sure everything was just so. He didn't want his site, however condemned to demolition it might be – the sacrifice in the owners' grand plans – to be deemed unruly. Smoothness of operation was most important even in the roughest environment. To be deemed a liability... well, it didn't bear thinking about the consequences. Joe still bled in his dreams. So, Mankev had summoned – no, he had politely asked for – the Namelesses. For a routine sweep, that was all. But of course, there was nothing they didn't know. And knowing that they knew took the buzz out of the management process.

'Miss Corinthia?' said Anon Nameless. She turned her head and saw two medium-sized men standing on the sand. They were dressed as locals, the only people who came to the beach at this time of day. At night, they dressed as tourists and sometimes behaved like tourists, except they were never drunk. Corinthia turned her head. 'If you wouldn't mind, Mr Hughes would like to see you.'

'I'm not due in yet. And who are you, anyway?'

'He says it's just a quick word. If you'd be so kind,' said the Mouse.

'Like I said, who are you?'

'Please,' said Anon, extending his arm to usher her off the beach.

'Are you the ones who did Joe over? Are you?'

'Please, Miss Corinthia.'

'Don't call me Miss.' But she went with them back to the Bulldog.

'I want you to convey a message to your dance partner,' said Mankev. He had manned up. He was a manned-up manager. The Namelesses weren't the only security experts that could exude menace. Mankev, the menace-exuding manager. He was back on form.

'Tell her yourself,' said Corinthia.

'Oh, I have… but you see, I want to convey it to you, too. I sense a certain hostility. A slight breakdown in communication… we are, it seems, a little light on trust…'

'Get on with, will you? Whatever it is…'

'Why? Are you in a rush? No? So, we can pause for thought. Ponder our working relationship.' He picked up a metal bottle, the sort carried by mountain climbers and slightly larger than the plastic water containers favoured by cyclists. 'Put it to what we might call the acid test.'

'What are you on about?'

Mankev swirled the bottle. 'You have to be careful about storing sulphuric acid,' he said. 'Twice the weight of water, you know, in its concentrated form. Eats into just about everything except carbon steel. One small splash and… hiss, you've got a mess. Just a few drops – goodness, how did they escape? – and your face is… well, it's not going to be doing too many *Boleros*.' He reached for the screw-top and Corinthia took a step back. Mankev kept his hand on the top and they both stared at it. 'There,' he said. 'As I said, no rush. Just something to think about. That's the message.'

Corinthia walked slowly backwards towards the office door, not taking her eyes off the bottle in Mankev's hand.

'Oh, and another thing,' he said. 'Nearly slipped my mind. It's the very reason I want the message to be… taken to heart. Why you two have got to be good, on top form, on best behaviour…'

'Best behaviour? We're strippers, for Christ's sake…'

'That's more like it,' he said. 'A little defiance in small doses – all part of the act.' He pointed the bottle at Corinthia. 'It's what sets you apart. As long as it's contained, held in check… why are you smirking?'

'I'm waiting for the third… It's the way you do things: in threes. Say it once, say it again and then a third time. It's the old Welsh windbag in you.'

'As I say, defiance contained is no bad thing, even to be encouraged…' He stopped himself in time.

'What's the one more thing?' said Corinthia.

'The owners are coming. Soon. So, I'll say this once and once only. Be good. Because this really is the acid test for you.'

Corinthia left the room and Mankev undid the screwtop and took a long pull on the still and chilled water. Melodrama was such thirsty work.

There began a waiting game at the Big Blue. When would they arrive, these owners? How long would Kaja's state of acceptance last? She was on improved behaviour, was less glazed of eye, less floating out at sea, less adrift, but at the same time she was hardly swimming strongly. Mankev would have settled for anything akin to gracefulness, but she was more like something in the last stages of floundering before going under. She would make it to shore only by being washed up there. A stranded stripper simply would not do. To have the stranded alongside the sullen, Corinthia's adopted mood, might not work, might disturb the dynamic, upset the chemistry of Mankev's *oeuvre*. It might not survive its unveiling before his employers and what a waste of time and effort that would be, and what a hindrance to his prospects of seeing his potential realised when the dumps on the Strip were razed and rebuilt as a playground to a different class of visitor.

Corinthia danced the nights away, the senses that had been reawakened by the very real incident with Joe – plus the follow-up insinuations and the imminence of the owners' arrival – growing more dulled with each night that passed without an appearance by them. It was a royal visit that looked increasingly like a figment of the manager's imagination. Corinthia lapsed into indifference at the same rate as the season grew towards its summer climax and *Bolero* continued to pull the punters towards the Big Blue.

Every night was a steaming night, but this one night was particularly hot. It seemed that any day soon the clouds would well up and, overloaded with vapour, burst over the island, but for the moment the night sky remained clear and the air sat heavy on Magaluf. The battered air-conditioning units rattled away but body heat within the club overwhelmed the thin trickle of cool current. Even before they began to sway to the opening bars, Kaja and Corinthia were glistening with perspiration. It was all part of the act.

Never had there been so many faces surrounding them on all sides. Only their narrow catwalk to the backstage area of the club was not packed with onlookers. So many faces, absorbed by every move the two dancers made. There were people who had come back for more – couples even – using *Bolero* as a stimulant. There were the first-timers, doubtful that this could possibly be as unmissable as its billing through word of mouth across the town promised. By the end, they wore the same expression of rapt concentration, and before their lust could give way to the embarrassment of being titillated in public, their mouths opened to roar their approval. Not all could raise their arms, so tight were they all pressed against each other – all part of the process of overheating and stimulating – but those that could clapped their hands above their heads. The entire sea of faces had the wide circle of open-mouthed approval.

Corinthia saw only a faceless mass. Circles of mouths within circles of heads. She rose from her prone position – from her downfall – with her chest heaving from the exertion of the past seventeen minutes and her ears ringing to the eruption of sound. Unabashed in her nakedness, she swept both hands up her forehead and back through her hair, to keep the sweat from her eyes. A shower of perspiration flew into the fetid air. Unmoved by anything she could see, she reached for Kaja's hand so that they might salute the faceless together. And as they arched their backs, ready to raise their arms, she saw him, a circle with no inner circle, a familiar face with a mouth held shut. Daniel Post Jones.

Kaja was thrown off balance when Corinthia did not move the hand held in hers, and she stumbled forward. Mankev in his office, watching on his laptop screen the output of the club's two internal CCTV cameras, immediately spotted the loss of co-ordination. He heard through the doors that separated him from the show the change from approval to alarm as the nearest onlookers thought Kaja might fall into their midst. He leaned forward in his seat and ignored her. He watched Corinthia. Instead of maintaining her poise and completing the show with a disdainful exit down the catwalk, she was frozen on the rostrum, staring into the audience. And then she dropped Kaja's hand and tried to cover her nakedness before turning and running off the stage.

Mankev remotely turned the cameras towards the crowd, but there was just a crush of people, turning their heads, oblivious to the moment, away from the central dais and looking for an exit of their own, seeking air that had to be fresher and less charged. Mankev's eyes darted from face to face on the screen, and his fingers danced on the keyboards, zooming the cameras in, panning left and right. Nobody stood out. He took out his phone and summoned the Namelesses again.

Chapter 18

All was quiet in the west. Without its source of human warmth, Tallis Hall seemed to go colder on the inside. Daniel kept the range alive in the kitchen, to be able to cook meat and boil or roast the produce from the garden, but for many weeks after Megan's death, it was a thin trickle of smoke from the chimney and he was a reluctant stand-in for his mother over the stove. He accepted the role on the understanding that Lady Phyllis would hire a new cook soon, but she deemed his fare satisfactory and the household continued to eat his lamb broths and mutton stews, and the weeks passed and the seasons changed and nobody new came into the house.

Gabriel worked in the fields from dawn till dusk, alone in the company of his cattle unless Her Ladyship appeared, which she did frequently enough to put a spot of colour permanently back in her cheeks. She would discuss with him which of the beasts were ready for market and she would walk the land talking about hedging and fencing and water and increasing the size of the herd again. She even went to market with him and together they studied the bidders, read their style and knew their limits. She bought a bull, barely raising a finger to bid, but coming away with a prize specimen. She called him Cromwell.

The farm business ran at a tidy little profit, putting money in the bank and before too long, prime beef on Daniel's kitchen table. Even the reluctant chef admitted that the aroma from his oven competed with the scents from his preferred place in the walled garden, now Gentle John's domain. The meat reserved for domestic consumption arrived in the butcher's van, completing its brief circuit of the area, from being livestock in the fields around Tallis Hall to slaughter, hanging and division into sides so weighty that Daniel couldn't raise them on his own from their hooks in the cold store. Gabriel declined to help him, stating that he would concentrate on the cattle while they still had breath. Instead, Gentle John would help with the manhandling of the carcasses and the preparation of the cuts.

It was Lady Phyllis who eventually tackled the issue of the missing ingredient in her house of men. One afternoon, she found herself in what she called her viewing gallery, the empty guest room on the first floor of the north extension to the back of the house. The largest window faced straight out over the walled garden, but if she took two steps back and turned to her left she could look out of a side window and survey the fields where the cattle roamed. And to her right she could look across the back of the house and into her son's room in its corresponding position on the south extension. He tended to keep the side curtain drawn even by day, because he had seen her looking and what he was working on was not ready for inspection. He was writing a personal account of his war, a development of the rough diary he had kept, a memoir interspersed with the clinical observations of an artillery officer. These were technical – a detailed analysis of the wisdom of the gunnery manual, with measurements and drawings assembled to form a critique. At the risk of seeming immodest, he included some of the adaptations he had made in the field – ad hoc and unauthorised at the time, but improvisations that had made him more accurate than the more obedient adherents to the rule of doing it by the book. He had emphasised communication and co-ordination with observers in forward positions and especially in the air, seeing the contribution the Royal Flying Corps could make long before it became standard practice. His memoir included excerpts from his correspondence with the top brass, reports on certain specific actions, including the testimony of his men, but he also transcribed into the work the odd poem he had written and inserted some of the more abstract sketches he had made of the landscape and of his guns at work and rest.

He had looked up from his desk to see his mother reverse into view and stare at him. His writing was deeply personal, strictly for his eyes only, and he felt hers boring into his, even though they were separated by the entire width of the house. She had looked at him for a full minute before turning to look towards Gabriel's fields. He had pulled the curtains and they had remained closed.

On this afternoon, she ignored her son's room, now hidden from inspection. She knew he wasn't there. She could hear the rhythms of his stolid labour outside. Having checked first on the Herefords to the left, she only now turned to face front, into the garden. She surveyed the scene. Daniel was lifting carrots and John was cutting asparagus. They were working without talking but the sound of soil moving and the harvesting of vegetables carried to her room. She saw and heard them laugh when Daniel pulled up a root twice as big as any other and waved it in the air.

'I believe it is time,' she announced five minutes later, her words making them both start. The gliding widow had made her customary entrance, unseen and unheard, into the garden. 'I believe it is time,' she repeated, 'to look ahead.'

Gentle John was caught out on two fronts. He had been made to jump by her arrival and he was thrown by the direction of her thoughts. She had always been a creature of the past, for whom today was of interest only when it became yesterday, but of late she had been confounding predictability. He had imagined that a life without Megan would drive his mother back into isolation, back into the airless shadows of her room, but quite to the contrary, it seemed to have reactivated her. She had begun to move again, through her interest in Gabriel's cattle and quite possibly, it seemed, through Gabriel himself. Incidentally, thought the last of the Tallis-Brown offspring, what an unlikely first port of call the second Jones son was on any voyage of recovery, and especially hers. Gentle John sighed. Second this, last that – what did any of it matter? Except it was evident that a connection had been made and, if that were the case, then anything was possible and he, her only son, shouldn't be so very surprised by anything else she did. And who was he anyway to be confused by past, present and future? He, her ignored son, head down in his writing, delving into a past that nobody cared to remember, assembling his recollections that nobody should ever wish to see, closed within his four walls? Who was he to have a view from within his shelter, his four-walled hiding place?

It was nevertheless just a bit disconcerting to find the figure of his mother in the place where he felt safest, within the walls that Daniel and he had built. On the other hand – and heaven knew, Gentle John irritated himself by constantly weighing up more than one side in any debate inside his head – he really shouldn't be caught out by finding her here, in her late husband's second folly. Sir Gordon's cattle and bricks, as once recounted by Megan fondly – with only a trace of teasing as she used to retrieve memories of times when Her Ladyship hadn't been quite so withdrawn – had after all arrived together. Lady Fierce had been disdainful of the livestock back then, but the new herd of Herefords were of significant interest to her now. Perhaps the second element could work too, cows and bricks in restorative harmony. She might roll her black sleeves up and prod the soil. Perhaps, but in all truth Gentle John was thoroughly disconcerted because he remained absolute in his belief that whatever else had remobilised his mother, he would not be included. And yet, here she was, in her black and floating on air in his space and emitting a phrase he would have sworn she had never used before. If his ears hadn't deceived him she had just said, 'Look ahead'. And there was more. 'Yes,' she said. 'It is time to find you a wife.'

They travelled to London together. None of the absurdity of it was lost on Gentle John. Lady Fierce and he, a stand-in for Gabriel, were going off to market, to buy not a cow for the fields, but a wife for the house. What would they look like, the widow from Wales and her son in his mid-twenties, heading for town? What would they do there? Present themselves at court, some grotesque replica of the mother-daughter double act of the debutante world? John Tallis-Brown, coming out.

He accepted the challenge of being taken under escort to the wife market because it coincided with an invitation, via the publishers to whom he had sent the first four chapters of his memoir, to the War Office. It seemed his analysis of gunnery protocols had sparked an interest. Or hit a nerve. Perhaps he was guilty of treason. Perhaps his questions – his divergence from the manual – were regarded as an act of sabotage. The tone of the note did not seem to suggest he was about to be hanged, drawn and quartered at Tyburn and he was more intrigued than fearful – at least, of the military test ahead – when he set out with his mother for London.

They sat in silence in their first-class carriage most of the way, Lady Phyllis facing the front and staring at the passing countryside, Gentle John with his head down, sometimes dozing, more often too agitated to sleep because of the urge to bring out his manuscript and carry on writing. He couldn't with his mother there. To have it so close to her seemed strange. How easily she rattled him. On the other hand – as always, he couldn't stop the other side from presenting itself – her presence here meant that she couldn't be plotting elsewhere. She couldn't be planning a failed medical, or going through Megan's great ring of keys to find the one that unlocked his bedroom. It was perhaps better to have her here, as his chaperone. He cleared his throat to quell a chuckle. But what was he doing here, going along with whatever her plans were for him – presumably something to do with him propagating more than just parsnip seeds? He had always thought she regarded him as the end of the line, the buffer on the track that would put a halt to any more Tallis-Browns, but here she was, on the hunt for a wife. And women like his mother did not make such plans without accepting the possibility of procreation. Cromwell, her bull, had made her something of an expert in the field of insemination. Could Pembroke John live up to Hereford Cromwell?

He looked up briefly, unable to keep the smile off his face. They were pulling into Reading. Not long to go. She raised an eyebrow. 'I was just musing on you… as a farmer,' he said.

'And your musing… amused you.'

'So it seems.'

'I have been thinking of you lately,' retorted his mother.

'Again, so it would seem. Since we find ourselves here on this… adventure, I take it I must have been in your thoughts at some stage.'

'I may have been wrong about your heart,' said Lady Phyllis, looking him not in the eye, but at Berkshire outside. 'It appears yours is the exception. As in its operational efficiency.'

'Well, that may be something… a small mercy…'

'Don't be impertinent, John. The Tallis valve has been a grave issue… and please don't construe my choice of word as an attempt at humour…'

'You are truly changed of late,' said John. 'If I'm not mistaken, that was an attempt… more than an attempt. A bit macabre, but…'

'As I say, John – don't be impertinent.' She twitched.

'You're smiling,' he said.

159

'I most certainly am not. I am merely on the brink of a second admission of fault.'

'Goodness.'

'About your heart. You have one.'

'At the risk of repeating myself, so it would seem. And as you said, it appears to work.'

'I don't mean its physical properties. I have conceded on that point already. You are a Brown in the matter of a steady beat. No, I mean heart, as in to have courage. I have underestimated your qualities. The war… I have never asked about it. Your war…'

'I'm not sure…'

'Of course…'

They did not speak until the train was slowing on the approaches to Paddington Station.

'I'm not sure I can talk about it yet,' said John. 'But I am writing about it…'

'I know,' said his mother.

'But how…?'

'Do you think I do not know what goes on in my own house?'

'You haven't…'

'Read it? No, I haven't. But one day I should like to.'

'One day, but…'

'Of course.' She was smiling again.

John was not. 'Mother, do we know what we are doing here?'

'It's a long time since you called me that.'

'But do we? Do you?'

'I was rather hoping you might take charge. As for my purpose, I have come merely out of curiosity to see Smithfield Market. As you may have noticed, meat is my salvation. Other matters of the flesh, I leave entirely to you.'

She kept to her word and left him to his own devices. There was no presentation at court, no gathering of the eligible, no dance cards to be marked. He was just a minor aristocrat, one that chose not even to use his title, in the London of 1924, a city never fully to recover from the Great War, but brighter of spirit than at any time he had known it. He went to the War Office and found the contents of his manuscript spread over a large table, in front of two colonels and a brigadier.

'We had to run a check on you, Tallis-Brown,' said the first colonel. 'You appear to have slipped through our net somewhat…'

'This,' said the brigadier, indicating the military pages of the manuscript, that seemed to have been set apart from the more abstract elements, 'is not without interest…'

'Pure sedition, of course,' said the last colonel, but with an exaggerated gruffness that suggested they were more tickled by it than outraged.

'And then there was this…' said the brigadier.

'In damned French, of course…'

'No, not without interest, Tallis-Brown.'

'We just wanted to express the gratitude of His Majesty's armed forces.'

'Better late than never, what.'

'So, on behalf of… belatedly…'

'Do get on with it, Plummer…'

'As I was about to say, we thank you.'

The two others nodded curtly. Gentle John had been invited to sit down and he now sensed he had been dismissed. He stood and rather awkwardly saluted.

'No need for that,' said the second colonel.

'And of course,' said the brigadier, 'this cannot be published. Not yet. A nation in recovery and all that. Exposure of certain inadequacies… well, it won't do.'

'The more… the more artistic elements of course are of a less sensitive nature,' said the first colonel. 'You are free to do with them as you will.'

'I rather saw them as an ensemble,' said Gentle John, choosing his French with care. 'I felt they might complement each other...'

'We rather see them as a potential embarrassment and would take a dim view...' said the second.

'As we say,' interrupted the brigadier, 'we should rather you didn't put them in the public domain quite yet.'

'The greater good and all that.'

'That will be all.'

With his literary project on hold, John went without gentleness to his publishers, ready to give them a piece of his mind. He was soothingly told that there was something of an obligation among publishing houses to turn over material of a sensitive nature to the authorities. There were several works similarly affected and – how could they put this? – by more established writers than yourself, sir. Everything would be returned, uncensored, and it would be shipped back to the author. They were sorry, but they, too, saw its miscellany as its worth and if the military observations were not allowed to sit alongside the artistic interpretations, then they would have to await the day when they could. Resubmission when such a relaxation came would be welcomed.

The dogged side of Gentle John supposed there were publishers that were not so compliant and that he should persevere. His more docile side accepted the situation and in a strange mood of deflation and vexation he returned to the company of his mother, who was having, it appeared, altogether more success in her dealings.

'Harold, this is my son, John,' she said in the tea-room of their hotel in Bloomsbury. The presentation by Lady Phyllis of this Harold by his first name made Gentle John think that his mother had been on something a little stronger than tea. 'John, this is Mr Harold Taylor.' They shook hands. 'I am in Herefords and Harold is in refrigeration,' continued his mother. 'And we have been getting along warmly.'

They dined in the hotel that night. Harold Taylor was a self-made man, a meat-supplier to the Black Country. He lived in Walsall and he had cold-storage facilities in Wolverhampton and Dudley and had plans to expand from the heart of England in all directions. The three of them ate early so that the budding business partners, who seemed to be hatching some joint venture at breakneck speed, might reconvene at Smithfield Market before dawn the next morning. And in the evening of that next, long day, they ate at Harold's hotel, this time joined by Olivia, Harold's third daughter and the last woman in the Taylors' Walsall household. Two older daughters, Geraldine and Charlotte, had been married off to prosperous merchants – 'and doing very tidily,' per Harold – and his wife, Imogen, had been lost to malaria, contracted while living in India as a child.

'She had a terrible struggle, did Imogen,' said Harold, now in his fifties and more than happy to change the subject and talk about the conservation of meat by chilling it, or better still, freezing.

'Pretty little thing,' said Lady Phyllis after that first dinner. Gentle John said nothing but was not surprised to find himself having Olivia to himself at dinner the next night.

'I don't think it inappropriate for two adults in these circumstances to be on their own,' said Harold with a wink. 'I'm referring naturally to you and me, Lady Phyllis.' It was with a slightly strained smile that Her Ladyship left the hotel with Harold for a night at the New Theatre to see George Bernard Shaw's *Saint Joan*.

Olivia Taylor had had her father's Black Country lilt educated out of her. She was surprised to find that John, equally neutral of accent, could speak Welsh – surprised and then relieved, because they found that her attempt to wrap her tongue around the language broke the ice at dinner. *'Mae'n bwrw o hyd ym Maenclochog... It rains a lot in Maenclochog,'* reduced her to giggles. *'Gwrthgyferbyniad,'* she had learnt by the end of her fish course of Dover sole, or *'lleden chwithig,'* as she tried. They recognised that they were being set up by their single parents and it provided a second topic of conversation. By the end of their soufflé, they both agreed, to ape a phrase used by the person whose nickname she already knew – Lady Fierce – that despite being brought together through refrigeration, they had been 'getting along warmly.'

Gentle John returned to Pembrokeshire without a book deal but with an advance on Olivia. Harold and his daughter were delighted to accept the invitation to Tallis Hall, ostensibly for the man of meat to run his eye over the estate's herd. In reality, the four parties knew exactly what was going to happen. Good men were in short supply and an eligible aristocrat was a bonus for the Taylors. Gentle John liked Olivia. Lady Fierce, satisfied that her matchmaking was heading painlessly towards the couple's engagement, was able to put a space even frostier than the most frozen carcasses in the Taylors' storage between herself and Harold, who seemed to have been working on the assumption that she was as much up for sale as her son. The presumptuous parvenu and his hopes were dashed as soon and as resolutely as Olivia began to make plans for her future with Gentle John, for her life as his Lady Tallis-Brown.

Chapter 19

The Namelesses found Corinthia and Post within minutes, tracking them down to a small patch of scrubland, a gap between the houses where once a bakery had stood before it sagged to the ground in a fire. It was a piece of scorched earth that set the tone for the Strip – the gateway to vice in most people's eyes; ripe for development in Donna and Ian's. Post and Corinthia were standing five or six paces off the congested pavement, still busy with the flow of people heading back into town. She had her hands held out towards him. Anon and the Mouse watched as, almost against his will, he took them. They did not speak.

He had been scouring Magaluf for many long days, starting in the centre of the promenade and working his way outwards. He had seen her many times, disappearing around corners, ducking into a shop, and he had run after her, only to discover that he was chasing a ghost. Several women gave him strange looks as he ran up to them and then halted in disappointment. Here was living proof, they concluded, that Magaluf, as they had been warned, was full of danger. One or two had even reached for their pepper spray, but he had held up his hands and apologised profusely. He thought he would have better luck at night, thinking that she would be visible at work, but he ended up trapped in crowds of drunken youngsters and he could not find her. The more he was caught in a sea of people, the more alone he felt. What had he been thinking? Almost as a last resort he let himself be carried in the flow of revellers heading for the Strip and there he discovered what drew them so far beyond his search zone. He had found her at last.

The last stragglers in the clump of punters from the club passed the scrubland and suddenly their hubbub gave way to relative silence.

'Don't make us do it, Ms Corinthia,' said Anon, pulling out the metal bottle and shaking it.

Corinthia dropped Post's hands and stepped away. 'No, no, it's cool,' she said. 'Please...'

'Who is he?' asked the Mouse, nodding at Post.

'He's an old friend. He's just arrived... look, he's nobody...'

'A nobody. Hardly a ringing endorsement, is it?' said Anon.

'Or an old friend. Seems we may have a divergence here...' said the Mouse.

'Who are you?' asked Post.

'Oh, we're nobody. Isn't that right, Ms Corinthia?'

'Or we're new friends. Something like... but basically, you don't need to know.'

'All you need to know is to stay away. You are a diversion...'

'We have a divergence and a diversion, which is unfortunate, isn't it, Ms Corinthia?'

'This is a time for walking a straight line with single-minded purpose. So, tell him to go,' said the Mouse. 'Or we'll have to show him the door.'

'Please,' said Corinthia, 'let me...' But Anon simply shook the bottle again. Corinthia's shoulder slumped. 'Go,' she said to Post. 'Please go.'

Post looked at the Namelesses and assessed their menace. He stepped back and raised his hands, not high in surrender but as a gesture that he was about to obey, that he posed no threat. He forced his mind to function, to recover from the shock that had reduced his speed of thought to sludge. Not asking for rocket science, he pleaded with himself. Just some basic Welsh.

'*Ydych chi... ti'n eisiau mynd?*' he stammered.

Corinthia stared at him. And then shut her eyes and went back to school *'Ie,'* she said.

'That's enough,' said Anon in a different voice now, stepping forward.

'Ond nid wyf yn gallu,' said Corinthia, allowing Anon to take her by the arm and lead her away.

Post nodded, just before the Mouse doubled him over with a short sharp blow to the solar plexus. 'Don't know what you said, old friend,' he said, kicking Post in the ribs, 'but this is for taking the piss. Now, you be a good nobody and stay away. Got it?' And he kicked Post one last time for good measure.

During their period of consolidation, of maximising the potential of the clubs they already owned on the mainland *costas*, rather than extending their business empire, Donna and Ian had to face the issue of leaving. Not as in their own departure, but that of the country they had left behind and its leaving the European Union. Donna loved the irony of it all, of being an instinctive Leaver, under the lasting influence of the 'Up yours' spirit of the Valley Commandos, and yet being at the same time the most obvious beneficiary of all that a common market offered. She was a Welsh bigot prospering in Spain. She liked the word 'bigot' although she wasn't sure, in her new age of going places and becoming a better Donna, she should be particularly proud of applying it to herself. She was a slimming, trimming Donna of body – two stone down from her peak fighting weight, from having taken to the pool that Ian seemed to have abandoned – and a growing, improving Donna of head. The pair – this double Donna; not Don and 'I' – decided to seek advice, as they so often did, on the internet. Donna did not speak Spanish. She had no need in her club world populated by Brits to go beyond self-improvement in her native tongue. It was the language of the internet and Donna was tempted to think that the debate over

167

Europe was largely irrelevant. She had gone from little Wales to fully global and wondered if there was anything in between to interest her, a Welsh woman of the world.

Just to be sure, she consulted her selection of bloggers and vloggers. She enjoyed the shock jocks of the right and the anguished sisterhood on the left. They all had their views and Donna came to the conclusion that it was probably in her best interests to have no view at all. The old country was leaving. Why should new Donna give a damn? She turned instead to the DfL, her true vlogger of choice, a self-declared born-again son of Wales, who didn't give a damn about anything. He had this easy relationship with the absurd – pipistrelle bats in a national park were his latest source of material – that made Donna chuckle. 'Blind bats are seeing us off. Never have silent creatures been heard so loudly... gas the little bastards.' The ex-Valley Commando liked her pet bigot.

She wasn't so sure any more about her Ian. He was disrespecting his diabetes, taking less exercise and taking fewer precautions with his diet. He said he was bored, which set alarm bells ringing in Donna's head because that usually meant he was on the lookout for gratification. His needs were as excessive as ever, his desires more perverted. Donna knew he was veering towards the plainly illegal and sensed the danger that he now presented. It had cost her a lot of euros to buy the silence of the last pair of girls from the Marbella club. She knew how easy it was to download images on to the internet. One properly organised sting – one secretly filmed session of Ian at his worst – and it would be out there for all to see. Not even the Namelesses at their most persuasive would be able to stop it.

Ian knew he had gone a little far in Marbella and he had to pretend to be penitent. He settled down to the business of expanding into Magaluf. Sodom was calling to him. Sod the lot of 'em. Penitence was his price but he could sense a prize. He was not well, but his downfall would have its benefits. Magaluf. Ian was on his way. He would carry Donna with him, take inspiration from the side of her she could not deny. It was her saving disgrace. Dear Donna. He loved her most of the time but for just a weeny bit of it… well, in those precious moments he saw himself folding her – fold by fold, as it were, because they both had to face it, she was always going to be more bloater than flatfish – into a freezer. Over we go, darling, that's it. Bit uncomfortable? Never mind. Soon have you all tucked up. Donna *pliée*, as the French might say. Plied Donna. Plaid Cymru in the freezer, a slab of Welsh mutton, fingers frozen in the act of trying to claw their way out. Donna's digits, fishy fingers.

And, as he repeatedly stressed to himself, for much more of the time he loved her to bits.

It was with some relief that Donna discovered that Ian's boredom for the moment seemed to be related to a lack of activity on the business front. A deal to occupy him was better than allowing him to dwell on his 'swill', as she named his dark side. Or was it? What was she saying? Dirty Donna was a little weary, too, of the period of consolidation. She, too, was ready to sink. She would decide when the swill would swirl. It was the dialectic of their shared depravity. You self-taught wonder-cow, you. Double Donna's dialectic. His swill, her swill. The swirl of the swill, you two-faced double-Donna. She was well up for some trouble, too. Just don't let on, Devious Donna, especially not to the perv, because the anti-Christ still had some grovelling to do.

'There's this place in Magaluf,' he told her one morning. 'A bar with clubs on each side.'

'Mallorca?' said Donna. 'That means going offshore. Is the timing right?'

'Well, they're on the wrong side of town – and Magaluf isn't exactly salubrious at the best of times. But there's a planning blue tag on the area, apparently. They want to give it a makeover. Put up a hotel with casino… that sort of thing. It may be worth taking out an option.'

Ian moved with a speed that Donna hoped wouldn't turn into recklessness. The sums, she asked him? Had he worked out how many tourists were travelling abroad nowadays? Times were changing, she warned him. Not that she cared. She could make it work. She could sense a fix. As she knew he would, he carried on regardless. It kept his dark side at bay, he told her. Almost sheepishly. As if. The wolf in sheep's clothing. She could feel the heat in him beginning to rise.

He didn't bother with the option. He met Mr Coslett and bought the properties on the Strip outright and they installed Kevin as manager. And all was going well, even if the Namelessess were required to sort out an errant bouncer. All was exceeding expectation. Especially when Mankev opened up the private video link from the Big Blue to their home on the mainland and Ian saw *Bolero* for the first time. Don't-let-on-Donna would have told herself by his reaction that this spelt imminent danger, but she didn't because the leery old Commando found herself as lured to the show in Magaluf as her Sodomite. We're going to Gomorrah tomorrah. Let the swill swirl.

Up went the '*Cerrado*/Closed' sign at the Big Blue. It caused considerable trouble for security, but the performance of *Bolero* that night was strictly private. Two free drinks per person were offered at the Naughty Naughty and the Big Blue's other dancers were transferred for one night only to the club on the other side of the Bulldog. There was an imbalance between the one club, heaving with a restless and overcrowded audience and a double troupe of artistes, and the other, empty except for Donna and Ian, sitting side by side, close together in front of the stage, Corinthia and Kaja off it, awaiting their cue, with Mankev and the Namelesses in the office at the rear. The Mouse leaned over Mankev's shoulder and turned off the screen on his laptop. Jesus, thought the manager, did they have no curiosity?

Kaja was more spaced out than usual. Joe was making slow progress in hospital. She was condemned to doing this seventeen minutes of shit for ever. She had taken an extra little bluey and was barely able to perform. Corinthia was fully alert to the arrangement before her and sensed the peril Kaja was in. She helped her through the act. In doing so, she made herself more the flowing heart of the performance, generous and still haughty, supportive and yet vulnerable. The routine ended and there was silence.

Donna was so turned on she could not speak. She could feel Ian almost shuddering in his excitement, the heat pumping out of him. Corinthia helped Kaja to their feet and even as they turned to walk off, she knew it would not be allowed.

'Stop,' said Ian and reached into his pocket. Is this where it begins, thought Donna? But all he pulled out was his phone. He sent a brief message to the office and Anon soon appeared. Ian pointed at Kaja and ordered with a backhand flick that she be taken away.

'I'll stay,' she said, but Ian repeated the flick and Anon jumped on to the rostrum and pulled her away from Corinthia and down the catwalk. They left the club through the storeroom and side door. The Mouse came into the club and stood in the shadows.

'Dance it again,' said Ian. 'No need to dress.' Donna was repulsed by the look in his eye when he turned to her for approval but she couldn't stop herself from nodding and standing to join

171

him at the edge of the stage. They pressed themselves against the side of the dais, within touching distance of the dancer. Nobody had ever touched before. This would be different. The Mouse moved forward because Corinthia did not move. She looked around for help but there was nobody there. Only these people who were going to do something terrible. If she screamed nobody would hear a thing in the bar and club next door. People there were having fun at full volume. She looked into the unblinking eye of the camera overhead. Mankev had just turned his screen back on, but he was the last person to interfere. He sat and watched. Corinthia felt a trickle down the inside of her leg but it seemed only to make the pair more absorbed in her.

'Please,' she begged of the Mouse, but he leapt effortlessly on to her platform and she felt herself pushed forward. The music began again. 'Please,' she said again. Nobody was listening to her. They were watching her.

The music stopped. Post stepped away from the sound system behind the bar and into the half-light of the floor. He had slipped in when Anon and Kaja left and had worked his way around the back of the club through the shadows while the Mouse shepherded Corinthia into place and while Donna and Ian had eyes for nothing else but their prey. Post was carrying a rucksack, perched high on his shoulders, and was wearing a loose, dark jacket over his shirt, with sleeves so long they covered his hands. He looked anything but a knight in shining armour.

'Oh my God,' said Donna, breaking the silence. 'It's the hunchback of Notre-fucking-Dame.' Tmesis, she thought. Or was it? 'Who the fuck are you?' she shouted. 'For fuck's sake, the Mouse. Sort it.'

He was already on the move, moving back into the shadows and circling the room. When Post saw him, he was only eight feet away and closing in fast. Post seemed to shake and Donna wouldn't have been surprised to see him wet himself, too.

Instead, giant rubber gloves seemed to drop out of the ends of Post's long sleeves, followed by metal rods. As the Mouse moved in, Post reached out and touched him in the chest. There was a spark and the Mouse flew back and landed in a heap on the floor.

Donna was so stunned she didn't move. Mankev in his viewing room didn't move, either. He was not supposed to have his screen on. How was he supposed to know what was happening? He was almost too excited to react but he forced himself to reach for the keyboard and zoomed in on the action. With a roar, Ian rushed at Post. Nothing could beat a man's desire abruptly interrupted as a spur. His face twisted in rage, he hurled himself at Post only to be catapulted back by another prod from whatever the weapon was that Post had protruding from his arms. Ian joined the Mouse in a tangled heap.

Donna then noticed the hesitation. Would this intruder, this walking fucking Taser, attack her? What a quaintly old-fashioned twat. Little did she know that Post was wondering about how many shots he had left. The tractor battery in the rucksack wasn't exactly new and he hadn't had time to check its charge. He had discussed cattle prods with Charles II and in theory he knew it would work, but he had felt something of the zap go out of his weapon when he downed the second man. He knew that this foul-mouthed Welsh woman – Valleys, if he wasn't mistaken – had spotted his hesitation.

Corinthia leapt into action, throwing herself off the stage and, in all her nakedness, wrapping her legs around Donna's back and scratching at her eyes. Donna was sent into a spin and while she was turning blindly, Corinthia jumped off and ran to Post, grabbed his arms and pointed the prod into Donna. 'Fry the cow,' she shouted.

'Stand clear,' said Post.

The last splutter of a charge went into the target and Donna slid to the floor. Post dropped the prods, removed his rucksack and gloves, took off the jacket and wrapped it around Corinthia's shoulders. They ran to the side door, slammed it behind them and disappeared into the night.

Mankev watched as Donna staggered to her feet. He turned the camera to find the Mouse, who was slowly coming to. Ian was still not moving. He watched as Donna knelt down by his side and felt for a pulse. She lowered her head and it covered Mankev's view of Ian's face. She might have been giving him the kiss of life.

Donna looked at Ian, breathing evenly, his eyes shut. He was so much more handsome this way, without that leer, without those thoughts twisting his mind. She had gone far enough with him. Look where it had led. To this, all through lust, hers as well as his. He had saved her and he had polluted her. Well, there was zero-balance for you. Donna Hopkins was self-made better than that. She leant close to his mouth, feeling his breath on her cheek. She moved both hands into place and, knowing full well that her head was obscuring the view of the camera, she tightened her fingers around his nostrils and mouth and waited, leaning her bulk against his chest when he began to contort, for the moment when he breathed no more.

'Shall I call the police?' asked Mankev, walking into the club a few minutes later.

'Don't be a twat,' said Donna. And then she recovered her poise. New Donna took over. 'I take it you have a doctor who's… tame? That can do you a favour…' Mankev nodded. 'Tell him to say that Ian lost a brave fight against diabetes.'

Part 3

Part 5

Chapter 20

There was a brief spell at Tallis Hall when the garden lay untended. Gentle John, his dreams of being published now on ice – his book closed, as it were – stayed in his room. The curtain was still pulled across the side window and Lady Phyllis could not see if he was brooding or making plans. She feared his introspection would always hold sway over any inclination to look ahead. She should know, the black widow, better off in the shadows. Except, she had stirred and it was time he did likewise. Let the light in, boy. She sighed. The possibility that their house might be opened up and restored as a family home seemed as remote as its position on the map, a bleak house on the very edge of the page. He was an infuriating man. What would his wife make of him, of this place?

He did not brood for long. The garden was empty while Daniel was still confined to the kitchen – and that wouldn't last long either. Olivia and Lady Phyllis would hardly allow their family seat to be run so improperly. The post-war state of making do in the house would give way to the efficiency that the matriarch had brought to the farm business on the outside. Gentle John would have to pull himself together soon.

It was the rooks that drew him back to the light afforded by the window overlooking the garden. They came from the copse that grew out of the bottom of the steep-sided hollow five fields away, a dingle on the edge of the estate. The occasional nervous swoop by a single black bird had become an invasion. With a human presence among the beds reduced to Daniel's brief early-morning harvest, the birds had grown in impudence, barely bothering to circle and reconnoitre the feeding ground below before landing heavily in the walkways between the beds and taking their fill. They left so loaded that they could barely clear the walls and wheel away for home.

Gentle John declared war – and he was fully conscious of his choice of words – on them. They became an outlet for the something that gnawed at him, his frustrated literary career, he supposed, although he was hard pressed to define what those ambitions had been in the first place. Perhaps it didn't matter. The landing of the rooks in their squadrons and the raucousness of their caws drew him to the window. He observed their habits and then he moved, exhausting Seiclops on a fast-about trip to the gun shop in Haverfordwest. He could have chosen from the household armoury – there were four Purdeys in the Tallis Hall shotgun cabinet – but he made a concession to the thunder that still shook his dreams and declared this an all but silent war. Death delivered with a phut of compressed air.

With his purchased air-rifle, he needed to hit his targets full in the chest or head. A glancing shot to their side was deflected by the birds' thick wing feathers. It was not lost on him that as he reverted to a life of military precision, he was thinking more of *Nawr Te* the sniper than he was of Olivia the fiancée. It wasn't long before the wily rooks avoided the killing ground where corpses were hung on wire strung along the walls – and what an evocation that was for the former gunner – but while they were in his sights, he found a level of concentration not felt in years. It wasn't lost on him either that he could have cleared the garden of predators merely by going into the enclosed area and resuming work there. Each time he picked up a corpse and added it to the lines of the dead on the walls, he told himself to stay and bend his back over the soil, that enough was enough. He should put down his gun and pick up his spade, but, might he be forgiven, Gentle John was enjoying himself.

When his spree came to an end, he reappeared in what Lady Phyllis could describe only as something approaching good spirits. He set about making the house and its gardens fit for a wedding. He cleared and he weeded and he mowed, and he built a giant bonfire of branches and corvine corpses and fed it for two whole days, a last burst of manual labour before he accepted his place as the overseeing head of a household to be worked by others.

They were married on a beautiful late-summer Pembrokeshire day and held their reception in the grounds of the Hall. Olivia was transformed from Lady Phyllis's 'pretty little thing' into a stunning bride, much admired by the Taylors who outnumbered the Tallis-Browns and the Joneses – all four of them combined – fifteen to one. The Midlanders scattered themselves around the gardens, breathed in the aromas of honeysuckle and mock orange and plied themselves on Tallis Hall's restocked cellar. Gabriel joined them and it took a sharp word from Lady Fierce to keep him away from Georgette, Olivia's cousin, who was not averse to being manhandled in Wales – just not by a drunken herdsman. Gabriel reluctantly let Georgette go and returned to his bottle. When the Taylors congregated at the front entrance to say goodbye to the couple as they boarded the trap bound for the Castle Hotel in Haverfordwest, there was a slight pause while Daniel extricated himself from the arms of his brother, who, without this fraternal support, slumped to his hands and knees in the courtyard between the back of the house and the walled garden. Daniel jumped into the driver's seat and, with the bride and groom tightly packed in the rear seat, Seiclops set off.

'In the annals of love-making,' said Gentle John later that night, 'I fear that may not have merited a chapter of its own.'

'It seems we are starting out together…' said Olivia with a

smile. 'As with all things new, it may take some time.' Olivia had come to the bedroom on her wedding night with a certain nervousness but with a determination that overcame shyness. It had been a surprise to find that her husband in his mid-twenties was much more timorous and totally inexperienced. To have to take the lead was unexpected, but not without its appeal. The question of what to do was still largely for a young woman without a mother to find out for herself, but Olivia knew enough about libido to be sure that she was not lacking in that department. She paused in their bed now and put a hand on John's bare chest. 'I think it is… and please, I am far from implying… I am not judging in any way… I am bound nevertheless to confess that your innocence was unexpected.'

'It seems I may be a man out of his time,' said Gentle John. 'I believe it's plain to see I'm a peaceful fellow… and yet I went to war. And in those years…' He stopped talking and put a halt to the caress of her hand as it travelled south, raising it instead to his lips and kissing it.

'And in those years,' picked up Olivia, 'you did not do what most men in more normal times do. You did not sow your wild oats.'

'Not even when the war was over. I have sown only my parsnip seeds and my asparagus…' They both laughed.

They went to London and stayed in the same hotel where they had first dined. And that night Olivia noted that John was making progress with his tumescence. She worked as best she could on it, almost wantonly by the end, and managed – not without a fleeting image of herself as a milkmaid among the Herefords trying to draw milk from a cow's soft teat – to extract an ejaculation. It left her exhausted and slightly aching of forearm, which struck her as slightly unladylike, but none the less confident that in the city of love where they were bound, she would receive firmer gratification.

They travelled by train to Folkestone and from Boulogne to Paris. Gentle John believed he was ready to revisit the rolling landscape of Picardy, green again of pasture and yellow of cornfield, with saplings in the devastated woods already higher than the lifeless stumps, but there was still enough shell damage in the villages and towns they passed to make him shrink. The slow-moving train passed signposts on the roads to Arras, Amiens, Albert. They crossed the Ancre river. 'A' was for the ache of memory. Would he never move on? 'A' for amour. He roused himself when Amiens was behind them, to tell Olivia a little something of his small place in all that they were passing, but her head was lolling against his shoulder.

They stayed in Paris for six days. They explored the capital on foot, climbing into Montmartre and crossing the river to see Napoleon's tomb at the Hôtel des Invalides. They danced in the Latin quarter and they nodded off at the Opéra together and they strolled the *quais* of the Seine and the corridors of the Louvre and Versailles, tiring themselves out and replenishing themselves with fine food and good wine. Olivia had brought a dowry to the marriage and a certain taste for the high life, that she assured her husband they were well able to afford. She was an extravagant tourist by day and an increasingly restless wife by night, because in their enormous bridal bed in the Hotel Westminster on Rue de la Paix they slept. It was bad enough that he did not approach her physically, but now he withdrew spiritually. It was as if the train had left him on the Somme. He seemed to retreat into some impenetrable depths. Olivia had known these troughs were there, but had hoped that she would be granted access and she would coax away the demons and bring his innate goodness to the surface. She had wanted to believe that what lay beneath would be ardent. It seemed she had misjudged his urges. It seemed she had been very wrong. And never mind what lay within. What hung below remained equally without life. She reprised her role as the coy virgin and when that elicited nothing more than a fond embrace, she pressed him a little harder. She reached for him but he drew away. She tried him drunk after dark and she tried him sober in the most romantic light of day, with the shutters a quarter-opened, that he might gaze upon her in all her immodest, youthful splendour. Nothing.

She waited for her frustration, her vexation, to settle before she spoke to him. She stifled a sigh, she quelled her tuts. She prevented the mockery forming in her mind at the sight of his sagging asparagus from spurting from her mouth. The Olivia that was still resolved to be dutiful knew this was a situation best approached through discussion, however delicate the matter, however embarrassing – shameful, she couldn't stop herself from suggesting – the lack of function. It wasn't exactly a problem shared, being far too one-sided for the responsibility to be evenly distributed, but it was better, she repeated to herself, to acknowledge the 'thing' and find a resolution. She waited and then turned to him, the soothing, understanding wife in the city of love, but he was already asleep, his back to her, his knees tucked up towards his chest.

They returned to Tallis Hall and Olivia felt the walls of her home close around her. She was the young lady of the house, the mistress of this dystopia. She was an English castaway in Little England beyond England, a rose in a land where everything was battered by the wind unless it was sunken below the surface. You could survive here only by being drilled downwards, out of view. She forced herself into the open, walking from Tallis Hall across the fields to the sea – anything that was different, anywhere but the enclosed space into which Gentle John retreated. Gentle John, she now sneered. Her John without genitals.

On the way back from her escapes to the coast, she passed

through the pastures where the Herefords grazed, and she paused to watch Lady Phyllis and Gabriel at work. What an aristocracy she had joined, where the widow in black strode the fields and prodded her beasts, while the master eunuch fussed in his beds up at the house. The only beds where anything happened.

She was watching Gabriel at work one day, isolating a couple of heifers from the herd, when Lady Phyllis came up behind her.

'Dear God,' exclaimed Olivia. 'You made me start.'

'I don't think he's being so very dear to you,' said Lady Fierce.

'Who? John?'

'Or God.'

'Do you think I have been forsaken?' asked Olivia, unable to keep the faint sarcasm out of her voice.

'I am aware that you are being denied… fulfilment.'

'How could you possibly…?'

'How would I not know what goes on – or does not go on – in my own home?' said Lady Phyllis.

'So, you know. But how was I to know?' asked Olivia, her levity giving way to a more plaintive note. An unattractive tone, thought Lady Fierce. How quickly the façade crumbled to reveal an unappealing neediness. On the other hand, at least it also revealed a dependency and a reversion to a pecking order that this pretty but petulant little thing had dared to challenge.

'And more important, what do I do?' asked Olivia. Definitely a little desperate, reduced so quickly to pleading. Lady Fierce was being consulted. It satisfied her.

'I may have made a miscalculation,' she said. Magnanimity – not exactly a bosom pal, but it was time to soften the pout on the young wife's lips. 'I was firmly of the understanding, given the inherited frailties of two deceased children, that John would be no more robust. And yet it seems he has the Brown heart.'

'It is not his heart that is of concern to me…'

'Precisely, my dear. I just wanted to clarify the situation. He has been given a reprieve, but it is in keeping with the destiny of this family, that what is given – perhaps by your dear God – here, is taken away… well, let's say "there".'

Olivia couldn't help but laugh. '"There",' she said. 'Well, that's one way of putting it.'

It was Lady Fierce's turn to make the sound – her strangulation – that passed for a laugh. 'Blessed with a pump, an organ that works, and cursed with another that doesn't.'

'Oh, for a sound pump,' said Olivia and they both laughed so much that Gabriel, thirty yards away, looked up. It was a sound not heard in the Hall for many a month.

Those months slipped by and the two camps became more clearly defined. There was the group that gathered around the herd and there were the gardeners, and somehow a kind of peace grew. Meat and vegetables and fruit were provided for the table and in a time of economic stress across the world it seemed to suffice for the moment. Deep in their isolation, the occupants of Tallis Hall were nourished.

The heatwave of May came as a surprise. Daniel and Gentle John were more accustomed to reinforcing their late-spring produce against the gusts of wind and rain showers, that still came in off the sea and found a way into their haven, than they were to watering parched beds. The sun beat down for a full week and everything shone bright green until the leaves began to droop and the gardeners had to fill their watering cans and keep the drought at bay. And every night while it lasted, Lady Phyllis would stand at her bedroom window and stare out over her son's workplace, thinking her thoughts and giving nothing away, even in total privacy, with only herself for company.

The moon this night was full and bright enough to cast shadows in the walled garden. Lady Fierce stared without expression –

and without starting – as Olivia appeared, coming through the slightly warped door, set in the middle of the scooped wall and that required a little shouldering to open, and walking slowly into the middle of the enclosure. She was wearing her palest long summer skirt and blouse, that both looked white in the moonlight. She was bare-footed and was holding out her left hand behind her, as if beckoning somebody forward. Gabriel appeared and went towards her. She took him by the hand and they kissed. He broke away only to begin to unbutton her blouse. She sat down slowly on the thick board that contained the earth of the central raised bed and leant back, watching as Gabriel watched her. Her breasts came into view and she leant further back, pulling up her skirt and then reaching for the buckle of his heavy leather belt. Lady Phyllis watched without expression as he thrust into her. Olivia raised her legs, entwined them around Gabriel and lay flat, feeling the watered earth against her bare back. She released her arms and placed them on either side in the bed, squeezing her hands tight against the asparagus spears that twisted and broke in her grip, releasing their watery juice. Olivia turned her head, ignoring Gabriel and stared straight up into Lady Phyllis's room. And then into the bedroom she was supposed to share with her husband.

Lady Fierce stepped back, knowing she had been seen. She looked to the side, out of the side window, along the back of the house and into the side window of her son's room. The curtain was not closed. She could see her son. He was looking straight ahead. He turned to face his mother. Or not her, but to accept somebody else. An arm appeared around his neck and Daniel came into view, pressing himself up against Gentle John and undoing the buttons on the master's shirt. John now did stare straight at his mother and then closed his eyes, a look of calm ecstasy on his face.

Chapter 21

The Bulldog stayed open even as the arrangements for Ian's disposal were being made. Donna called it a funeral but the truth was that she just wanted to be rid of him – of it, his corpse – as quickly as possible. It didn't take long. The tame doctor signed the death certificate and 'I' was gone, repatriated at no mean expense for cremation and dispersal. That was more like it, thought Donna – dispersal not disposal. Less cruel. Just as final, she supposed, but that was the point, wasn't it? Filthy Ian reduced to ash and cast to the winds beyond DNA examination. Beyond contamination. The cinders of a certifiably diabetic, a diabolically dirty man.

Donna did not go back to Wales with him. It would have been a complication, with no doubt a family she did not know, there on their rain-lashed posh ridge over Cardiff, tear-filled of eye, and with all their questions about how and why, and all the while with their grabbing hands held out, no better than beggars, for a slice of the business he left behind. Donna was having none of that. She was the surviving partner. It was all hers now, as tightly screwed down as the lid on her 'I' in his casket for the flight home and his final glide into the flames of the crematorium in Thornhill. 'Im in 'is urn and Donna, the sole earner. All hers, including this three-part operation on the Strip of Magaluf. A bar and two flanking clubs, of which she did not approve. They had been 'I's' idea. 'I' for 'is idea. No lapsing now, Donna. Pick up your 'h's', girl, pack your bags and head back to the mainland. Even before she discovered Mankev's mistake, she was of a mind to mothball the Strip. Bollocks to *Bolero*, she

186

found herself humming. Mind your language, Hopkins with an aspirated huh.

Mankev's mistake. He had recorded the output of the cameras. The last *Bolero* in Magaluf was on the record – or at least on a memory stick in his safe – with its own little tragic postscript, the real-life death of Ian. That life and death had really gone together on the stage he managed was not lost on Mankev. He had unwittingly produced – but there now for him, and him alone, to see – his very own snuff movie. Decidedly, he stressed to himself, strictly for his own amusement. But even to dwell on it for a second was all too tempting: two live dancers, one live cattle prod or whatever it was that had electrified the after-dance imbroglio, and one electrocuted dead owner. A live death; real-life and really snuffed. It was too good to delete. But it was purely for his own delectation. The last thing he would ever do would be exploit it for personal gain. He knew the Namelesses and recognised that blackmail would be utter folly. Perish the very thought of it. Except, of course, he had had the very thought. It had sprung into his dreams and pinged him to life every night since. And the memory of it sat on its stick, under a coded name, just another file of accounts within the accounts, safe within the safe. There but not there. To be enjoyed but never used. That would be ridiculous.

Donna ordered the Namelesses to sweep the joint before she shut down the Strip. She was not an islander. She was a mainlander. The Bulldog and its outbuildings were an earner, no question, but they were dirty little businesses. Ian's masterplan to give Magaluf its makeover, with his casino and hotel, had always struck her as fanciful. And way beyond their means, unless he had been thinking, plotting behind her back, of raising capital for the island venture by selling the core businesses on the mainland. She had no reason to believe Ian had been duplicitous, but she liked the word and it suited her to think he had. Everything that had happened to her in this Magaluf den of iniquity merely confirmed that she was better off without it. Without him, too. A new life beckoned, back on the mainland she knew. She gave everyone a month's notice and ordered the Namelesses to give the premises and the books a thorough going-over. She contemplated asking her inquisitors to exert a little pressure on Kaja, to see how much this stripper B knew about the flight of Stripper A, but Anon assured her the distress of the partner on learning that she had been abandoned had to be authentic. Nobody could wail that much without it being real. Anon in the end had given her a simple, single slap and Kaja had fallen back into her junkie's trance. Red-eyed and dead-eyed. It had to be real.

Kaja knew nothing of Post's escape-plan, but she was well aware that her innocence would be difficult to prove. As soon as she knew – on the night itself – that Corinthia had escaped, and before the Namelesses were sent to conduct a search of their own, she went into her friend's room and looked for her stash of money. It was under a floorboard in the wardrobe. Kaja took the bag of cash and carefully put everything else back in place. She was a little surprised not to find a passport in the room. It wasn't the sort of thing they carried to work each day.

The role of hysterical addict, too unappealing for public display, kept Kaja on cleaning duty for the short time the Bulldog remained a going concern. She dried out over her mop and bucket. The only chemical she used was bleach for the toilet bowl. She was clearing her mind, careful to keep herself poor of appearance. It wasn't difficult. Withdrawal pinched her looks and made her grimace. She left before the month was up, walking off the Strip for good, helping Joe out of his hospital bed and leading him slowly away, hobbling down a corridor in a less dramatic breakout. They headed for a new life, clothed, unthreatening and almost entirely tax-paying respectable, as owners of a small restaurant on the colder coast of the Baltic. Donna decided not to give chase.

It didn't take the Namelesses long to find the address on file, the house in the northern suburbs of Cardiff, the place to be contacted in an emergency. Corinthia had written down Park Crescent when she joined Mr Coslett's operation. Post's home was on the radar. Having been through the former owner's quaintly old-fashioned filing system, it took Anon slightly longer to open his safe, but he had cracked bigger and securer repositories than this. The combination lock was beyond him but with a combination of power tool and force he soon had Mankev's secrets deposited on his desktop. And there lay the memory stick, its buried secrets easily disinterred, the manager's passwords easily cracked, the contents of the forbidden recording coming back to life on his screen. Mankev's mistake.

Corinthia left Magaluf under the cover of two hen parties returning to Manchester from Palma Airport. That she was not known to the bride-to-be in either group and that she was not in either of their uniforms didn't seem to matter. Pink T-shirts with 'Katie' on the back, and purple for 'Jaqs does Magaluf' had been compulsory on the outward journey, but such had been the personal devastation across their six days that the rule of being in costume could no longer be applied. The Katie of the first party still wore the remains of a veil, but it was as if it had been used as a kitchen gauze to sieve purée. It was impossible to see the Katie in question behind it, so dense were the remains of a good time in front of her face. And such was the general state of exhaustion among the combined group of twenty that to be head-down and shuffling was the norm. Corinthia, stone-cold sober and fully alert, but with the hair of a peroxide wig hanging in front of her face, sloped away from Magaluf, just another hungover tourist.

Post took the slow route home: a foot passenger on the ferry to Denia on the Spanish mainland; by coach to Valencia; plane to Brussels and to Cardiff by train. He had dressed Corinthia, put cash and the ticket to Manchester in a handbag he bought her, and had brought her food, but they had barely spoken. She had stayed in bed in his mid-price hotel room, curled up in a state of shock, or wide awake, feeling the strangest kind of embarrassment in his company. Post sensed it and left her alone, talking to her only when it was time to put her in a taxi to the airport. So repeated were his reminders to her to keep her wits about her all the way through Departures, he hardly said goodbye.

'Come on, Post,' she said. 'Why would they bother? I'm just another bit of meat to them.'

'They'll bother,' he said. 'It's about loss of face.'

'And why do you bother?' she said. 'I've let you…' She couldn't finish and Post stood, flustered, unable to react. And then he pulled her towards him and hugged her tight. 'You haven't,' he said. 'You haven't.'

'Haven't what?' she whispered in his ear.

'Haven't… whatever it was you were going to say you had.'

She moved her face a fraction of an inch into his neck and kissed him. 'Let you down…'

'You haven't.' He didn't let go until the phone rang. He gently broke away answered it. 'It's the taxi. Oh, I nearly forgot… your passport.' And he pulled open a drawer on the bedside table and took it out.

'How the…?'

'After the night we were talking and were… interrupted, I followed you, And the next day I went in and retrieved this.'

'You sneaky...'

Post nodded. 'I stalked you,' he said.

'And saved me...'

'We're not out of this yet. Look,' said Post, 'I'm going to say it one last time. Keep your eyes open. They'll be after us.'

'Because they lost face.'

'Exactly...'

'You know what they threatened to do to me, don't you?'

'Not... not the details...'

'Talking of losing face... they threatened to throw acid in mine...'

They paused. 'Which is why you take care,' he said. 'Look,' he said, 'I couldn't find a mobile when I went in your room.'

'They took it.'

'Well... can you get one, once you're home?' She nodded.

Post felt in his pockets for a bit of paper. 'I'll jot down my number.'

'Don't bother,' said Corinthia.

'What?' he said, suddenly alarmed.

'Got the same one?' He nodded. 'I remember it,' she said. 'I forgot it, but now I remember it, clear as anything.'

'How could you...?'

'Oh, don't worry about that, Post Jones. I've got your number.' She reached for the bag he'd bought, the only luggage she had to take. 'Never had you down as a stalker, mind...'

It still crossed her mind, once she was disentangled from his hair and out of range of his scent – the musk of Post Jones, who'd have believed it? – and once she was shuffling forward in a line, bewigged and bewildered by the recurring thought that all it would take was a splash of acid to convert the absurdity of all this into a burning, agonising reality, that she would be better off on her own. Go to Manchester and start afresh. Go back into a safer world of shared anonymity without responsibility. Go with a gentler flow than this cascade of nonsense – no, these droplets of face-melting torment.

When she landed in Manchester, however, she caught a shuttle into the centre of the city only for the purpose of buying a new mobile. She banished thoughts of heading anywhere other than south and went to Piccadilly Station to catch a train that connected with another and found herself south of Crewe, bound for Cardiff. And once there, she changed again and went almost to the end of the Coryton line, alighting on Platform 1 in Rhiwbina, walking out past the library and up into Park Crescent, and letting herself into Post's house with the key he had dropped into her bag. And far from going with the flow of a careless squatter, she busied herself around the house. She went down to the familiar parade of shops and stocked up on food – and stocked up on greetings of 'Welcome home, darling' from older but still familiar faces. She thought she might bump into her mother. She even thought about going to Pentre Close, of going... she stopped herself from saying 'home'. She didn't have a home. She went, instead, back to Post's place and started – could she believe it? – to dust. Stop this 'fussing', she said to herself. But she carried on. You're playing home-maker, she warned herself. Nest-building. It was too Spartan and too ordered to require a thorough clean. In fact, she thought, to be a home it needed to be scruffed up a little, but she sprayed the surfaces and polished away and went from room to room, exploring every corner, opening every door and every empty drawer, turning on the hot water, putting down her cleaning cloths, closing the curtains, lying back in a hot bath and relaxing. 'Safely landed,' she texted to the number she knew by heart.

The Mouse did not sit and case the house. He recognised Park Crescent for what it was, a little suburban concrete croissant, empty by day but under constant surveillance – not from CCTV, but through unseen all-seeing eyes behind the lace curtains of the bay windows. Better not to attract their gaze. If the stripper and her knight were here, the curtains of the surrounding houses would already have twitched. There would be talk, chatter in the air. Better not to be part of the gossip. The Mouse cruised the Crescent once and came back later, when the cars were filling the spaces against the kerbs, when routines in the kitchen were taking over from good citizenship at the front window, when it was entirely unremarkable for a weary-looking homeowner to walk up the path and go to the door at the back of the house. What was slightly unusual was that this occupant, having tried the handle, seemed to have forgotten his key. The Mouse bent down to pick the lock.

'On my way,' texted Post two days after Corinthia's return. It meant he was not just at the outset of his journey from one end of the continent to the other, but on the last leg. When she heard the scratch at the back door she almost ran to it and threw it open, but neither rest nor her declining sense of security in a place called home had fully lowered her defences and she stopped at the bottom of the stairs and looked first. Even though the lower half of the back door was of frosted glass with vertical lines, as chosen by Maurice back in the day to replace the original pane he'd cracked with the backswing of his garden hoe, she knew that it was not Post, but one of them. One of her pursuers, a huntsman, a destroyer of faces.

Her phone and her stash from Post were in her bag on the table in the kitchen, into which the back door led. Corinthia calculated time and distance and noise and she reached slowly for the latch of the front door. It closed behind her as the Mouse opened the back door and walked into the kitchen to find only what she had left behind in the kitchen of a silent house.

Anon opened the office door just after Mankev discovered that his secret was now his mistake. A strange calm came over the manager. He weighed up his options and acknowledged that a survival instinct was in play – an urge to run, scream, attack. The best form of defence. Part of him knew it was an act of folly even to try, but what else could he do? He'd only wanted to slip away. The secret was not a threat. He'd never have used it. Let him go. Others had managed it. Why not him? If a manager couldn't manage it, well, it didn't say much for his managerial skills, did it? But he knew he wouldn't make it. The moment he saw the remains of his stuff on his desk he knew his game was up. And here was Anon, soft as you like. Quiet as a coffin-bearer. Should Mankev offer him money? Buy his way out. Guess what? That would be declined – politely even, but most certainly not accepted. So, that was it then. Everything from that moment on was a frank acceptance of reality. Anon moved forward and Mankev knew it was for the kill.

His body floated into Cala Falcó three days later, face down but still an upsetting sight for the children playing on the shore. Their mothers decried it as yet another example of everything that was going wrong on the island of Mallorca. The police found no trace of foul play and concluded that the man had taken his own life, perhaps as a result of the sudden collapse of his business on the outskirts of Magaluf. They had been there to question the staff, but they had all gone and the shutters were down. '*Cerrado*/closed'. The mothers preferred to argue, and did so at length under their shades on the beach, that a line should not so easily be drawn under such a matter. How many more times would they be exposed to yet more leakage of sewage from around the corner, from the devil's playground, into their haven?

Donna returned to her villa on the mainland in time to be nowhere near Mankev when it came to his removal from her employ. She issued a statement, including a quote from herself: that he had been a loyal servant of the company, a manager of great experience and energy. He would be sorely missed by his many colleagues and friends. If anybody said anything like that about her, Donna decided, she would come back and haunt them. Haunt them down like dogs. Widowhood, she had to say, was proving good for her wordplay.

Anon stayed in Magaluf until the Mouse returned and presented his report from Wales. There was little to say. The Mouse had waited in Cardiff, but it was clear the birds had flown. They waited again, for fresh orders. Donna assessed her options. A third death would complete a holy trinity of revenge. Donna of old would have pursued the skinny tart to the ends of the earth in order to have her fill of retribution. Her full fill. A fourth would be her full effin' fill of ful-effing-filment. As it was, new Donna could make do with two. A new life awaited, of singleness and single-mindedness. She sent the Namelesses back to Puerto Banús and settled back by her pool, ready for a life of consolidating, of doing her lengths and becoming a better person.

Part 4

Chapter 22

Tallis Hall emptied quickly. Gentle John and Daniel left for London at first light the next day, in such a rush that as the departing master of the house tried to stuff the pages of his manuscript into a case, they all spilled to the floor. The military addenda – the apparently unpublishable material – were the most scattered. John looked at his strewn work and all the rewritten, reworked lines and considered leaving the whole lot where they were. He was keen to be gone. He sighed and picked up as much as he could in three hasty armfuls. He took one last look at what was left – the diagrams and calculations of an artilleryman in the field – and left them. If these supposedly sensitive sheets had a purpose it would be as nesting material for the mice. Military tittle-tattle for the rodents.

They found digs in Clerkenwell, within walking distance of the Thames and easy reach of St Paul's, Fleet Street and the City. Daniel felt far removed from the capital at its most grandiose and industrious. They took separate but equally damp rooms in a bleak block, part of the Farringdon Road Buildings. They shut the door on the smaller, more odorous room and set up home in the larger, and settled down to do nothing except quietly and without complaint accept that this was most likely to be their lot: poor of means, rich in affection. Gentle John told Daniel that if the worst came to the worst he could always find work at the nearby Mount Pleasant Mail Centre.

'The poshest postie in London,' said Daniel.

If doing little was the stoical plan, it didn't stop Daniel from seeking something that might fill part of his time. He had hours and hours to while away, so much time on hands unaccustomed to being idle. Painstakingly, he began to put the manuscript back together. Not without difficulty, he began to read, sometimes mouthing the words to himself while running an index finger, that still bore the ingrained soil of home, under Gentle John's handwritten lines. Since so much of the technical content had been abandoned, he removed what little else remained.

'I've taken the liberty of removing the last of the gun stuff,' he said, dropping the rebuilt manuscript on the stained table in their room.

'The esoteric detail...'

'The boring bits,' said Daniel.

'So, you're my editor now, are you?'

'I'm your censor. Or I'm doing some weeding...'

'You don't think it needs the gunnery content to offset the more personal view?'

'The soppy bits are good,' said Daniel. 'Really good. You don't need... *cudweed*...'

'Balance...'

'Balance... the war does that. That's the balance against the 'you' in it all. The bloody war. And the poetry. There's that too. It's a... *ategu*...'

'Complement.'

'A complement to the prose. There's so much here that's strong. Why didn't you ever let me see it?'

'I don't know. Perhaps I felt I needed a more detached eye to see it first.'

'So, tell me then, what happened to that plan?'

'I am where you see me.'

'Well, this is what I see – and say. Enough of this detachment. We need to sell you heart and soul.'

'Are you sure?'

'No. But I'm going to give it a shot…'

'You're talking like a gunner already.'

'I'm a simple gardener. I've done some weeding. Now I'm sowing. So, I want a crop… of words. There are some gaps to fill in. One hole in particular. You know exactly what I mean, don't you? Man of secrets, let it out. There's a story to finish. Something to do with the French? It's bad enough trying to think in English, but there's something in French… isn't that right? Something you're not saying… You know exactly what I'm talking about, don't you?'

'Is there a document in French there?'

'Not that I can find.'

'Well, then.'

'But there are references… to something. We don't need the French to explain; we don't need anything but you. Your story. So, get to work, master.'

'Don't call me master.'

'Get to work, slave.'

'Yes, master,' said Gentle John, reaching for the neat – and slimmer – pile of his pages.

Daniel requested a meeting with the publishers who had rejected the work. It was a starting point, even though he fully expected it to lead nowhere. Why should they change their mind? A start and a brick wall at the same time. He had to be prepared for such start-stops in this life they had chosen. Chosen? Had they had a choice? Or were they simply being blown along, so reduced, so repressed by their previous existence that they had been light enough at last to be carried away on the prevailing wind? How much of them was left to be able to make new roots?

Instead of being kept waiting, however, Daniel was shown straight in. A pair of elderly men in starched collars and heavy suits indicated that he might sit.

'Are you Sir John's agent?'

'I'm… I am his representative. His appointed…' Daniel was struggling with the words he had learnt.

'Do you know, Sir John?'

'Very well, sir.'

'Good Lord, man, we've been trying to track him down. Given up the ghost, hadn't we?'

The second publisher grunted. 'Even sent an emissary down to Wales. Came back with his tail between his legs. Said he'd had a "damned frosty reception".'

'Lady Phyllis?'

'Her name was mentioned.'

'May I ask why you sent someone to Pembrokeshire?'

'It seems Sir John has a champion. A Mr David Jones, poet and artist. Most talented, if a little…'

'Idiosyncratic…'

'Exactly. But unquestionably talented and a good judge of talent in others. And it so happened that we showed him Sir John's work… minus the…'

'Sensitive material…'

'Precisely. Minus the sensitive material.'

'The boring bits,' said Daniel.

'Well said, sir.'

'And Mr Jones considers the verse in particular to be of singular merit.'

'On its own?' asked Daniel, 'or as a complement to the prose sections?'

'As both,' both the publishers said.

'And if Sir John could be persuaded to eschew the more military aspects…' resumed the first.

'The esoteric material?' said Daniel.

'Just so,' said the second.

'Then we should like to make him… make yourselves an offer to publish.'

'"Gentle Songs of Fire",' said Daniel.

'Sir John's idea?'

'His gardener's, actually.'

A contract was signed, a small advance made and the book appeared. It sold in sufficient numbers to remain in print. It was said that it exerted an influence – among so many influences – on David Jones's 'In Parenthesis', published years later. 'Gentle Songs of Fire' was never a best-seller, but the royalties allowed Gentle John and Daniel to get by in Clerkenwell. And then, when its success prompted interest in the life of the author, enough to escape for a second time.

They ended up in Marrakech, Morocco, drawn there by tales heard while travelling south through France. They listened to a fellow traveller, talking of the light on the edge of the desert, of the spell of the Atlas Mountains, and the sounds of the souk. When this storyteller left the train in Cahors, his two fellow travellers stayed aboard and kept going, out of France and into Spain, and from there to Morocco. In Marrakech, where they finally stopped, not another word was written – not on the subject of war or the peacefulness into which they now retreated. They returned instead to the soil, joining the project begun by the French artist, Jacques Majorelle, to create a walled garden of seclusion and great beauty. There, they lived and worked, capturing water and treating it with a reverence far removed from what they had often felt about the rain that prevailed in Pembrokeshire. They turned sand into soil and made it fertile, and with such contentment that they never saw what they did as arduous toil. And in the Majorelle garden in Marrakech many years later – and at peace with the world, especially their walled oasis – they died, one after the other in the space of a few days.

Olivia and Gabriel fled to London, too, where they rented a small studio flat in Blackheath. Their passion lasted as long as her full allowance from her father, which was longer than she might have thought. Harold heard nothing from Tallis Hall and assumed that no news spoke of harmony rather than upheaval. In the late autumn and in the hope that he might be invited to Tallis Hall for the festive season, he wrote to Lady Phyllis and asked after the couple.

'Your daughter is no longer here,' came back her reply, almost by return of post. The words were written on an embossed card, above a signature, complete with title, that filled more space than the announcement that shook Harold to his core. He packed immediately and appeared in person at Tallis Hall, the first leg of his journeying between Walsall, Pembrokeshire and London over the ensuing months – the three-sided road map of this love quadrangle, as explained to him with a candour that was as brutal as the welcome he received at Tallis Hall. The speciality of the house: Lady Fierce at her frostiest, treating him with undisguised contempt. She did not invite him into her home, but stood at the front door – he noted she opened it herself – and gave him her eye witness account, allowing no interruption and beginning to close the door as she delivered her conclusion: 'Your daughter is a harlot and my son a degenerate. It might be said they were made for one another. And yet it would appear they are not. Haven't we done well, Mr Taylor? Well, they have made, so to speak, their bed... or not as the case may be. So be it. But I shall have none of it. They are not welcome here. And neither are you.'

Harold retreated straight back to the Midlands, sorely tried by events but unable to deny that if that were the tenor of the house Olivia had briefly inhabited, then he had some sympathy for her. His mixture of vexation and understanding was further confused by a sense of relief – that he had been spared a similar exposure to the chill that emanated from the lady of Tallis Hall. To imagine that he had in his deluded dreams of grandeur flirted with such a creature. To think that he had once contemplated courting the dragon that now reigned with absolute authority over a household shrivelled to just one. Lady Fierce, ruler of upstairs and downstairs, and left with nobody but herself.

Still with no clue as to the whereabouts of his errant daughter and – this was the part that truly wounded the Harold unable to quell his longings for a higher station in life – her cowhand, he went for her in the place he knew better than he would ever know the pathways to the elusive entrée to high society. Her purse. He would draw her out through impecunity. He did it with the pain of a father that loved this youngest of his children. He had some sympathy for her plight – if plight it turned out to be – but it was, when all was said and done, an act of betrayal. She had dishonoured him and her late mother. His Olivia had brought disgrace upon the family, sullied the good name of the Taylors of Walsall, Wolverhampton and Dudley. He stopped her allowance and within days of Olivia being unable to draw on funds, he received a letter from her, begging him not to cut her off, pleading with him to come and hear her side of the story.

Harold went down the side of the triangle from Walsall to London and met her in a restaurant in Dulwich. She was sitting at a table, looking tired. She did not rise to greet her father and he did not stoop to kiss her. She asked after her sisters. He told her they were well, that family life suited them, that they were doing well in society and their husbands were prospering in business.

'Unlike me and mine,' said Olivia.

'Unlike you and yours, most certainly, it would appear,' replied Harold. Olivia picked up her teaspoon and put it down again. She put her hands in her lap under the table and then put them back on the table.

'Do you know… have you heard… where he is?'

'Me? The father of an adulterer, the father-in-law of a…? Should I be the one to know of his whereabouts? He has vanished. And perhaps it would be better if you did the same.'

'That would be easy, wouldn't it? Be rid of the problem.'

'That's exactly what you have made yourself.'

'All my fault. Of course, it is. How could it have been any other way? A husband rendered incapable by the war… and with inclinations that turned him even further away from his wife… It was not easy for me.' Olivia stopped. 'How much do you know?' she asked. 'Have you seen… her? Did she tell you?'

'Lady Phyllis put aside her revulsion and gave me a brief account. I cannot imagine what it took for her to relive the moment. The pair of you… the four of you… the disgrace, the shame you have…'

'She'd have enjoyed every moment, from the witnessing to the recounting…' said Olivia. 'You do not know what they are like. That family. Her. Him. And you. Yes, you, father. You placed me with them. You made it happen. You are partly to blame.'

'How dare you…'

'I dare because I was left there…'

'You listen to me, young lady… you have no right…'

'No right? I had the right to be treated as a wife. That was my right. You don't know what it was like… to be so alone in that house.'

'It's not all about… you were the wife of…'

'I wasn't the wife of an aristocrat. I was a trophy, put up by you and claimed by her… Her Ladyship.'

'You were his wife. You think you are the first woman to be unhappy in a marriage?'

'You married me off to a non-man.'

'It's not all about physical… about intimacy.'

'Oh, it is, father,' said Olivia. And she pushed back her chair and let him see her swollen stomach. 'It is.'

'You're… you're with child…'

'It's a shame such powers of observation deserted you when you were searching for a husband.' Harold could only stare at her bump. Olivia stroked her stomach. 'It was consummated, you know,' she said. 'The non-man did manage, briefly, to… be a husband.'

'Are you saying that it is his?'

'I'm saying that I am with child and that I am still the wife of Sir John Tallis-Brown.'

'Will you go back to him?'

'Ah, if only we knew where he was. And until we do, I shall remain in the care of a faithful servant of the noble house and together we shall sit and pine for his lordship. And pray that he returns safely to both his sanity and his home. In the meantime and in his absence, I shall require the means to live. A mother-to-be… I shall need your support, dear father.'

Once the outrage of the social climber had been eroded, Olivia and Gabriel were able to live on what Harold provided as a generous father. Harold recognised that he had been easily manipulated and, as a widower that had always doted on his last child, disapproved of her cynicism, but he hoped that she had inherited his inherently soothing nature and that it would be an emery board to her sharpened nails. He could never set aside the more thorough disapproval he felt towards Gabriel. He saw his obvious attractions and knew the unfortunate circumstances that had brought them together, but he also recognised something more deeply disturbing in the man, some force at work that was darker than the roguishness of a rustic opportunist. Harold was not obliged to do anything for the fellow and, given these additional misgivings, he was sorely tempted to do precisely nothing. But perhaps he sensed the menace that would rush to fill the financial void, and he sought to protect Olivia by putting some time and space between her and this Gabriel. He pulled a few strings and found him work at Smithfield Market, not a stone's throw from Gentle John and Daniel during their brief sojourn in Clerkenwell, and certainly no further than the walk from the fields that Gabriel had left to the garden Gentle John and Daniel had abandoned.

They never met. Gentle John and Daniel were moving in publishing circles, about to leave for France on their long journey to Marrakech. Daniel was a porter in London's meat market, a night worker on his way home, on the other side of the river, by the time the book world stirred. He was going back to the woman he revered, whose body he craved even as she grew rounder. He was intoxicated by Olivia. The passion did not flow both ways for long. Olivia grew irascible in her pregnancy and instead of using her solitude by night for rest, while Gabriel wheeled his carcasses around the market, she tossed and turned, increasingly resentful at the prospect of bringing a bastard into a judgemental world.

The work gave Gabriel something to do. Manual labour was good for him. Less fortifying was the culture of a breakfast-time pint at the end of the shift, a custom he resisted for as long as he could. Olivia's temper shortened at the same rate as her waistline expanded, however, and he slipped off his wagon, and once he had yielded to temptation he was soon in freefall. Blinded by love and now blind drunk. The lover intoxicated by passion became the intoxicated porter that staggered away and did not see the birth of his child. Olivia may have sown the seed in her father's mind that her child might yet be Gentle John's, but Gabriel knew that when it came to seed, only his was in play. And yet the combined might of his lover's passion and the pride of a father-to-be proved no match for his weakness and he was gone within seven months, the second man in Olivia's life to leave her in just over a year. He simply vanished, perhaps murdered in an alley for the few pence he had on him, or dead from a stumble into the Thames. Either way, he would have been in no condition to save himself.

Olivia went to see her father. She should have known by now that her homecoming was a doomed mission. She arrived to find he had suffered two strokes, a mild one a fortnight earlier in the home of his eldest, Geraldine, and a more serious one at Charlotte's, his second daughter. The two sisters, with their respectability to keep polished, couldn't be doing with a father reduced to dribbling and lolling, and just for once they were not inconvenienced by the return of their little Livs, as once they had called her. They almost had to admit they were pleased to see her. They had Harold transferred back to his home and installed their returned sibling by his side. Livs was home; Livs would tend to him. Olivia found herself running a big house at last, preparing for the arrival of her baby and nursing her father towards his departure.

With the same obstinacy that had made him a self-made champion of cold storage, Harold held out for a long time. Olivia did not mind. She gave birth to her son at home, much against the advice of the stern midwife ordered in by her sisters, and Harold was the first to hear – if he could – the cries of young Charles Taylor. Olivia took the family name again, not wishing to hear the surnames that had led her to this. She wanted to have nothing to do with either the Tallis-Browns or the Joneses. The forename she chose was similarly anything but a John or a Gabriel, the non-men that had touched her life – who had touched her. Charles was regal and yet it could be turned into Charlie, her right Charlie that she chose to call him in her father's room, where they set up home by day. The mother and nurse, with her infant and her invalid.

'Positively unwholesome,' was Geraldine and Charlotte's take on the domestic arrangement, but Olivia didn't care and if truth were known – which it was but never acknowledged outside their own company – the older sisters didn't either, so grateful were they that Harold was off their hands. They didn't actually defuse the gossip that swirled at first around the return of Olivia, but neither did they pour fuel on it. Olivia was reintegrated into the family home and enjoyed a neutral status, a harmless place between the infamy of being a fallen woman and the charity that went with looking after the bedbound father. If Harold had an opinion on the matter he was unable to express it, but Olivia told him – she found herself telling him everything – that if he were so very troubled by her chattering presence at his side or by Charlie and all his sounds, he could always shut his eyes and slip away. It seemed Harold did have an answer after all, because he hung on, childlike in his dependency and as free-flowing of bodily juices as his grandson, for a full decade.

'Am I right in thinking,' said Olivia to him one day as she smoothed his bottom sheet, 'that you may once have countenanced taking matters a little further with Lady Phyllis?' Harold of course did not reply. 'I thought so,' she continued. 'Well, that would have been interesting. You do realise, don't you, that she was the man of the house? Lady Fierce was Sir Phyllis, really. I liked her in a very strange way, you know. She was what I think they call a character. But, no, you silly old thing, she wasn't for you. Sir Phyllis. Syphilis, if you ask me. Sorry, but I mean it. She'd have driven you mad.'

The sting in the tail was not so much Harold's eventual demise, that came one morning with a soundless extinguishing of his barely-a-flicker existence, but in the aftermath, when Geraldine and Charlotte went to war over what he had left behind. By then, their husbands, thanks to their wives' power of attorney, had been through much of the Taylor treasure chest

– and not merely to assess its worth, but also to spend it in their misguided efforts to beef up the meat empire of the Midlands. They were no Harolds in business. To preserve the finest cuts had defined his approach to work. 'Cut' to the sons-in-law was to strip an asset. Meat poorly tended went off, and the remains of a life's work soon stank. No sooner had Harold been transferred one last time – out of the cold storage of the mortuary and into the cemetery, next to his wife – than the big house had to be put on the market to cover the debts already accrued by the next generation's mishandling of their inheritance.

Olivia was left with a lump sum barely bigger than a year's worth of the allowance that Harold, at his most horrified, had bestowed upon her and her cowhand. She settled for it without argument, preferring to start afresh rather than take against her sisters in the open. She had already vowed that Charlie would have nothing to do with his cousins by them. He was doing well at school and had his own friends. As determined as she was to avoid her sisters and their kin from then on, Olivia was nevertheless equally steadfast in her belief that she should not to stray too far from home again. Pembrokeshire had been a disaster and London had been even worse. She would stay in the Midlands and put her experience as a carer to good use. It wasn't exactly ever going to be easy for a single mother to step into the outside world again, but it was decidedly easier in the build-up to war in the late 1930s than it had been when she fled her husband, only to be abandoned by her lover, in the 1920s.

She volunteered to be a nurse and ended up as an ambulance driver. She worked all the hours going, a slave to duty. How different she was, she thought, as she eased herself out of uniform and into her bed in the makeshift accommodation at the hospital, from the sultry young woman that had departed for Tallis Hall. The only trace left of that time was on Charlie's birth certificate, where it was written – with a secret glee that she admitted to feeling only to her incapacitated Harold – that the father of Charles Tallis-Brown was Sir John Tallis-Brown, husband of Olivia Tallis-Brown, née Taylor. She was now Livs Taylor, ambulance driver and he was Charlie Taylor, an evacuee – and this was the only bit that made her wonder – on a farm in mid Wales. For one insane moment, out of that equally demented affection she had once held for the matriarch, Olivia thought of packing Charlie off to Pembrokeshire, but she had an image of him standing with his little suitcase at the back of Tallis Hall, with Lady Phyliis looking down on him. She thought invasion by the Nazis would be preferable.

From further north in Wales, her son offered reassurance in his regular letters that all was well, that he was with a group of boys he knew and that their hosts, the Evanses of Llanllwchaearn – 'Lanluckyarm,' according to Charlie – were generous and kind. It allowed Olivia to do her bit without conscience and she rose to the challenge, diligent in her work and good fun on the rare days when the drivers and nurses could let their hair down a bit. She was in her mid-thirties and quickly regained her ease of movement now that she was on the go. She was dubbed the 'Belle of the Blitz', which she wasn't sure worked as a compliment until a grandfather with a broken leg told her that it did, because she was the girl that would see them through it all right.

'I'm more like the Bell of the Blitz,' laughed this new Olivia, racing to and from the hospitals that served Birmingham and Coventry. The war revived her. She was revitalised by it. On the night of November 14th 1940, she was picking her way through the streets of Coventry, strewn with masonry and roof tiles when a high brick wall, weakened by the inferno raging inside the warehouse it surrounded, collapsed on her ambulance. The sound of her bell was immediately silenced. The war that had taken her out of neutral and brought her back to life had also killed her.

Chapter 23

The Second World War also reached Tallis Hall, but not before an echo of the First resonated through the house. When the door closed and Lady Phyllis found herself alone in her house, with no son and no servants, she resigned herself to a life of seclusion. And in that loneliness, she looked back on those that had abandoned her, finding fault with everybody, from Now Then senior and Megan and their three sons to her own husband and their one surviving son. Perhaps she even blamed her two children that had died, for they too were part of fate's conspiracy to leave her like this, frosted and bitter. She went from room to room, still able to glide silently through her house, and found the spray of papers across the floor in Gentle John's room. She felt most disinclined to go through the menial business of tidying them, but before she could turn her ramrod-straight back on this remaining detritus, she found herself bending and scooping them up. She took them to her own room and sifted through them, discarding page after page of arcane military diagrams and jottings, and was about to bundle the whole lot together and take them down to feed the single fire she was prepared to keep going in her solitude – in the kitchen – when she came across a page thicker than the rest, written in French.

It was the last time she left the house, to go to the reference section of the public library in Haverfordwest, and from its shelves to extricate a little-used French dictionary. As painstakingly as Daniel set about editing Gentle John's manuscript, she now translated this page of French. It was a citation describing the actions of her son in the early days of the

German Spring Offensive of 1918. He had been seconded to the French, to fortify the flank that would ostensibly not move in the face of the attack they knew was coming, thanks to information gleaned from German soldiers taken prisoner. As it turned out, his role changed in a matter of minutes as he scrambled to cover the retreat that became almost headlong as the Germans broke through and advanced to within shelling range of Paris. Gentle John's field gun detachment felt the line coming back towards them. They lowered their barrels to the near-horizontal and fired at the stormtroopers that for once they could see with their own eyes. They were more used to firing at an enemy out of sight. And when the enemy continued to advance and his own guns came under mortar fire, he organised the withdrawal of the wounded and then charged at an advance party of eight German soldiers, sent ahead to observe the state of the defences. He shot two with his revolver, clubbed another to death with a spiked trench club he had picked up near Ypres, and hauled one back as a prisoner. The remaining four Germans ran back to report that the defences were heavily manned. The ensuing pause allowed the French and their small contingent of allied gunners to regroup and reset a front line with a reinforced rear zone. The citation concluded with the recommendation that the actions of said Sergeant John Tallis-Brown be honoured with the award of the Croix de Guerre. A heavy stamp on the bottom of the page confirmed that the recommendation had been accepted and that the medal for bravery had been duly presented.

Lady Phyllis left the citation unfolded on the table, held down at its top corner by the French dictionary, but still on display. The library wrote to Sir John, or to whom it might concern at Tallis Hall, suggesting that such a valuable document should not be returned by post. If arrangements could be made for its retrieval the library would be most grateful, and in its acknowledgement of the honour, perhaps a small civic celebration might coincide with its collection, they wondered. Lady Fierce never replied and never left the estate again. The citation was put on display for six months before daylight began to fade the ink and it was slipped out of sight, into the archives of the local museum.

For the better part of two decades thereafter, Lady Phyllis was able to repel all invaders – 'all' being some minion from a London publishing house, to whom she gave short shrift, and the equally unwelcome Harold Taylor. This dreary butcher, desperate for details of the ruptured marriage of his daughter and her son, was soon sent packing, too, but when Hank Swift arrived in the first weeks of 1944 she opened the door and ended up letting him in. If she was surprised to see a captain of the United States Air Force on her doorstep, she did not of course show it. A frosty welcome was her speciality of the house and simply because she was out of practice did not mean she had lost her touch. She presented him with her most withering front. He, on the other hand, could not conceal his consternation when his thump on the door and his rat-a-tat on the knocker were answered. They had been delivered out of force of habit, formalities, something you did before entering a property that was not yours in normal circumstances. He understood that the amassing of Americans in their hundreds of thousands in a land on the other side of the Atlantic, far from his home in Bangor, Maine, in the build-up to the invasion of Europe, defined circumstances far from normal, but he also believed in the righteousness of the American way of life and its thoroughness. If he had received intel that the house would be empty, then he fully expected it to be exactly that, as in unoccupied. Rat-a-tat out of courtesy, but what the hell was this old woman doing standing before him?

'I'm sorry, ma'am, it was my understanding that this property was unoccupied,' he said, trying to recover his poise.

'Then why knock on the door?' came the glacial reply.

Captain Hank was further discombobulated. 'It kind of just happened,' he said. 'It slipped out… I was momentarily lost in the fog of war,' he tried with a smile, remembering that a sense of humour was the way to the Limeys' hearts.

'I do not have one.'

'I beg your pardon, ma'am?'

'A heart… to which you are trying to find your way.'

'Ah. Tell you what, ma'am, can we start again?'

'Shall I shut the door?'

'No need.'

'Then we shall not have restarted.'

'I'm sorry, ma'am…'

Lady Phyllis looked at the young American – he was thirty-four – and wondered if the war could ever be won. She looked over his shoulder to see the small convoy of Jeeps, packed with servicemen, and presumed it could. 'I take it Tallis Hall is to be your billet.'

Captain Hank breathed a sigh of relief. 'Those are my orders, ma'am,' he said.

'You may tell your men that I shall tolerate no noise beyond ten o'clock and that I shall be recompensed for all breakages.'

'You're staying?'

'Do you imagine I am going to hand my home over to children without adult supervision?'

'Ma'am, these are men of the 42nd Airborne Division and we do not require…'

'What is your rank, young man?'

'I am Captain Hank Swift, ma'am.'

'Well, Captain Swift, you may well go on to win the war against Hitler and the Nazis, but there are battles you will lose along the way. I take it you are a student of military strategy?'

'Two years at the Army Air Forces School of Applied Tactics, ma'am.'

'Then you decide if this is to be one of them.' Captain Hank looked at the old woman in black and guessed she had to be in her eighties. 'I am seventy-six years old,' said Lady Fierce.

'I guess we can… make arrangements to accommodate you, ma'am.'

'Your Ladyship.'

'No kidding.'

'Do I appear to you somebody with a bent for "kidding"?'

'No, ma'am, you do not. No, Your Ladyship, you do not.'

'Once is enough.'

'Ma'am? Your Ladyship?'

'Once the title is acknowledged we may settle for something a little less formal.'

Captain Hank was tired and war was muddled enough without this bullshit. 'What do I call you? Ma'am.'

'You may call me Lady Fierce. Everybody else does.'

For a few brief months, life returned to Tallis Hall. The American airmen brought ancillary services with them, cooks for the kitchen and engineers who spent most of their time hiding bulldozers in the woods. Once the runways on the airfields across Pembrokeshire had been upgraded and sometimes extended to take the B-24 Liberators, the heavy machinery was best concealed. The invasion of Europe was going to happen any day soon and everybody knew it, but secrecy remained the absolute order of the day. The Tallis Hall estate was a perfect place to hide machines and men.

Captain Hank made a single exception, ordering an earth-mover out of the trees and into the walled garden. It required a breach in the wall, but a working party was organised to repair the damage once an open space was cleared and the machine had been returned to its hiding place in the wood. What had been cleared was a sheltered expanse where the men could rest or 'play some ball', as they put it, out of the wind. He kept the lady of the house briefed when it came to such plans and even asked for her advice, but she offered none and already knew everything. 'I can see with my own eyes what is happening in my own home, Captain.'

The men who congregated in the garden to smoke and play in the spring sunshine were at first spooked by the presence at the window. Superstition was a strong force among aircrew that made sorties out into the ocean. The Battle of the Atlantic against German U-boats had largely been won, but there was still the occasional rogue vessel from the original wolfpack to pick off, and there were still fishing trawlers in need of protection, and convoys to escort. Besides, there was the invasion ahead, and nobody was under any illusions that it was going to be anything but perilous. Airmen remained superstitious and the widow at her window unsettled them.

It was almost a relief to see her move, but they soon realised they were about to be in even greater danger. With all the earth-moving in the overgrown garden – the engineers had left a couple of the raised beds where there seemed to be perennials like Jerusalem artichokes and asparagus – the rooks were back, circling the house and daring to land and peck away for worms and seeds, despite the presence of so many humans. They had been disturbed in their nests in the wood by the arrival of the bulldozers, and it was as if they took to the air to see what the invasion of their space was all about. The airmen did not see fellow-fliers. They didn't like the arrival of these harbingers of doom and did their best to chase them off and were already thinking of asking the captain if they could open the armoury and take some potshots at the birds. They were observing them suspiciously again and muttering as the rooks flopped heavily into the far corners, but turned their heads at the same time as a sash window was opened, not without resistance, in the house. Lady Fierce stepped into view and took aim with Gentle John's air rifle. The men, even from twenty paces away, noticed that the hands of the gun holder were not steady and the barrel was waving in the air. They dived for cover.

The Captain's hand steadied the gun and smoothly pointed it upwards and then pulled it calmly but firmly out of Lady Fierce's grip. 'I think, ma'am – Your Ladyship – we had better leave this to the military,' he said. He noticed the flash of defiance in the old woman's eyes, but then saw her drop her shoulders. She nodded and stepped back from the window. 'The men, I guess, are conscious that pretty soon they'll have Germans trying to shoot the hell out of them… and they'd rather wait… if you don't mind.'

Lady Fierce was about to turn away from him. Instead, she pointed to the gun. 'It belonged to my son,' she said. 'He fought in the Great War. He was in the Royal Artillery.'

Captain Hank looked at the weapon. 'Artillery, eh? I guess this was a little light relief for him. Was he any good with this?'

'It seems he was. With all sorts of guns.' Her voice dropped to barely a whisper. 'He was decorated. He was quite a hero, you know.'

Not always such a Lady Fierce, thought Captain Hank. 'Did he… did he make it home, ma'am?'

'He came home,' said Lady Fierce with a tiny nod of her head. 'And then he went away again.'

On his way out, Captain Hank removed the Purdeys from the shotgun cabinet and distributed them, plus the air rifle, among the men and for a few days they blazed away in the walled garden of Tallis Hall, killing rooks or sending them back to their treetops above the bulldozers. And no sooner were the surviving birds resettled there than the machinery below burst into life, ready to rumble towards the transporters that would take them all the way down to the south coast of England. From there, they were loaded aboard ships bound for Normandy. The aircrews were also gone soon afterwards, their Liberators climbing away from the coastal airfields of Pembrokeshire, heading for the skies over France, some to fall from it, most to be part of the air superiority that allowed them to land safely wherever the Allied advance over the coming year would let them. None ever came back to Pembrokeshire.

Just before he left at their head, Captain Hank handled the guns one last time. 'Better get rid of these,' he told one of the Liberator gunners. The shotguns were placed under the tracks of a moving bulldozer on its way out of its wood. 'But not this one...' The gunner cleaned the air rifle and wrapped it in oil cloth and Captain Hank carefully placed it in the compartment under the window seat in Gentle John's old room. Lady Fierce never found it.

The rest of her life was spent losing things. The stick she now needed. The matches to light the fire. Her land, that she sold off to the Hall's surrounding farmers. And when that last deal was done, she began to lose her marbles too, falling steeply into an infirm old age, muddled of thought and shaking of hand. Without her cooks and her waiters – the airmen on the rota to deliver her food had called it 'The Run' - she grew thinner than ever.

Stooped and frail, she slowed to a halt. She heard a rat-a-tat. She ran to the window of her bedroom. She could hear a growing roar. It would be a Liberator, looming out of a mist off St Brides Bay and taxiing up the driveway to her Tallis Hall. She skipped down the staircase and to the front door, and prepared to throw it open and shout, 'Welcome home.' Why was she shuffling? What was this fog before her eyes? Why wouldn't this key turn in the lock? She made a last effort and threw back the bolts that were not there. Captain Hank was back. Her son, John, jumped down, too, a pilot in the air force. Who'd have thought it? 'Out of the fog of war...' whispered Lady Phyllis Tallis-Brown to nobody but herself, slumped in front of the kitchen fire that had gone out. She let out the strange, strangled sound peculiar to her – Lady Fierce's last laugh, her death rattle.

Part 5

Chapter 24

Corinthia intercepted Post at Rhiwbina station. He wasn't on the first train from Cardiff Central, nor the second, but she saw him on the third. It wasn't difficult to scan all the passengers in the two carriages. Post had his finger on the button to open the door, but when the light came on and the ping sounded, Corinthia pressed first and pushed him back into the carriage, causing the only other passenger wishing to alight to mutter about letting people off first. Corinthia had wondered if an about-turn was the right way to retreat. She could have hauled Post out of the carriage and they could have waited on the same platform for this same train to go up to Coryton and come back again on its same track. She decided instead to get on board and carry on and then come back in the opp... what she really decided was that she was starting to think like Post and the worry of it cut through her fear of being pursued by that man in the house in Park Crescent. She pushed Post hard back into the train, put her arms around him and took a good breath of him.

They watched warily as they came back through Rhiwbina half an hour later and didn't relax for the next twelve minutes to Cardiff Central. They were still cautious on Platform 4 there, waiting for the connection west. They'd thought about running away to London, but opted instead for somewhere – they didn't yet know where – in the other direction.

Corinthia found work serving in the bar of the Wrecked Schooner between Newgale and Solva. It was a tiny pub with a large beer garden, designed for the Pembrokeshire seasons, its interior easily heated, to keep the small community of winter drinkers warm, and with this outdoor area that could seat the many scores of summer tourists that came to enjoy the views over St Brides Bay. It had recently been taken over by Mali Williams from Pen-y-Cwm on the road leading back to Newgale, and her Dutch husband, Jan, and Corinthia was just the person they were looking for as their newly acquired business became ever more popular for its good food and its beer from a micro-brewery in nearby Roch. They also needed more hands because the forecast, as best as it could for Pembrokeshire, told of good weather to come in June.

Almost next door to Mali's old family home was 'Evans's Everything', a shop that existed for nothing specific but was generally and genuinely loved by all that came to Newgale for an active holiday. They could hire anything to do with sport on the beach and in the sea, or to do with cycling or walking inland. Visitors could take their own gear to the E'sE, as the shop was known, to be repaired or to be part-exchanged for new. In the E'sE, nothing was too difficult, and Post was put to work in the back – in the Sweatshop, as the other repair workers called it. It was anything but, being under the sun and yet in the breeze. It echoed to the sound of enthusiasts at work, to their drilling and hammering, but also to their laughter and music.

There was the formal rack – of bikes and boards, each with a cardboard label bearing handwritten details of the repair to be carried out – and there was the Preseli. This was the mountain of 'stuff' that Pete, the owner of the E'sE, couldn't help compiling. It contained leftovers from previous repair jobs, that might 'come in handy one day,' according to Pete, or 'treasure' salvaged from junkyards and clearance sales all over the county. It was basically worthless, but it was a paradise for Post. Within a week of starting, he was the go-to man for parts that weren't in stock or that couldn't be delivered in time by the suppliers. Post could find the missing bit and broken holidays were made whole again.

It wasn't slave labour and the E'sE workers were regulars at the Wrecked Schooner. Nor was it all toil in the pub. Mali encouraged the staff to organise a rota that allowed them in daylight hours to climb down a precipitous cliff path to a tiny pebbled beach and spend an hour at play. Post and Corinthia met there early in the evening and washed away their grease and oil, before she returned to work and he went up to their caravan in a field, a quarter of a mile inland from the E'sE. The caravan belonged to the Davieses of Upper Cwm Farm and was the exception that proved the rule that Pembrokeshire was being tarted up from top to bottom as a holiday destination. The 'Van, as Ethel Davies referred to it, was as much a wreck as the Wrecked Schooner was not. Corinthia had examined it with extreme distaste after it had been 'recommended' to them by Pete. 'If you like a challenge, Post…' had been his words. She had rubbed a finger over the green mould that covered its exterior, revealing part of a name.

'It's a Tiffany 33,' she announced when all had been revealed. 'As in, built in 1933, by the looks of it.'

'It's perfect,' said Post. Within three days of finding it, he had stripped it of all its furniture and fittings, scrubbed every surface and rebuilt what he felt was necessary. This meant his traditional Spartan style ruled, but it left the interior with more room for the two of them. And for the king-size mattress that Corinthia asked him to buy and that would be the only new item in their home. The ancient water heater was taken apart and reassembled, and there was hot water from the tap over the sink that was the only part of the kitchen he kept. If they needed heat by which to cook, they would use the fire pit he dug, eight paces from the Tiff, six from the hedge. For a more thorough means of cleaning themselves, he went into the Preseli pile of junk and found a hose, a sprinkler head and a galvanised tub, and rigged up a gravity-fed shower. Corinthia called it the 'trickle', and told him it would do only as long as the weather held. There was no curtain around the cold-water trickle, but skinny-showering was part of the adventure, she confessed. Besides, there was nobody to watch, apart from a herd of seven Friesian cows.

The arrival of the mattress was a turning point. It took Post an hour to squeeze it through the Tiff's door and it filled the living space. That night they took sirloin steaks, provided by Mali, and cooked them over the fire pit. They baked potatoes in the ash, drank a bottle of wine, chosen by Jan, and then eased away from the fire. It was warm even at night and the spell of good weather had turned into a heatwave that showed no sign of breaking.

'That new mattress…' said Corinthia.

'Yes?' said Post.

'We'd better test it, I suppose.' They went inside and undressed each other.

'I'd forgotten why we called you Post…' she said.

'It was my presentation on post-industrial Wa…' whispered Post.

'You sure?' she said and slipped her hand lower. 'I reckon I know the real reason.'

The Tiffany 33 was in sound working order on the inside, but Post had not yet turned his attention to the underside. The moorings were slightly unstable and as the lovers began to move, so did the Tiff, to such an extent that Corinthia had to stop, thinking they were about to roll down the field. They spent the next half-hour forcing the mattress back out through the door and laying it in the open. They had been too hot before they were rudely interrupted; now they were soaking in perspiration.

'Damn it,' said Corinthia, throwing herself down. Post lay by her side, not touching her.

'Damn it,' he said, too.

They cooled in the open air, naked on the sheet over their new mattress, on their backs, staring up at the stars. Post reached out and felt for Corinthia's hand. He moved from her hand to her hip. A log settled in the fire pit, sending up a small shower of sparks before a last flame curled around the wood.

'Damn,' he whispered later, when the glow from the fire was but a dull orange.

'Damn,' she whispered back, 'that was good.'

It was so hot that the fence around the beer garden at the Wrecked Schooner was a hindrance. On top of the cliff, the pub had what tiny breath of wind came its way off the sea, but the whisper couldn't penetrate the barrier that had been built precisely to keep it out. The enclosure was still packed because visitors were quite happy to drink their way through their discomfort and talk about the weather. The crowd was young and nobody could remember a flaming summer like this one. They talked about the heat and they drank to keep cool and Mali and Jan did a roaring business, but they all agreed that a little more movement of air wouldn't go amiss.

Post visited the Preseli pile and emerged two working days later with three sections of what Pete dubbed the 'Creation'. It was loaded piece by piece into the back of the E'sE's ancient Land Rover, and taken up the hill to the Wrecked Schooner, where Post began to assemble it before the pub opened for its busiest period, Friday lunchtime. The long-weekenders that came down to surf found not the sea but a lake without a ripple, never mind waves. They took to the pub instead. Post chose the corner of the beer garden where, only a fortnight earlier, he'd built a barbecue from old oil drums. It was redundant for the moment because nobody had an appetite for anything that gave off more heat.

The Creation grew. Steel prongs, welded to a plate on the ground, supported the front of the bike frame, while a contraption was attached to the rear – a circular cage guarding a metal propeller, two feet in diameter, on the inside.

The lunchtime crowd came in, supplemented by Pete's entire workforce, who had been given the afternoon off, partly to witness the Creation's maiden voyage, partly because it was too hot to work. Post climbed aboard and, facing out towards the millpond sea, pedalled. The propeller turned with a whir that made everybody not already intrigued turn their head and catch the flow of air. Post pedalled faster, heating up while others cooled. From Platform One-and-only at Rhiwbina to here in Pembrokeshire. From Christmas lights to summer breeze. From looking for Corinthia to finding her. From longing for her to loving her. From 'Do Something' in the diary to having done something. Corinthia came out with a tray of drinks and stood in the draught. She placed the large tray in front of Pete, dipped her fingers into his pint of lager and flicked them at the machine. 'I name her "Fanny",' she shouted.

The heatwave broke a week later. The volunteer cyclist doing his stint on Fanny – it still made everybody titter – and facing out to sea was the first to notice the change in the sky to the west. For weeks, it had been a hazy blue, the horizon never clearly defined. The only clear thing had been the effect of the sun, scorching everything on the land. Drought and climate change and global warming had taken over from 'lovely spell of weather'. Now there was a change, a swelling in the sky of cloud, pillars of white, but grey where they grew out of the distant water. The cyclist shouted 'Storm ahoy,' and everybody looked over the fence to see what was coming their way. Two hours later, there was no need to pedal. The sun was still bright but a breeze was blowing, increasing in speed by the minute.

Post sensed it in the workshop at the back of the E'sE. For the first time, the Preseli began to chime as little twists of metal began to move. He asked Pete if he could take five and jumped on one of rental bikes and set off up the road, turned right on to the bridle path and sped through the open gate and across the fields to the Tiff. They were in the habit of leaving the mattress on its side, raised on three logs to keep it off the ground, but there something far more than the dew of dusk in the air. He wrestled the mattress back into the van, poured water over the ash in the fire pit to stop it from blowing over the clothes on the line, removed them, checked everything else was secure, and then headed back to the E'sE. Everybody had stopped. They were on the Newgale beach staring out into the bay. The sea had come back to life and waves not seen for a month were making their sounds, not heard all this time. It was the sky, though, that drew their eye. The sun was slowly heading towards the clouds but they were coming its way at a lick. When they met, with four hours of normal evening light left, day turned to night and, almost as abruptly, the wind seemed to gather new strength.

Pete ordered everybody home to batten down the hatches and suggested they meet up in the Wrecked Schooner later. There might be a show to enjoy. Post rode straight there, to dismantle Fanny and put her in Jan's shed, where the landlord stored the beer-garden furniture over the winter. Corinthia was at work, making good the inside of the pub, which had hardly been used lately. Post helped Jan with the parasols outside. They wondered if they could leave them, with their canvas panels folded down and secured by rope ties, outside. Each pole was held in a concrete base, passing through a hole drilled in the middle of the heavy wooden table it shaded. A gust of wind gave notice of a growing violence and they stacked the parasols around Fanny in the shed. Jan went back to his kitchen, and Post stood alone at the fence, looking out to sea. Corinthia came out and stood behind him. She put her arms around his waist and together they raised their chins to the wind.

Post hardly ever drank, but on this one night he joined Pete and the gang as they toasted – repeatedly – the rage of Mother Nature. It didn't take much to unleash a pagan ritual in the E'sE workers and soon they were having a right old singalong, and Post went along with them. By the time Corinthia finished serving, he was drunker than she'd ever known him.

'I love you all,' he shouted to the pub as Corinthia steered him towards the door at midnight. The E'sE roared back their love for him, too, and he fell into the storm outside. 'But I love you most of all,' he said to Corinthia as she followed him.

'What?' she shouted against the wind and the rain that had already soaked them both. Post wiped his long hair off his face. 'I love you,' he shouted.

'If you can remember what you've just said in the morning, I'll take you seriously,' she said. 'That'll be a bloody miracle.'

'What?' shouted Post, staggering a little.

'Nothing,' said Corinthia. 'Let's get you back to the Tiff.'

'I've got wheels,' shouted Post, pointing at the hire bike.

'You're in no fit state…'

'Come on,' shouted Post, putting one leg unsteadily over the top tube and patting the saddle. Corinthia laughed and more daintily put her leg over. 'Remember this?' said Post into her ear.

'You weren't drunk back then.'

'But I loved you just as much back then, too,' he said.

'Yes, yes,' said Corinthia. 'As I say, if you remember tomorrow… first thing, let's get home safely, right?'

'Let's go,' said Post and he lurched forward and they set off down the hill to the start of the bridle path. In the heatwave, they could cycle along it smoothly, but now it was alive as a raging conduit to the sea for the water lashing down on the surrounding meadows. They dismounted and pushed the bike through the torrent, the high hedgerow to their left forced down towards the horizontal by the wind. Branches bounced up and down, and they had to advance with an arm held up to protect their heads.

They found the Tiff on its side, its rusted underbelly exposed to the storm. The fire pit was an ashen pond, with grey water spilling out. The galvanised tank of the shower lay in the hedge, and through the howling wind they could hear the rain drumming against its upturned bottom. Their home was ruined.

'Oh my God,' said Corinthia. 'What the hell do we do now?'

'Come on,' said Post, picking up the bike and starting to walk on.

'Where are we going?'

'Wherever the wind blows us,' he shouted.

They pushed and hauled themselves and the bike across two fields, heading inland, until they came to a road. They got back on their machine and didn't think of right or left, but simply allowed themselves to be blown along, with scarcely any need to turn the pedals. And so it was, soaked to the skin and starting to shiver, that half an hour later, Post and Corinthia were borne on a storm through the gates of Tallis Hall and up to the front door of the house that hadn't been lived in for over seventy years.

Chapter 25

Spanish lessons were going well. *Clases particulares.* Donna had her own teacher, Javier, who gave her conversation classes by Skype.

'*Buenos días, doña Donna.*'

'*Buenos días, Javier,*'

'*Qué tal?*'

'*Muy bien, gracias.*'

'OK, so repeat after me: *los murciélagos de Murcia...*'

'*Los murciélagos de Murcia...*'

'*Y el jamón de Jaén...*'

'*Y el jamón de Jaén...*'

'*Muy bien...*'

'*Muy bien...*'

'You can stop now, Donna...'

'Oh, I see... what did they mean?'

'It's not so important. I just like to hear your Welsh voice make Spanish sounds.'

'Stop it, Javier.'

Javier was fitted in after two hours early in the morning of running the clubs. Remote control, Donna called it. The sending of quiet emails from home to keep the racket – the noise, the music, that is, and not any gangland activity (heaven for-effing-fend, thought *Doña* Donna) – at full volume on the *costas*. Running the clubs and swimming her lengths. Her pool; her think tank. While she went up and down through the crystal-clear water, she went back and forth through her options, coming to the conclusion during the last set of four in her daily one hundred – on her back, arms slowly turning like a wind turbine – that she would take the one marked Cut and Run. Not that she was partial to the 'run' half of the equation. Donna was not fleeing. Donna didn't do backward motion unless it was by backstroke. But there was no getting away from the reality of being a post-European trying do business in Spain. The clubs weren't what they were. The Brits were staying away, turning into 'staycationers', like something out of the 1950s, all sand-in-the-spam sarnies and huddling for shelter behind a windbreak, forcing the lid off a jar of whelks. Donna was being forced to contemplate selling – or, as she preferred nowadays, divesting herself of her portfolio in the sun.

Swimming came before a return to the laptop. If she was leaving it would be with an enhanced self-awareness. About diet. If Donna was going, remember, it was not backwards – not back to a diet of burgers and chips or kebabs. No Doner Donna. Chef Sofía was her guide to better food. She didn't interact with this guru of haute cuisine, but listened and learned. Absorb, Donna, and then pan-fry. And then settle down for a little siesta to the sound of home – to this bloke who at least in this time of reconfiguration (and she made a mental note to use the word again) made her smile. This DfL. Down from London, but BiW. Buried in Wales. This blogger bloke – her vlogger – did brighten her mood. And that helped, didn't it, to help her through her grieving process? Well, not exactly her grieving as such – not as in clawing at the coffin, sobbing and wailing and… what was it?… gnashing of teeth. Donna couldn't be doing with any gnashing, or wailing or even sobbing. God, she loved being on her own. But there were appearances to keep up and Donna let her DfL – she thought of him as hers – do her anguish for her. Vicarious. She'd picked that up, too. Go on, DfL, Donna's new bestie, you have your little rant while Doña D dozes. Forty effing winks. That's it, off you go, vlogger bloke.

'This is the Vlog of the DfL, and if you think that sounds like something that hasn't been decoded by the bleedin' Enigma thingummy, then quite frankly I haven't got time to explain. I'm not going through it all again. No "Previously on the DfL's Vlog…" here. Keep up or ship out, as we say in deep space.

'Anyway, to any of you up to speed, welcome back. To everyone else, well, better late than never, eh? For you, this is the grand entrance, as it were. The DfL coming down the staircase of your life. Well, maybe not so grand, what with the recent mishaps and all that. You know, the setbacks. The little SOS.

'Well, never you mind. Suffice to say – sorry if that makes me sound like some of the right bankers I used to work with, when they were really up themselves… suffice to say, there's been a development…

'So, to any of you out there who may have caught the "Mayday, Mayday…" of yours truly, well, there's no need to dial the intergalactic 999. There we were, a bit adrift in space, and suddenly we've caught a bit of… what is it? Gravitational pull. That's it. Gravity, wonderful thing. We're on the move. The Dfl, people. The Down from London. That's what they call me in the place I'm going to have to get used to calling 'ome… and 'ere I have to rub me eyes and confess I can't hardly believe it myself. Home is Wales. Bleedin' Wales, pardon my Cymraeg – that's "Cym" as in "Come" and "Raeg" as in Reigate without the "ate"… See, I've written it out for you. Bear with me while I hold this board up. There: "Come + Reigate – 8 = Cymraeg". Cymraeg, as they call their tongue in these parts. Or part of these parts. Look, it gets a bit confused – Welsh, English… all you need to know is I'm one of 'em. Would you effin' believe it?'

The Blitz came to an end, and once the threat from the Luftwaffe had passed, Charlie Taylor returned from Llanllwchaearn to Walsall, only to find a bombshell of a different kind. The family home was in the process of being sold. What would a minor, and an orphan at that, be doing rattling around in such a big old house? It was no place for a young man on his own. Besides, and rather more pressingly, his elders and betters, his guardians, his aunts Geraldine and Charlotte needed the money. They were his elders certainly, but they were up to no good. They stayed out of bankruptcy only because of the wartime black market in meat. They had gone from being pillars of their community to profiteers. Guilt made them take it – what was 'it', he wondered? Their shame? – out on Charlie, who went back and forth between these relatives for the remainder of the war. They were long years, in contrast to the vow he quickly took that as soon as he could, he would join up and leave what remained of his family and never return.

It was strange for a son that had met neither his real father, Gabriel, nor the one on his birth certificate, John, that they should all share the experience of what to do at eighteen in a time of war. John had gone, by his postal route, to it; Gabriel had been spared. Both had faced the matter of what to do when that birthday came. Charlie was absolutely certain that he would go, but he found himself in the same position as a third party at this eighteenth, his unknown uncle, Daniel. Both able and willing and eighteen, but both with no war to go to. Charlie stuck at his schoolwork through the early 1940s, but was denied his escape to danger by the ending of hostilities in Europe in May 1945. Such was his determination to be free of his aunts, though, that he left anyway, heading for London, where he started afresh.

It was a life singularly without an episode of high drama, but a life nevertheless of merit – of devotion to friends he made at work in his high street bank in Chiswick and to one in particular he met there, Naomi. They married in 1957 and at regular intervals into the 1960s had three children, the second of which, after Godfrey and before Eric, was a girl they christened Alice. Alice was respectability itself, like her father and mother. She surrendered the Taylor name she shared with her father – who now preferred Charles to Charlie – when she married Conrad Shaw, but her life as Alice Shaw, wife, was very much as it had been as Alice Taylor, daughter. She lived a similarly solid life, comfortably off and with a decent chap by her side. Conrad was in insurance and they lived in Putney.

The birth of their son, Alfred, in 1984 nearly killed Alice. For nearly forty years, the Taylors and Shaws had made steady progress with barely a ripple to disturb their lives. But Alfred nearly did for his mother, leaving her in need of a blood transfusion, and confining her to hospital for a month after his extraction. The word of their doctor. 'Delivery' was not how he described Alfred's arrival. This start proved to be a taste of what was to come. Perhaps he was starved of oxygen to the part of his brain that was trying to absorb all the good bits from his parents; perhaps there was the skipped presence of Gabriel in his make-up. Perhaps the never-known great-grandfather was keen to play a trick from beyond wherever his grave was, and leapfrog the generations and reintroduce himself to the family down the genealogical line. Alfred was born into an age of deregulation in the world of banking and finance, and into the Mark II of this deregulated world he would step as a worker. 'Step' was not how his introduction would be remembered. He had been extracted at birth and now he would 'infect' the workplace, as his bosses on the QT would one day put it.

He was a wild child and he became an unruly man. He was utterly legitimate and Alice would never have let a 'B' word stronger than 'blighter' slip from her mouth, but inside her head she screamed 'little bastard' at her son, every day starting with the very first, when he had nearly killed her on arrival.

'My old mother, bless her, never said a dickie bird. Maybe she never knew. I wonder. All part of the mystery. All part of the surprise. Which, I can tell you, it truly was. It being – and here it comes, people… drumroll, please… I am the owner of a pile. And where would that pile be, I hear you ask? Well, for the sake of arguments, let's call the dump it's near, 'Ave-a-lot-less. 'Cos it has. A whole lot less. Threadneedle Street, it ain't. Anyway, you go through this 'Ave-a-lot-less and you keep going until you nearly fall into a sea of hippies, all standing round looking at the sea proper and talking home brew and magic mushrooms, and you hang a right and go inland a bit and there it is. My gaff.'

The child grew, a constant menace into his teens until he abandoned school and home at sixteen and cut out on his own. He could have tumbled into the alcohol that had done for Gabriel, but he found his own addiction. He loved money, did Alfie, and set out to make himself a mint. He joined the City during its reconstruction in the Noughties – 'Weren't they just named for me?' – after the crash of the early 1990s.

'So, where d'you work now, then, Alfie?'

'Oh, you know, in the City.'

'So we 'eard. Good on ya, Alfie Shaw.'

He had joined the City. He loved the phrase. He loved it more than if he had been offered terms by the City – Manchester City, any City in the newly formed Premier League – and given a stonking great weekly wedge. Not that Alfie was much cop at football, although – don't get him wrong – he loved Crystal Palace as much as the next South Londoner. But he loved the City more. EC, that is, as in Eastern Central London. He loved the moment of going from his city to the City; through the portal into a new world. It didn't matter that he was an L-plate learner, a sub-apprentice, an on-trial probationer, a maker of a brew, an intern. He worked in the City. And he worked his way up in the City, from nobody in the Stock Exchange through Bonds and Equities and Foreign Exchange to being a somebody in banking. A right little banker. Who would ever have known that ferret-faced Shaw had such an eye for a deal, that skinny little Alfie would fill out and grow into his Jermyn Street suits and run his own section? Young Shaw, eh? A bit wide, a bit lairy, but undeniably an asset. Keep his section on the QT, but let's give him his head, shall we? Alfie Shaw on the QT, aye aye, in EC1.

'*Naturellement*, as we say in Welsh, the gaff ain't quite what it seems. Or what it was. It has seen, as they say the world over, better days. Still, no bother. Except there is. Don't think I don't appreciate this little bonus in my dotage – well, not so much dotage as early retirement, shall we call it – but there's a bit of an issue. It's in such a state that it makes 'Ave-a-lot-less look like bleedin' Palm Springs.'

In his section – the QT section – not-so-young Alfred Shaw in his shiny suit put together his packages. His film schemes, his offers of a stake in deep-sea diving, in housing stock in Dresden underwritten by the German government; his bundles and his prospectuses and his investment portfolios – and all so very tax-efficient. He moved everything he could into those places where they became even more tax-advantageous. They called it in the office 'doing an Alfie Shaw'. Going offshore. And just as he gave his name to the process, so he became known by his method. He was called Offshore, because that was how he made his name. Alfie Offshore, like having his own designer label in the City.

'DfL's Vlog, stardate blah-de-blah… So, this pile I've got, is it haemorrhoid or nest-egg? Now there's a question…'

Far from doing it all on the QT, this Alfie Offshore went VL, for very loud. FF. Effin' fortissimo. He was a child of the digital world and was a ready convert to home-made, desktop-published self-promotion. Alfie began to blog online – to vlog – with all the expertise, to begin with, of a second-hand car dealer in small-town USA, making his own advert to go out sub-primetime on his local cable network. Brash in his sales patter and a bit harshly lit by the lights of his office, Offshore was a bit wearing on the ear and scary on the eye. But he toned himself down – 'I need to turn down the dimmer on me,' he said – and he improved, particularly when his fortunes began to fluctuate and then go into decline. Here was a tale of rise and fall, told in Alfie Offshore's own particular way.

'There was a time when, if somebody had said to me, "DfL my son, there's a ruin in Wales and it's all yours," I'd have said, "Very kind of you, squire, but no thanks. I've got enough bricks and mortar on the books." Not that I'd have been that blunt about it – always mind your Ps and Qs, I always say – but, know what I mean, you can have too much of a good thing. Not that it's relevant, because by the time I'm having this chat with this bloke who's been chasing me up hill and down dale – as we say in Wales – my portfolio, as we used to say back in the days of plenty, was down the swanny. So, when he says I'm the owner of this mansion, I think, well, gift horse and all that… maybe I'm quids-in again. Little did I know that I'm about to be – and may I be forgiven for slipping into the language of my forefathers – up the Cleddau without a paddle. That's Welsh for being up shit creek.'

He had made his mint in the deregulated bonanza years in his beloved City. If anybody had told him that there was no such thing as something too good to be true, he'd have said that he wasn't doing Ponzi schemes or pyramid selling. He was merely a salesman of tax efficiency. And he was rewarded accordingly, his bonuses – he called them his *boni*, to bring out the Latin in him – taking him into the bracket of the seriously rich.

The problems started when the taxmen began to redefine tax-avoidance and it turned out, after all, that something that had appeared too good to be true was exactly that. And the new truth was that tax was now payable on all that excess of goodness. And back-dated and with interest added. Alfie Offshore's schemes were suddenly and eminently taxable and taxed and very taxing for him. Nothing was now on the QT and Offshore was on the street. He was packed off with a sum to buy his silence and a promise – slightly vague in its expression – of protection from any criminal liability should the tax investigations turn even more forensic.

His additional problem was that far from being merely the designer of his many schemes, he was also their guinea pig, their purchaser, their exploiter. Soon, it wasn't just his former clients that were being pursued, but Offshore himself. He insisted that doing an Alfie Shaw had been an office joke, not a scam. He claimed that his name was Alfred Shaw, never Alfie and not at all offshore.

'Oops, I used to say, there goes another one. The apartment in Monaco this time. Take the keys, HMRC. All yours. There might even be a bottle of Bolli in the fridge. Have it on me. What can I say? Well, I'd like to say there's plenty more where that came from… but the portfolio – as they say, people – grows slimmer by the day.'

It was said that the BBC were thinking of offering him a slot on *Working Lunch* – until their due-diligence probes revealed that his slide into impoverishment might have an impish charm in its recounting, but what he had been up to in his career and what remained of his assets were a little suspect. More than a little 'out there'. *Working Lunch* opted not to go on air with Offshore. Alfie would have to develop his own career in broadcasting. Which was tricky, because any seed money, any programme budget had gone the way of everything else in the portfolio. There was nothing left.

'Rumbled and rolled over, all the way to Mr B. Well hello to you, matey. Can't say it's a pleasure, but there you are. Mr B for Bankruptcy. Has a certain finality to it, doesn't it, people? Well, we gave it a go. I called them schemes; they called them scams. You takes your pick and you pays your money. And you did, people – and I thank you for it. And sorry for any inconvenience along the way. I suppose we knew the score, didn't we? Well, you didn't know my score. How could you? I was never entirely honest with you, if truth were known. Truth and Honesty, my middle names? Not really, people. This is my confessional. The truth is – honest – I veered a little to the dark side. I couldn't help it – well, that's what I'll tell the judge. Those two little imps had me well hooked. Those other two Bs. The twin Bs that came before Mr B. Love 'em, Bungs and Bonuses. The *boni* of my life. Well, bye bye, *boni*. It's official, people. I've hit the big zero. What have I got? Zilcho. Mr B has me collared.'

It would have been a cartographical point of interest had the Landsker Line ever been definitively marked on the map. The salient around Tallis Hall was intriguing enough – this English name in its bubble, sticking out into Welsh-speaking Pembrokeshire – but the house also had another line creeping its way. The boundary of the Pembrokeshire Coast National Park. The firmest line was of course the path that hugged the coast for 186 miles, but the boundary of the Park drifted inland by as far as several miles in places and in a slightly more abstract land-grab. Since Tallis Hall had been unoccupied for longer than either the National Park or the Path had been open, it had never really been a bone of contention – whether it sat within or without.

Times were changing, though, and Pembrokeshire was growing in popularity as a destination as people chose to spend their pounds at home rather than see them suffer in their conversion into euros that wouldn't go far abroad. It was excellent for the local economy of the westernmost point of Wales, but there was a hitch. When it came to the user-satisfaction section of the holiday experience, the National Park found itself in need of an upgrade. In short, Pembrokeshire needed to be smartened up, given a makeover that wouldn't smother its natural gifts but would make the 'visitor experience' more rewarding. If people were prepared to take a risk and brave weather that was slightly more bracing than Mediterranean, then they needed to find a warm welcome and top-notch facilities.

It was in keeping with these findings that a survey was commissioned into every property – and particularly every neglected property – within the National Park's curtilage. And Tallis Hall, it was discovered, was near the very edge but firmly within the boundary. There were not enough hotel beds within easy reach of the sea. It had enormous potential as an investment opportunity, and it projected the very sense of neglect that the new Development Plan was addressing. The owner of Tallis Hall had to be found.

'So, out of the blue, this geezer, right, he comes and says he's from the – and wait for this... he says he's from the Pembrokeshire Coast National Park. And I say, some mistake, surely, because I'm strictly Clacton for me hols, mate. And he says, well, according to their records... And I say, "Oh yes? And what records are we are talking about here then?" And he says: the records that say that my mum, Alice Shaw, was the daughter of, let me get this right now, Charles Taylor... and he, my grandad, right, was the son of none other than Sir John Tallis-Brown. Says so on his birth certificate. So, I'm thinking... OK, you're royalty or near enough, Alfred Shaw. Or Sir Alfred Shaw as I now am, don't you know. Fair enough, I can handle that. Always felt a little blue-blooded. People have always said, "You, sir, are a gentleman." Or words to that effect. Could have been: "You, sir, are a right rascal." But it's the 'sir' bit that counts. Sir Alfred Offshore. Even got a double-barrel, ready to go.

'But I'm thinking at the same time... OK, but you're the Pembrokeshire Coast National Park. What have you got to do with the new me? And he says it's the house... and I'm kind of waiting for him to say, "It's the house, sir... " but he doesn't and I'm left thinking, "House? What house?" I think it's pretty well documented right here that this Alfred has no houses left. And he says, So-and-so Hall. Forgive me if I keep it to meself for the mo.

'So, I say to him: "Don't get me wrong, but where's So-and-so Hall? And more to the point, where's the sting? 'Cos I've been through it a bit of late – you may have noticed – and you dropping in out of the blue is a little too good to be true. And they don't exist, things that are too good to be true." In fact, I might use that as the family motto on the coat of arms I reckon I must have. Beware Things Too Good To be True. Bit long, but I think we can squeeze it in. Turn it into Latin. *Nunc Dimittis,* or something. Anyway, fair dos to the man, he says it straight, that he's not here entirely as a bearer of good news. And I thought to myself, "Aye, aye, thought as much."

'But for the moment, people, let's just park it there, right. I'm your phoenix for now, resurrected and all set to be plonked in the House of Lords. With a pad in Wales to boot. Let's just rub the old sun cream in that and sit back and enjoy it, eh? Ah, Sir DfL, signing off. Now, where's the butler... ?'

Chapter 26

The rooks had won the battle for Tallis Hall, filling every one of the large chimney pots with their nests. Leading into the house off the courtyard, Post and Corinthia found a door that had half-fallen off its hinges, and they slid through it and went straight through the house to the main hallway. The rooms exposed to the west were full of damp and the ceiling had come down in the dining room. The wind howled upstairs, telling of broken windows and holes in the roof. Post ran from room to room, with Corinthia, not wanting to be left on her own in the dark, right behind him.

'Why would a non-smoker like you carry a lighter around with him?' she asked at the top of the main stairs above the hallway.

'Just in case,' said Post.

'Just in case you find yourself in a haunted house in a storm…'

'Something like that. Come on, we need to light a proper fire and get you warm.' He lit a handful of twigs and straw that had fallen down the chimney in the hall and held it in each fireplace they came to. The smoke refused to be drawn upwards. They went down into the kitchen last and there they found that the flue from the range, too slim to accommodate a rook's nest, was clear. There was coal in the corridor to the basement back door on the north side of the house. It had spilled out of decomposed hessian sacks. There were candles in a cupboard in the scullery, thick with cobwebs.

'Time has shtood still,' said Post, suddenly less sober than he had appeared during the emergency.

'Say that again.'

'Shtood still. Stood shtill.'

'You need to lie down, Post Jones.'

He stayed awake long enough to drape his clothes over the hob cover that was now warm in Megan's old domain, before lying flat out on her kitchen table and beginning to snore. Corinthia kept watch, feeding the range and turning their clothes and lighting fresh candles until day's light began to appear through the windows, thick with dust and more cobwebs. Sitting in Megan's old carver, her head dropped at last and she slept too.

'Captain's Vlog… blah, blah, blah… OK, people, here goes. I know I've kept you in suspenders long enough, as the saying goes… so here it is. Or rather, here I am, suddenly Lord So-and-so of near 'Ave-a-lot-less, no less, with that question nagging away: what's the catch in all this, then? And the bloke from the PCNP, as we in the know about the Pembrokeshire Coast National Park like to shorten ourselves to, says: "Well, yes, your highness (not that he quite said it like that), there is – how can I put it? – grounds to suppose we may have an issue to resolve." So, I'm on full alert already. Up go the sensors and, there it is, the rat. I can smell 'im.

'Lucky for me, 'e goes off into his alphabet soup of the NPMP for the National Park Management Plan and the LDP for Local Development Plan and CS for Community Strategy and the LCA for Landscape Character Assessment and the SA for Sustainability Appraisal and the SEA for Strategic Environmental Assessment and the HRA for Habitat Regulation Assessment… and I'm thinking BS. Not bullshit, but Breathing Space. As in, needing one, and a bit sharpish. 'Cos what he's saying is, there is a requirement to bring properties – my big pile, by way of example, as he put it – up to standard. "In short," he said, "we're smartening up our act."

'Well, here's my dilemma, as them old Greeks used to say. Me and Mr B. Me with my zilch and this old house needing loads of wonga. If I put it on the market, guess what? Mr HMRC – Mr P for Park ain't the only one who can swim in the alphabet soup – would take that. We'll be having that, thank you very much, Sir Offshore. Another house gone. Lovely while it lasted – all five minutes of it.

'And then it comes to me. My light bulb moment. Sir Offshore, my son and heir, I say to myself: what did Mr P just say? Just rewind a bit, me old guardian of the Park. I was only half-listening 'cos of the need to find me a BS. But what was that? HRA? Habitat Regulation Assessment. Now call me what you will, but I bet chiropterologist wouldn't be among the first insults to spring to mind. But I am, you know – and if I say it myself – a right one at that, a proper little chiropterologist. Now there's a confession, eh?

'Nah, look, the reason I know, between you and me, is because in my old spread in Berkshire – number four on the list of repossessions – I had, if truth were known, what they called a planning issue. A PI. And as soon as Mr P for Park said the word 'issue', up they went, my antennae, sensitive as a pair of bat's ears. And that's it, people. Bats. Chiropterology. Bats and more bats. Find bats and there's nothing you can do on the planning front. There was a time, of course, when I did think differently about the little darlings. "Blind bats are seeing us off," I might have said. "Never have silent creatures been heard so loudly... gas the little bastards." I might have said that – and I wouldn't be proud. That was when I was going through my anti-bat phase, a time of life not to be envied, I'm sure you'll agree. Wouldn't recommend it to my worst enemy – so, I'm talking bad because I've made a few in my time. Enemies, that is. Anyway, it's my bat-bad period. Can't say everyone must go through this phase – it's not like puberty – but it can happen to the best of us. But now, and thank you for your concern, I'm well through it. Clean out on the other side, in the uplands of bat love. I'm a bat-lover person, people. This is my mantra, as we say in Mantraville: when it comes to the matter of smartening up – even if it's in Mr P's National Park, there can be no such thing – no smartening up of any act – until the bat issue is resolved. Planning Issue? There's no PI if you've got a BI. See a bat and tools are downed. New motto on the coat of arms: "Bats Are Best." What did me down in Berkshire might do me good in Pembrokeshire. Precedent, as a judge once told me, "binding on or persuasive for… " and I've always been a stickler for the law. So, bats are my BS. Find bat shit and I've got my breathing space. Better still, find a bat. A pipistrelle would do nicely, as we chiropterologists say.

'Course, there's no way I'm going down to the ruin – even if it's my ruin – to find proof of bat. You know, I gave it a butcher's and I've got to say, between you and me, it does need… well, smartening up wouldn't be the start of it. So, no, I didn't actually go down looking for bats. Who do they think I am, Sir David Attenborough? Fellow peer, by the way. Nah. It's better to do it this way… like this, what you're watching – if anybody is – by means of technology. Bit expensive, but even a penniless aristo with Mr B as a best mate has to have space to breathe in… Yeah, yeah, Mr T for Taxman, you find it matey, you can have it… and here it is, a few bob later, faithful followers… I give you: Batcam. There, if I swing the old laptop round to face you, you can see what I think in the business is called the "output". So, I'm putting it out there: Batwatch.'

The upstairs rooms overlooking the walled garden – Gentle John and Lady Phyllis's – were in much better condition than anything at the front of Tallis Hall. Less battered by the wind, the windows at the back of the house were more or less intact and the roof had all its slates. Vandalism had not been an issue.

The farmers that had bought the land from Lady Phyllis seemed to have respected the property's role as an exhibit in a time warp. The passing years and the weather were solely responsible for its dereliction.

The garden was thick with brambles. An ash tree had come down in the 1970s on the south side and dislodged three feet of bricks along a section near the American repair job, but the rest of the wall was intact. The farmers had cleared the trunk on their side of the wall, but the crown of the ancient tree, silver and brittle, still lay where it had tumbled into the enclosed garden. Corinthia wandered around in the sunshine the day after the storm. White clouds scudded across a sky that was crystal clear. She spotted something in the soil poking its head out of the weeds and grass in the middle of the enclosure and she bent down to examine it. Seeing it was one of so many, she pulled it out of the ground.

'What's this?' she asked, hearing a weary Post, stiff of back, walking into the garden. He was looking for water.

'Looks like asparagus,' he said. 'It must have self-seeded and kept going all these years. About the only thing that has. Bit woody to eat.'

Corinthia took it back and held up the spear, hard of stem, with a slightly drooped tip. 'Reminds me of you, you old drunk.'

'Not so drunk that I can't remember,' he replied.

'Remember what?'

'You've forgotten?'

'Forgotten what?'

'What you said.'

'Oh, I remember.'

'And so do I.'

'So you say.'

'But I do.'

'And?'

'And so… I love you.'

'Oh,' said Corinthia.

'Always have done.'

'Through everything?'

'Through thick and thin.'

'Just as well then.'

'Because of all this?' said Post indicating the derelict house and garden.

'No, not because we have no clothes to wear but these, that our home is a caravan on its side in a field and that we slept on a kitchen table in a ruin…'

'Why "just as well then?"'

'It's just as well… because, well!… just because…' She reached up and hugged him and when she released him, they stood stock still, looking at each other, right in front of the Batcam, placed out of their sight in the silver, brittle branches of the fallen ash tree.

Chapter 27

Donna was drooping on her bed. The sun was beating down as it had been day after day. The air conditioning was on but it wasn't a question of thermostatic control. She was simply out of sorts. Doing her lengths had lost its appeal, and chef Sofía was really starting to annoy her with her *sardinas* and *boquerones* and *pulpo*. One more deep-fried dish of *calamares* and she'd be turning into a bloody squid. And Javier, she suspected, was using Spanish classes as a means to case her joint. Case her, as well. 'Let me see a little bit more of you, Donna.' If truth were known, she was done with pervs. If truth were known, she was done with the clubs that were starting to lose money, and maybe she was done with Spain. If truth were known – Donna had picked up the phrase from her vlogger, the DfL who was sort of keeping her going at the moment – she was bored out of her mind. She turned on her side and turned on her laptop lifeline, hoping to drop off with a smile.

'Captain's blah-blah…

'Well, look what the cat dragged in. No, not me – Viscount DfL – but something very interesting, I think you'll find. Bear with me. I'll show you in a mo. Just to recap, first – here I am at the controls of the hottest Batcam in the county of Pembrokeshire, or Sir Benfro as we sirs of the Welsh shires like to say in our native tongue. If you recall, I'm on the lookout for the little beauties of the night, that might spare me forking out on my new gaff – new but sadly old, if you know what I mean.

'Anyway, I was just saying "*Bore da*" to the Batcam this morning, ready to stand it down for the day, when 'ello 'ello, what's this I see? Not pipistrelles, I hear you say. Not by a long chalk. You don't have to be much of a bat-man to see that these are not bats. OK, OK, I need to show you, don't I? Let me turn the screen round and… find the right bit on the recording… here we go. So, what do you think, people? Look what we've caught in our little net. Two beauties, aren't they? Ah, isn't it sweet?

'Or is it? What's a lord of the manor to do when he finds strangers in his castle grounds? Let's face it, when all's said and done, we're talking trespassers here. Illegals. It is, as Sherlock Holmes might have said, a conundrum.'

Donna was suddenly wide awake. There in front of her were the *Boleros*. The stripper and Taser-man. Her and him. Her nemesis. Her neme-fuckin'-sis. Well, downfall could work both ways. Bored Donna gave way to old Donna, leader of the Valley Commandos. She reached for her phone and mobilised the Namelesses. She plunged into her think tank and churned up and down and thought her thoughts, mostly to do with the joys of the maiming game. Wherever So-and-so Hall near 'Ave-a-lot-less was, she'd find it. Donna was going 'ome.

The Mouse and Anon were restless, too. To be a Brit in Puerto Banús was no longer to be trusted. The big money now arrived by superyacht, with their own security on board, including divers. The scene had changed, from laid-back wealth on display amid an easy-going swirl of onlookers, to a tighter exclusivity where the watchful mega-rich built a protective wall of 'Do Not Enter' around themselves. The Namelesses were no longer treated as part of the new bubble. Where once they had been known to all and forgiven for their slightly eccentric enterprise on the waterfront, now they were litter to be cleared away. They were moved along by large goons that outnumbered them ten to one. The displaced pair thought about planting a limpet mine on a couple of hulls, but settled instead for following four of the biggest off-duty guards to La Anchoa bar, in a street behind the waterfront. They gave them an hour of drinking before approaching them.

'We think you should move on, now, gentlemen,' said the Mouse to the heavyweight multinational protection force.

'As in, hear that?' said Anon, cupping an ear with his hand. 'That's your masters' dog whistle. Time to run along now, please.'

There was no need to translate. The four bodyguards were quickly on their feet. And just as quickly they were down again, knees buckling and heads snapping backwards beneath a five-second flurry from the hands and feet of the Namelesses, who finished by looking up and directly into the CCTV camera, and taking a low, slow bow.

'I think we may regard that as burning our bridges,' said Anon, as they strolled away.

'Or is it burning our boats?'

'That's a good point.'

'If you burn your boats, there's no going back. You stay.'

'Which doesn't apply to us, does it? I take it we're kind of committed to leaving.'

'Probably the wise option.'

'So, it's bridges, then.'

'It may depend on when you burn them.'

'Come again?'

'Well, say you've got the enemy in front of you, on the other side of the river, and you cross the bridge and then burn it… well, it's the same, isn't it. There's no going back. But if you go over, engage the enemy, drop back and then burn the bridge, it's more an orderly retreat, wouldn't you say?'

'I would say. So, it's that one – Bridge burnt, option B, right?'

'I'd say so. We could always burn a boat or two.'

'What, now we're in the mood…'

'That kind of thing. What do you think?'

'Probably best not to.'

'You're right. Orderly retreat it is, then.'

In a further reassessment of their options, going back to Blighty presented itself through Donna's summons. Free repatriation. Home leave. They weren't particularly enamoured of the woman that kept them on their retainer and in more prosperous times they would have politely turned down the offer to do what they imagined would be no good at all to the *Bolero* Two. In a peaceful world, where issues might be settled amicably and without rancour, the Namelesses were sure they would side with the innocents, Ms Corinthia and her hunchback. Donna was a little out there at the red end of the Namelesses' gauge of acceptable practice. As business-like as she was in her commissioning process, this looked altogether more personal and the risk of being compromised by a miscalculation born of rage made them think twice. This was a delicate one and yet she would no doubt require them to be anything but. They were tempted to decline the offer of work, but they had to admit the incident in the night at La Anchoa might have left them a tad exposed. A little caught on camera. They had to be aware of knock-on effects, now that their cover was blown and local job opportunities had most certainly been put on ice, to say nothing of the matter of superyacht vengeance. The mega-rich tended to abhor loss of absolute control. Reluctant as the Namelesses were to back away from a scrap, they were trained to accept the wisdom of an orderly retreat, and they said yes.

It took them a little time to organise a passport for Donna. She told them nothing about her intel and how she had tracked down the Boleros, but she did share with them that when it came to presenting herself at UK Border Control, she might cause a bell to jangle. She was not, she hastened to add, on anything like the FBI's Most Wanted list, nor did she come with a High-Security alert – Do Not Approach Under Any Circumstances. She had done nothing too dastardly, but, she had to confess, she may have committed certain indiscretions, may have been guilty of certain misdemeanours, and that if she went back as Donna Hopkins, this unfortunate past might tickle the fancy of Passport Control. The Namelesses, with not a blot to the real names they never divulged, smiled to themselves at this Dastardly Donna and wondered what it had been about her ex that had made him so very unlikeable. What he had been that might rhyme with dastard. They were amused by how she was more embarrassed by her Pontypridd peccadillos – that they assumed to be financial irregularities, otherwise known as stealing – from her misspent youth than by anything she had done more recently. Here she was, all flushed of face over petty pinching, and yet she hadn't batted an eyelid when it came to snuffing out her skinny piece of nastiness. And they knew all about that, because the Mouse had come to just as Donna was putting her truly dastardly man out for good. The Mouse coming to, Ian going out. And she had commissioned them to get rid of Mankev without so much as a flicker of remorse. They had to admire her and they had to chuckle at her embarrassment.

She caught them smirking. 'Just get me a passport,' she said. 'I am not Lady Mac-fuckin'-Beth.'

It took them much less time to find their destination. 'Ave-a-lot-less was hardly the stuff of GCHQ. Derelict mansion between Haverfordwest and the sea. Search. Ping. Tallis Hall. Found. They booked their tickets and headed for the airport, there to meet Belladonna, the name they had nearly given in the new passport to their Welsh employer. They had chosen Anne Thomas. It was time to be serious. And any residue of a smile was wiped off their faces as it was they, and not their travelling companion, that made the UK passport officials pause. What was the nature of their business in Spain? How long had they been there? How long would they be staying here?

'Welcome home,' said their respective passport-checkers in the end, but the Namelesses did not feel particularly welcome. They felt a little over-scrutinised, a little too exposed to the cameras that followed them over the threshold and back into their country of origin.

'To be perfectly honest, Sir DfL, I said to myself, I'm not that bothered. You know, at first I thought my personal space was being invaded. Like I had a bad dose of the squatters. Or gypsies. Or imagine if my gaff turned into a, I don't know... like, some terrorist training camp.

'But I think I may have been getting a little carried away. Call it a knee-jerk reaction. The more I watch them – I've turned into a right little Sir Peeping Tom – the more I see a couple of kids doing no harm. And as long as they don't go and disturb my roosting bats, I've come to the conclusion that I'm going to forgive them their trespasses. So, I am chilled, people. Sir Live-and-Let-Live, that's me.'

Post and Corinthia rode on the bicycle made for one back to the coast and returned it to the hire-pool at the E'sE. Over the following few days, they commuted, as they called it, from Tallis Hall by running to the coast, heads down into the breeze that blew in the wake of the storm, swimming in the sea and reporting for duty as if nothing had happened. Post extricated their mattress from the Tiff and hauled it back to the Hall, lugging it up the stairs to Gentle John's old room. For a new item of bedroom furniture, it was looking decidedly worn. But it turned Gentle John's old haunt into their room, and here they set up camp. It wouldn't be for long. The Tiff had been righted and with some patching up of the floor, re-plumbing and reinforcement of the anchor-points, would be back as their official residence in no time. In the meantime, the big house would do.

Corinthia passed Post at the Tiff on her way back to the Hall. She was swinging along in the first unbroken sunshine since the storm. She was fresh out of the sea and looking forward to stretching out in the walled garden on her afternoon off. Post was under the Tiff, with his legs, a toolbox and some copper piping from the Preseli sticking out into the sunshine.

'Have you told Charlie boy about the Tiff yet?' she asked.

'I think His Majesty understands the concept of the mobile home and holiday opportunities for the masses, yes,' said Post.

'Well, you can tell His Maj that Nell Gwyn is going back to the palace for a bit of sunbathing… tell him his little orange-seller is well up for a squeeze.' And Corinthia danced away across the field. Post laughed and decided to finish the last bit of soldering and then follow her home. He heard 'Oranges and Lemons…' fading into the distance.

Corinthia spread a towel on the grass that covered the raised bed in the walled garden and paused, checking that Tallis Hall was as empty as ever. She pulled the T-shirt over her head and stood topless under the sun. She then slipped off her shorts and bikini bottom, still damp from her swim, lay down on her back and waited for Post. Ten minutes later, she turned over and drifted into a light sleep. She awoke when she sensed through her closed eyes a drop in the level of light. She thought Post would be standing over her and waited for the touch of his hands on her back.

'I must admit, I still had some doubts,' said Donna. 'Was it really you? But seeing you like this… I'd recognise you anywhere…' She began to hum the old Ravel tune. 'So, hello again, *Bolero* girl.'

Corinthia opened her eyes. She noticed for the first time,

as she tried to calculate distances to the opening in the wall or even up into the remains of the ash tree, that there were rhubarb leaves coming through the brambles, a few paces away from the old asparagus plant. She hadn't seen them before. She braced herself to spring into a starting position and make a bolt for the hole in the wall, but legs stepped in front of her. Four of them. Men's legs.

'Up, please, Ms Corinthia,' said the Mouse.

'No, no,' said Donna. 'Let's leave her as she is. Tie her hands together.'

'I'll scream,' said Corinthia as the Mouse dropped in front of her and tied her wrists together.

'Oh, you can scream all you like, love,' said Donna. 'You hear that?' She paused. 'That's the sound of fuck-all for miles around. You'll be just another screeching crow.'

'They don't screech. And they're rooks.'

'That's my little smart-arse. Stake her out. And gag her anyway.'

The Mouse pulled Corinthia's arms out straight in front of her and drove a stake into the ground with a rusty old lump hammer and fastened the twine that held her wrists to it. He stuffed a cloth into her mouth and held it in place with more rough twine. Worse happened behind her. Anon forced her right leg straight, down from the instinctively flexed position it had sought for a modicum of modesty. He then placed the tines of an equally rusted garden fork on either side of Corinthia's ankle and pressed the tool into the soil. He then straightened her other leg, prised her legs apart and drove a second fork around and over her ankle into the ground. By the very tools that Gentle John and Now Then had used to turn and break their soil, Corinthia was now pinned down in it.

'Face down, arse up,' said Donna. 'How any good *Bolero* should end.'

Post ran home and then more carefully entered the house, prepared to play his part in the little piece of theatre Corinthia had planned. He went quietly up to their room to collect a blanket. He looked out of the window and froze.

'Take your fill, boys,' said Donna. 'It's a peachy sight, isn't it? I mean it. Feel free to take her.' Old Donna was up for this. Old Donna was going to take revenge and when *Bolero* girl could take no more, Donna would drive one fork after another right through the bitch's back. 'Where's the hunchback?'

Alfred Shaw stared at his Batcam output and did not move a muscle. A little part of him said that he could stop this. Dial 999 and have the police send in a helicopter. A bigger part told him to sit back and enjoy the show. Batcam Plus.

Post grabbed his mobile phone and saw what he knew it would show. No signal. He tried to open the big sash window. It would not budge. He jumped on the window seat and pulled and pushed even harder. All that happened was that while he was trying to pull up the lower frame, the rotten window seat gave way and he collapsed in a heap.

The Namelesses were sorely tempted. Not because they were entirely evil – they were just bad enough through experience to have a loose take on morality in a combat zone. So, they were tempted. In the end, though, they did hold back. This self-control was not out of pity for Corinthia, for although it was there, it was easily overcome by the red-blooded badness in them, the lust that clouded their judgement and might have made them susceptible to being caught off-guard. Nor were they stopped by the sudden commotion from the bedroom window, where Post was punching holes in the panes, since to draw Taser-man the Hunchback from his cover was all part of the plan. What stayed their hand was their sixth sense. Their heightened awareness of security elbowed susceptibility aside. It was their area of expertise, after all, and something in their filters told them to hold fire.

'Remind me,' said Anon, 'how you knew they were here.'

'Who gives a shit?' replied Donna, deeper in her red mist by the minute.

'With all due respect, we do,' said the Mouse. Polite Mouse, but firm Mouse.

'The Down from London's Batcam,' said Donna impatiently, as if this should make sense.

One part of it did to Anon. 'Cam – as in camera?' he asked.

'As in here? Right here?' said the Mouse.

'Are we going to get started?' shouted Donna, but the Mouse and Anon ignored her.

'What d'you think?' asked the Mouse.

'I'm wondering why… why my insouciance is ruffled. Why I'm suddenly not inebriated by the scent and the temptations in this garden of delights.'

'It worries me when you get a little…'

'Wordy?' said Anon. 'Me too.'

'Shall I go and sort him out?' asked the Mouse, nodding towards the House where Post was still breaking glass. 'I kind of owe him – for what he did.'

'In a mo,' said Anon.

They turned away from the women and began to patrol the garden, scanning it with their expert eyes. They found the camera in the branches of the ash tree and Sir Offshore, the DfL back up in London, saw them peering at him. He couldn't help but slide back in his chair.

'Damn,' said the Mouse. 'There's no getting away from them, is there?'

'We live in a surveillance society,' said Anon.

The Mouse looked again at the camera. 'What d'you think?'

'D'you know… I'm thinking somebody's trying to tell us something. I'm just thinking we should… be careful.'

'I agree.'

'As in… orderly retreat.'

'It's becoming a habit.'

'But don't you think…?'

'I do. And d'you know, I like her. Ms Corinthia.'

'Me too. What about him?'

'I kind of admire him, too…'

Post looked at his hands soaked in blood and groaned in despair. He let them drop and watched the blood drip into the cavity beneath the window. There was something there, not absorbing the drops. He reached down and found the oilcloth, the protection that had withstood the damp of the years, that had been carefully wrapped around Gentle John's air rifle by the American crewman of the Liberators. He unwrapped the weapon and found a sealed tin of pellets.

Anon and the Mouse backed away from the camera. The Namelesses didn't run for their lives but they made a show of leaving the scene without causing any more damage. They pointed out the camera to Donna. That it was live. That they were being watched.

'Don't you think of leaving,' she shouted. 'You stay right here.' But the Namelesses had backed out of the garden and were away down the drive.

The Valley Commando didn't care. She looked over her shoulder, up at Post in his window and screamed, 'I'll give you twenty seconds to get your arse down here. Or this…' She heaved on the one fork and it came out of the ground. Corinthia tried to kick her with her suddenly freed foot, but Donna stamped on a flailing calf and pinned her victim back down with her foot. She raised the garden tool and held it high. '*Bolero* girl gets forked.' Donna was almost choking with rage but up came another sound, a cackle of a laugh, and she nearly fell over through lack of breath.

Post took aim and fired. The pellet struck Donna in the right buttock, still an ample target even after years of swimming in Spain. She suddenly could breathe in, with a short gasp of pain. At first, she thought it was a wasp sting, but a second pellet hit her just above the waist and she yelped and dropped the fork. She reached for it but a fresh round caught her in the wrist and she saw blood and fell over. Post rained fire down on her as fast as he could, reloading and chasing her through a bramble patch. There, she cowered briefly, scrammed by thorns and peppered by lead, before throwing herself back into the open and diving into the tangle of the fallen ash tree. Her desperate search for cover shook the branches and the Batcam was tossed around. The DfL saw Donna for a fraction of a second in big close-up before the lens lurched again and ended up pointing at the sky. His garden show was over.

Donna was aware that she wasn't being stung any more. She peered out from the branches and saw that Corinthia was still on the ground, but about to free her other leg with her kicking. Perhaps there was a lull while Taser-man – gun-man – was making his way from the house to the garden. Donna took a deep breath, put her head down, crashed out of the branches and charged. When she looked up, she saw only the tight circle of the end of Post's barrel. Corinthia was standing by his side, holding the two garden forks. Donna dropped to her knees with a sob.

'Who are you?' she managed to say.

'He's a bloke who talks to dead kings,' said Corinthia.

'What?'

'Charles II to be precise. On this occasion about… what is it?'

'Pressurised air and pneumatic accumulators and pellets with a muzzle velocity of approximately a thousand feet per second,' said Post, not lowering his weapon.

'He's a good man, too,' said Corinthia. 'A good man who's going to let you go. Me? I'd take your eyes out. But it's your lucky day. So, go.'

Donna rose unsteadily and limped slowly past the pair, giving them a wide berth, facing them all the way until she was through the garden wall. She then turned and began to run as fast as her wounds would allow.

'Is it loaded?' asked Corinthia. Post nodded. 'May I?' she said. Post handed her the gun. Corinthia took careful aim and fired and Donna left Tallis Hall with a flesh wound in her other buttock. She reached the end of the drive, just in time to throw herself on the bonnet of the Namelesses' hire car as it was doing a three-point turn. She slid to the ground. They thought about running her over, but stopped.

'Did you harm her?' said the Mouse.

'Harm her? I've been shot. By Taser-man. He's a luna-fuckin'-tic.'

'Don't bleed on the seats,' said Anon, getting out and pushing her into the back. She yelped as he gave her a last solid shove on her behind. She couldn't sit down and had to kneel across the rear seat. Face down, arse up. They pulled away and left for their respectively insecure worlds in Spain that night, never to work together again.

Post picked up the towel, Corinthia lifted her arms and he wrapped it around her, his hands leaving red marks on the cotton. She had bloodstains from the rifle on her hands. She gently took his and checked the cuts from the panes he'd broken. 'We need to clean these in the sea,' she said softly.

'Nothing too bad,' he said looking down.

'It's all bad,' she said. 'I'm sorry for getting you into this.'

'I'm not,' he said. 'This has made me do something.' Post began to walk towards the ash branches.

'More than something.'

'Maybe.' He was peering at the camera, twisting his head to see where it was pointing.

'You are a good man, Dan Post Jones. And one day you can rescue me when I have some clothes on.'

'I'll rescue you however you are.' He turned away from the camera and gave her his full attention. 'You're the reason I've come to life,' he said.

'Come on, get me out of here.'

Chapter 28

The Namelesses left Spain and headed for the Caribbean. They imagined they would run a diving school for young holidaymakers from the UK, combined with fishing trips perhaps for less adventurous parents. What they didn't want to do was appear on camera, or have anything to do with the world of installing them, dismantling them or viewing their output. They were seeking a life that offered security, but not in Security. They ended up looking after elderly Americans, something that they would never have imagined being of any appeal whatsoever to them. They had the lifelong mistrust – jealousy perhaps – that they and the vast majority of the personnel with whom they had served reserved for their Transatlantic allies. The Namelesses would have said they did not like the Yanks. But they discovered they did, after all. The UK holidaymakers they were seeking did not come their way, and instead, they found work crewing yachts for their retired Americans. The craft they manned were not the superyachts of Puerto Banús, but vintage sailing boats. Anon and the Mouse would never have confessed to loving anything – and remained reluctant to admit that they were quite happy now to be taking orders, delivered as polite requests, from their ageing clients – but they both acknowledged a lasting satisfaction from their new line of work.

They nearly made it in front of the cameras again. Piracy was rare in the Caribbean but it was always a risk, particularly when there were rich pickings on these high seas. Elderly couples, like Frank and Lucille Green of Hertford, Connecticut, retired from the insurance business and novice sea-farers, were not so frail that they could not lend a hand on board, but they would have been sitting ducks had they taken to the blue waters off Antigua on their own. As it was, they had their crew and when they were approached by a high-powered, speeding inflatable they found they were not in danger at all.

'RIB,' said the Mouse. 'Five on board. Sir, ma'am, go below deck. Three knocks and you can come back up. Until then, stay put. Please.'

The Greens did as they were told and witnessed not a thing with their eyes. Their ears told them there was a brief scuffle overhead. Then silence. They held each other's hands and wondered if all was lost. Were the Brits part of the gang? The masterminds? Were they dead? Knock, knock, knock. When they came back up, there were five men trussed up against the mast, with a few bloodstains on the teak decking.

'Oh, my Lord,' said Lucille. 'What do we do now?'

'Personally, ma'am,' said Anon, picking up a machete removed from a pirate's grip, 'I'd gut them and feed them to the sharks.' He threw the machete overboard.

'On the other hand,' said the Mouse, 'We can take them back to port and hand them over to the authorities.'

'Shall we do that?' said Frank.

'Good idea, skipper,' said the Mouse, picking a handgun off the deck. 'Is this for real?' he asked one of the helpless boarding party, pointing the weapon at him. The flinch told him it was. He pointed it away and aimed down at the inflatable, bobbing against the Americans' vessel. He fired three times and the RIB went down with a hiss. Lucille put her hands over her ears. The Mouse tossed the gun into the sea, and was about to kick the remaining arsenal of knives and another handgun the same way, when he stopped.

'Do we need some evidence?'

'Better had, I suppose,' said Anon.

'Won't these do?' said the Mouse, pointing a toe at the pirates. 'I'm sure we could extract a confession. By the way, don't worry, Mrs Green. They won't be going anywhere. If I say it myself, I'm good at knots, ma'am. As in, what you tie, not speed at sea. Although, we do have a little experience, don't we?'

'We do. The ocean wave and all that,' said Anon.

'As I was saying, Mrs Green, they'll do… Would you like to, um, train a gun on them?'

'No, thank you,' said Lucille. 'We'd be much happier if you did.'

'Bit small for us. We were gunners, you know. Royal Navy.'

'Gunners and then divers. And then…'

'Hush hush stuff…' said the Mouse.

'That's strictly for your ears only,' said Anon. 'You can't tell anyone.'

'Or we'll have to shoot you. That's a joke, by the way.' The Greens laughed. A little nervously.

Anon radioed ahead to give an unadorned report of what had happened and to announce their return to port. Frank was rather more effusive in his phone call to 'the folks back at the hotel' and word spread to such an extent that the *Liberty Bell* returned to port to find its pontoon crammed with family, friends, police, a reporter and a local news crew.

'We owe our safe return to these guys,' said Frank, standing in front of his boat. He was more composed now and his heart rate, that Lucille monitored with care, had slowed. She had insisted he take his time, to let himself and the confusion that had gone with the docking and the unloading of the captives settle down. Only then did she allow him to have his say. He'd used the time to prepare his thanks, and thought he'd timed his moment pretty well – to hold out his arm and bring in their saviours. Still staring at his interviewer, he beckoned the crew forward with his fingers, but they were gone.

Donna took to her lounger by the pool she no longer used and spread out. VC for Veritably Corpulent, she said, keeping up her utterances if not her appearances. She turned to cocktails between chapters in the books she read, and she slurred her way into her expanded vocabulary and waistline. She sold the nightclubs and made enough from the fire-sale – 'I've been rolled over,' she claimed when she made only half what she thought they were worth – to set her up for a life of comfort in the one property she retained, the villa near Valencia.

She went into the pool one last time. 'Dead drunk, by the looks of it,' was the unofficial verdict of the expat English doctor – Donna would allow herself to be treated by no other – who came to pronounce her well and truly drowned. Drunk and dead, Donna would have corrected him, conscious of her word order to the end. Drunk first, thank you very much, and, oops, dead. There's hubris for you, she would have said. Hu-effing-bris. At least she went with a splash, she would have added.

Epi-vlog

'Last entry of Sir Down-from-London. A sign-off, I suppose. Over and out, that sort of thing. Look, it's not exactly Captain Scott sitting in his tent waiting to freeze to death, but I thought I might say *"Adiós"*, as we say in Wales.

'So, after all the fun and games in the garden, I thought, "What have you stumbled across here, Lord Offshore, me old mucker?" What are you running here, exactly? A bleedin' theme park? Pardon my French. Murder-mystery nights in the haunted house? A whodunnit?

'Well, who did what? Who were they? As if I know. Not a clue. And let's face it, that's not really the way, is it, in the Whodunnit business? I say it again, "Who done what?" Answer: not a clue. Sort of misses the point, don't it? Doesn't it. Mind your estuary mouth, me old lordy-lordy.

'I therefore came to the conclusion, after much deliberation – as we used to say in the banking sector – that the best thing was to give it up. I mean, Batcams… really? I'm sure they're there – the bats – by the hundred but, d'you know, I kind of ran out of bat-steam. Sell the place and be done with it, I decided. But there's still old Mr B. Him and the Rev. The Inland Rev, that is. Money, Sir Alfred? We'll be having that, thank you very much. Your account is not quite settled.

'So, I gave it away. Tallis Hall, bequeathed to Mr P for Park. It's all yours, if you'd like it, I said to the Pembrokeshire Coast National Park. I was never going to be its restoration king, was I? What was I going to do with the place? And – wait for this – Mr B and Mr Rev said it was a most generous gesture. And talking of Bs, I've heard the old garden is already full of them. As in, beehives. Not bats, but bees. *"Mêl"*, as we say on our side of the language line. The Landsker Line. Land of honey.

'Anyway, out of the blue, the old Rev brings down the stamp saying, "Account settled". So, the National Park has my pile and I've got the monkey off my back. Easy as that. And since I was on a roll with all this transferring of titles, I decided to un-dub myself, as it were. Strip off the title. Sir Alfie Offshore. Never sat easily with me, to be honest. A bankrupt peer of the realm… it's not good for the image of the country, is it? So, no more 'Sir'. Call me Alffi, with two 'f's' and no 'e', if you don't mind. Welsh through and through, me. 'Cos I like it down here. I am still the DfL. Thought I'd give it a go. Between you and me, there's a little bit tucked away. A stash. A little bit of know-what-I-mean buried treasure. Call me an old pirate. Something for a rainy day, you know how it is. And talking of the weather, I'm off up the coast… there's a little scheme I've got my eye on. An Alf-finger in a pie. Renewable energy for the newly re-energised yours truly. Alffi Offshore lives. No more of this old windbag nonsense. Real offshore wind, that's for me. You can't have enough of it down here. So, feeling the power, I bid you *"Hwyl fawr"*. Alffi and out.'

Postscript

Post and Corinthia stayed in the Tiff through the autumn and winter. Post had to abandon the trickle and rig up a proper hot-water shower inside Mrs Davies's 'Van. He also had to build a kitchen. They had a damp time. Condensation poured down the walls of their home and the holes in the plywood floor gaped as the weather deteriorated. They didn't mind because it was strictly – Post, up to his elbows in the Preseli, had promised – temporary.

Tallis Hall was to be renovated and work would soon begin on its conversion into the Coastal Path Visitor Centre, with, according to their blurb, 'All-season Accommodation and – once the ever-popular bees are relocated to their purpose-built new home nearby – Performance Area.' The Visitor Centre, the VC, as well as being accessible by road, would have a special walkway to the sea and already had a whole programme of events in the planning stage. The VC couldn't wait to unveil their Performance Area. This PA was the VC's veritable USP. The walled garden was going to be the star attraction.

The walkway had to be attractive in its own right and properties along its path had been encouraged to present plans for improvements, all part of the upgrade of the groove in the landscape between the sea and Tallis Hall. Ethel Davies was granted planning permission to convert her old outbuildings into a residential dwelling. With the proceeds of the sale of the house in Park Crescent, Rhiwbina, Post and Corinthia bought the plot. Post redesigned a home of oak and glass and slate that removed most traces of the agricultural original, but whose plans were welcomed as 'a courageous example of what could be achieved through imagination and respect for the landscape', as the National Park Authority wrote in their annual report. There was a place for bricks too, and the Authority especially liked the conversion of the small farmyard into the new property's own walled garden, an 'elegant structure', affording not only privacy to the owners on their side of it, but also a foretaste to passing visitors of the main attraction that awaited them a little further inland. Corinthia suggested that they could apply for a licence and open up a watering hole.

'I'm going to be absolute in my belief that you are joking,' said Post.

'We could call it the Pit-stop, I was thinking,' said Corinthia. 'And we could have our own performance area, to pull the punters in. You know, strike up the old tune and I could get my kit off… the Strip-stop.'

'As I say, absolute in my belief that you are not serious.'

'Of course, I'm not. You are the only, only, only person who will see me with no clothes on. But we're going to have to able to talk about it, Post. You know, about what happened… You're not the best at letting stuff out. Unless it's to you-know-who. We've got to be able to talk, too. You and me.'

'I know. And I shall.'

'Right now.'

'How about… every time I see you when you're cleaning… when you put your rubber gloves on, I think of my big electric prod?'

'For a boffin, Dan Post Jones, you have a very dirty mind.'

They moved into their new home early the next summer. And on the first night they stared out of the big floor-to-ceiling window, that could not be seen from the walkway but that gave them an unrestricted view over St Brides Bay. Corinthia turned around and looked between her legs at the freighters and tankers at anchor in the calm waters. 'Ships in the sky,' she said. She nodded and her dark hair brushed the floor. 'And I agree.'

'To what?' said Post, standing upright by her side, his back stiff from digging in the garden.

'His Majesty just said it reminded him of… help me a bit here…'

'The time he reviewed the fleet off Portsmouth on the occasion of the arrival of his wife, Catherine of Braganza.'

'That's exactly what he said. And he said there was no finer place than this, right here, in all the land. And I said I agreed.' Corinthia stood up and ran a hand through her hair before holding up a palm, as if to stop somebody. 'No,' she said. 'That's between us. And for me to say.'

'What is?'

'Personal stuff.'

'Oh,' said Post. 'He's gone. Left the building.'

'I can't be sharing you with him,' said Corinthia.

'He's left the country,' said Post.

'I want you all to myself.'

'Won't be back any time soon.'

'Because I love you.'

'Completely gone.'

'With all my heart.'

Post put his arms around her. 'Just as well…' he said in her ear.

'Why?'

'Just because…'